LOVING CAPTIVITY

HUMAN PETS OF TALIN
BOOK 1

Copyright: RK Munin, 2021
Cover Illustration by RK Munin, 2021
ISBN-13: 978-1-962699-18-1

Warning: Author is dyslexic as hell.

Professional editing done by Amanda Brown at Amanda Brown Edits, LLC

So much appreciation to: Martha Collins who did the first read-through and put up with my whining, my constant questions, and my anxiety! You're a rockstar and a good friend.

And special thanks to: Lauren Meghoo who was kind enough to read my work, see all the mistakes and contact me to offer help. You have a big heart and a kind soul.

And, as with many writers, your reviews on Amazon, Goodreads, and/or Kindle help immeasurably, even if it's just clicking on the stars.

Thank you to all my readers!

CONTENT WARNING

-Several scenes are set at a slave market
-Talk of past abuse
-Threat of sexual assault and forced pregnancy
-Violence and fighting on page
-Graphic, consensual sex on page
-Family betrayal, one in the past and one on page
-Kidnapping
-Pregnancy
-Threat of abortion

DEDICATION

Thanks, Mom, for all the extra and frustrating hours you had to put in to teach my dyslexic butt how to read and write. You never once told me I couldn't do it. You never once discouraged me. When a high school English teacher told me I probably shouldn't waste time with college, you laughed in her face.

No matter how defeated I felt, you picked me up, brushed me off, and kept me going. I wish everyone could be as lucky as I am to have someone like you in their life.

CHAPTER 1

Sora

For the second time in her life, Sora waits to be sold. The first time was at sixteen, when her uncle sold her to a wealthy man in the Orimax system. Since humans are a bit of an oddity in that system, the alien that bought her thought it would be fun to have an unusual slave to show off when he traveled. She never had a specific job except to scuttle after him holding items, picking up things he discarded, and being ready to fetch and carry.

It wasn't hard work, but it was dangerous. When Master De got annoyed, he lashed out at anything close by, and she was often close by. She'd acquired a dozen scars over the years from his temper and had learned the hard way to drop to the floor and cover her face, waiting for his temper to expend itself.

Whimpering and softly crying helped, but pleading for him to stop only made it worse.

Now, after ten years, he's selling his slaves and has fired most of his staff. The rumors are he gambled too much and now owes money to several powerful houses. She, along with the rest of his dozen slaves, were shipped off to a nearby auction house. Because she arrived covered in bruises and welts from his last temper tantrum, she was held back from the others so she could heal a little and increase her value.

She's the last slave waiting to be sold that belonged to Master De.

It's a slow day at the auction house. Only a handful have stopped to look at her and inquire if she has any special skills. Master De never had her trained for any skilled tasks, but she has tried to showcase her ability to learn. No potential buyer seems interested in what she can learn, only what she knows.

She worries as the days pass and only low offers are made on her. Low offers are for disposable slaves, meaning there's a good chance she'll end up as a slave in a mine or bought by one of the cheap brothels. Both those options are a quick death sentence because half the time being sold to a cheap brothel ends up making you food for a species that accidentally kills when they mate because of frenzy or instinct.

"Can you cook?" a large insect-like alien called a Nimon asks her. "Do you know anything about Seffi food requirements?"

"I assisted my master's cook many times," she tells him, stretching the truth so far that if it was a string, it would have broken. "I have quick and nimble hands, good for preparing delicate cuisine."

"But do you know how to cook Seffi foods? I need a cook that knows how to kill and prepare Oniron."

She doesn't even know what an Oniron is. "I can learn quickly. If you give me access to a UniBase, I can do anything you request." She can tell by the way the Nimon strokes his palps together that he isn't pleased with her answer.

"I need a skilled cook now," he grumbles. "Your price is good, but I can't risk my house being poisoned by a cook that doesn't know how to prepare Oniron." He tucks his arms tight against his body and moves on.

Sora tries not to let her shoulders slump. Already the slaver who was contracted to sell her was annoyed by the delay while she healed. He finally gave up on having her fully healed. He grumbled at how weak humans are and put her out to auction still bruised and wounded.

She tries to stand tall and pretend her back isn't in agony and her vision doesn't swim when she moves her head too fast, but without any special skills, no one's interested in buying her. With every day that passes, she's more likely to be sold off cheaply to a cut-rate pleasure house, often referred to as meat bordellos.

She wants to cry, but no one buys weeping slaves. With a deep breath, she straightens her spine and looks around, trying to catch the eye of a potential buyer. She wonders if she should take off her clothes. Many of the slaves stand at their pole naked to let the shoppers better assess their health. She's only wearing a simple, shapeless dress that hangs to her knees. It has to be pulled off over her head and hung from where her collar chain attaches to her pole.

While she's debating the merits of being naked, a Leemron stops in front of her. Looking up, it's all she can do to keep from cringing back at the familiar face.

Leemrons have cat-like features and tend to be a friendly family-orientated species, but not this one. He embodies just about everything horrible about the slave market.

"Still not sold, I see," he purrs to her with a toothy smile. He runs many of the low-cost local bordellos and because of the nature of his clientele, he is constantly on the lookout for cheap slaves as his stock is depleted by clients. He likes small females the best. She overheard him talking to another buyer the other day when he mentioned the species his clients like the best. Humans were on the list.

Thankfully she's still too expensive for him, but if she isn't sold soon at the price posted, she's sure he'll be able to bargain her price down.

"I've had several interested buyers make inquiries today," she lies, casting her eyes down. He gives a coughing hiss, which she knows is the Leemron version of a laugh.

"And what skills have you told them you possess?" he asks her. "Can you pilot? Tutor children? Craft exotic metals or stones? Perhaps you can cook?" He laughs again when she flinches at the last word. He knows she doesn't have any skill sets. Unless a slave is highly exotic or a good breeder, a lack of skill sets equals a cheap price. Unfortunately, even though she could be considered an exotic in this area of the galaxy, humans aren't well-known enough to be sought after. She's too exotic to collect, apparently.

Except for brothel owners who like cheap products.

"Tomorrow is clearing day," he announces, as if she and every other slave didn't already know and aren't dreading it. Clearing day, also referred to as stock day, is when the bigger ships come in with any stock they want to unload. The market is flooded with new slaves, and old products like her usually have their price lowered just to make room. This Leemron is waiting for clearing day.

Clearing day might be the last day she gets to be alive.

CHAPTER 2

Searin

Searin, Prime Son and potential heir to the monarchy, tells himself he isn't sneaking into his friend's menagerie to cuddle his pet human, Mari.

Prime Sons don't sneak anywhere.

They stride with purpose and no guilt.

His actions are above reproach. He's simply checking on her while Tieno is away on a diplomatic mission. It's only polite that he looks after his good friends' pets, especially the sweet human who is always eager to crawl into his lap and give him one of her human clutches.

In a society where touching for anything but combat or healing is seen as a weakness, and affection is an unnecessary distraction, Searin can't admit to himself, let alone anyone else, that he's drawn to Tieno's soft pet for anything else but a practical purpose.

If he holds her in his lap, it's an efficient way to check her health. If he hugs her to his chest, he can feel her body temperature, her heartbeat, and assess her general well-being. Besides, humans need a great deal of body contact and petting to remain healthy, especially the females. He's providing Tieno's pet with something she requires.

That he's avoiding Tieno's house so the man's family can't draw him into a discussion or invite him for a meal only means he doesn't feel like interacting with fellow Talins today. It doesn't mean he's sneaking anywhere.

The little human makes a cheerful sound when she sees him and hurries over to the cage door.

"Prime Son Searin, I didn't expect to see you today." Her human voice is a much higher pitch than a Talin's and contains a musical quality to it. Although she is only the third human he's ever interacted with, he knows she's of typical size for human females from his research on the species. Even though all Talins tower over her, she never seems intimidated by any of them.

The Hiko bird in the cage next to hers gives a loud screech. She turns her head to scowl at it. "Hush, you," she calls out. "It's not food time yet."

The bird settles with a little squawk, and she turns her attention back to him. "It's an honor to see you, Prime Son."

"I've come to check on you while Tieno's away," Searin explains.

She gives a small pout. "It's nice to see you, but I miss Master."

"He's still gone," Searin tells her and unlocks the gate. "I'm here for now."

Her enclosure is the largest in Tieno's menagerie with an expansive outdoor space decorated with several flowering trees and elaborate garden adornments. Her indoor sleeping area is far grander than the little female needs, and she even has indoor bathing facilities with access to warm water for her delicate human skin.

"Then I'll be content with your visit," she says. Placing a finger on the door's display, he waits for the mechanism to recognize him. The door's biolock is keyed to very few, and he's one of those privileged enough to be allowed entry. Mari's much too valuable and easily hurt to let just anyone have access to her. Searin feels honored to be one of the few Talins Tieno trusts with her.

She takes a few steps back as he enters her enclosure and gives him one of her toothy human smiles. She's done this every time he visits and while he knows it's not a threat display, he can't understand why any species with such flat teeth would want to show them off.

"Did you bring me anything?" she asks, her eyes going to his belt pouch.

"I only brought myself this visit," he says. "But I'll make sure to have a treat for you next time."

"That would be nice!" she agrees, keeping her distance.

She doesn't approach him until he sits down on one of the Talin-sized stone benches in her enclosure. Once he's situated, she slowly crosses to him and crawls into his lap.

"You can cling to me, if you wish," he offers.

Her smile dims a little before she wraps her arms around his thick neck. She rests her head on his shoulder, near the exposed area where his chest plates meet his neck plates.

He goes perfectly still as her warm breath wafts across his skin. It's a pleasant sensation he's come to associate with Mari.

"I'm going to make sure you stay secure in my lap," he warns her.

She hums a sound that he thinks means agreement. Humans lack back plates or chestboxes to convey emotions. Oddly enough, they display emotions with their facial expressions, which could be hard to interpret.

"Was that acceptance?" he asks.

"You can hug me back," she agrees. "Thanks for asking."

"This isn't a hug," he argues as he wraps arms around her torso, careful to keep the defensive quills on his forearm down so he doesn't accidentally hurt her. He doesn't even need to think about keeping his claws retracted. That happens naturally as his hands stroke down her back. "I'm only doing this to keep you safe from a fall."

"If you say so," she says, and then he hears the sound that indicates humor. Tieno calls it laughter.

He can't understand what the little human finds funny, but he's happy that she's amused. "I do say so."

She's covered in Tieno's scent. He must have marked her strongly just before he left for the scent to linger.

The scent glands in Searin's cheeks swell and become uncomfortable as he fights his instinct to mark her and cover Tieno's scent. Not only would it be rude, but it might hurt her. Humans can become accustomed and even addicted to their owner's scent. Being exposed to another's can make them uncomfortable to the point of illness.

He wouldn't ever do anything that might cause Mari pain. And he certainly wouldn't betray Tieno's trust by marking her as his own.

They sit in silence for a while, and Searin feels a pressure lift from his chest. Visiting Tieno's pet human and holding her always does that for him and makes him feel some semblance of peace. When she's perched in his lap and twines her weak human arms around him, it's as if he can finally take a full breath, expanding his lungs after spending too much time forced to breathe shallowly.

"When will Master be home?" Her words make his chest tighten a little. He doesn't want her thinking about Tieno. He wants her to be content with just him.

"Soon," he assures her and gives her a little squeeze with his arms. By now he knows how much pressure is just right for her delicate frame and is rewarded for his efforts when she gives a little sigh of contentment and snuggles against him. Humans are a blessed group, he thinks, so free and uninhibited with their affection.

His mother started collecting humans a decade ago, but he's never been allowed near them. He was told it's because they're delicate and prone to panic when strangers are introduced. He thinks it's more likely that his mother is greedy with their attention.

Everyone knows humans bond to only one or two Talins. The last thing his mother would want is any of her humans bonding with someone besides her.

It's sad to think his mother might be so petty, but it's the most logical reason to keep him away.

That's why he never bothers visiting his mother's wing of the palace anymore. He visits the royal house but meets both parents in the center rooms instead of venturing into the private west or east wing.

Even then the visits are brief and factual. It's rare they'll even sit down. He speaks, they give advice, and he leaves.

Neither parent is interested in interacting with him outside of his duties. The only draw to go to the palace outside of work would be to let a little human sit in his lap and clutch at him. Being denied admission to the area where his mother's human pets are housed feels like a far worse injury than the cold interaction with his mother and father.

A rumble of curiosity sounds from the gate, drawing their attention to the male standing there. "And what's going on here?"

Mari gives a little cry of joy at the sound of the familiar voice. Sitting up she pushes at Searin arms. He lets go and means to set her on the ground, but she's already scrambling off his lap. She runs to the gate where Tieno is walking in with a small bag of something in his hand.

"Master!" She jumps into his arms, and he catches her easily, lifting her up to cradle in his arms. The moment she's in his arms, he starts up a soothing rumble.

Unlike when she was in Searin's lap, she doesn't simply rest her head on Tieno's shoulder. She nuzzles her face into his neck and clings to him with arms and legs.

As Searin watches her interact with Tieno, he touches the patch of skin she warmed with her breath only moments ago and tries to deny the bereft feeling rising in him.

"I missed you too," Tieno says as he rubs the scent glands in his cheeks into her hair. Once his scent glands are empty, Mari brings both hands up to vigorously rub Tieno's scent into her hair and scalp. Searin notices that Tieno's scent changes slightly as it soaks into Mari. The changed scent seems to draw contented sounds from both of them.

The moment between them is tender, and suddenly Searin feels like a voyeur. The brief time he got to spend with Mari pales compared to the affection she has for her owner.

When Tieno slides his gaze over to meet Searin's, he feels a little like a youth caught acting badly.

In an attempt to dismiss any sense of guilt, Searin stands tall and strides over to his friend without sparing a glance for Mari cuddled in his arms. He strikes his chest with his fist in greeting, the sound vibrating off his chest plates. Tieno shifts his pet onto his hip so he can return the greeting.

"Why am I not surprised to find you visiting my menagerie?" Tieno asks as he makes his way to the bench Searin just vacated. He sits down and sounds a rumble of humor as Mari grabs for the bag in his hand. She opens it and gives a delighted laugh.

"Don't eat them all at once," Tieno admonishes her as she pulls a small red fruit out of the bag. Searin can't remember the name of the food but knows it's Mari's favorite.

Tieno told him once he attempted to grow the fruit in the family garden, but the plant isn't native to Talarian. Unsurprisingly the plant didn't take, so when he can, he imports the fruit instead.

Searin knows for a fact it costs almost as much to import a small amount of the little fruit as it does to buy Mari an entire year of regular human feed. But considering the immense pleasure Mari receives from eating the sweet exotic fruit, Searin would probably spoil her in the same way.

"Thank you!" she cries out, then showers Tieno's face with lip presses. Once she feels she's shown enough affection, she settles down in his lap to consume the fruit with delicate greed.

Even when he brings her treats, she never graces Searin with any lip presses.

Unwilling to leave just yet, even though he knows Mari won't come near him now that Tieno is home, Searin leans against a nearby tree and regards Tieno with interest. "You're back early."

"Talks went well and a new contract with the Rekam station is now ready to be submitted to the Apogee Assembly and the monarch."

"That was fast. I didn't expect you to finish for at least another few rotations."

Tieno sounds another amused rumble. "My Delorta counterpart is newly mated and eager to return to her mate, which made negotiations easy."

Searin knows he should compliment Tieno on the rapid conclusion of his assignment, but all he can feel is disappointment that his good friend is back and Mari no longer needs him to visit or care for her.

"You've been gone for a while and I know Rekam doesn't have good training facilities. Come spar with me. You look weak," Searin challenges. He can feel the familiar tight tension building in his chest again and knows the only way to get rid of it, besides access to Mari, is to work his body to exhaustion.

Instead of responding to the barb, Tieno sounds a rumble of concern as he strokes his fingers through Mari's lush mane. Mari has stopped eating her fruit and is watching the two of them with wary curiosity.

"You're not happy," Tieno finally comments.

The whooshing snap of a mocking rattle sounds from Searin's back plates. "I wasn't born to be happy. Members of the Prime family are born to 'serve our people with honor and courage,'" Searin responds, parroting the monarchy slogan.

Tieno's gaze doesn't waver, and Searin finds he needs to look away.

He reaches down to pluck a flower out of a nearby pot and then leans over to tuck it behind Mari's ear. She sometimes decorates her hair with colorful things, and he hopes the gesture will make her happy. She gives him one of her human smiles, but he can tell it's not a real one.

When she feels genuine happiness, her smile is wider and the skin around her eyes crinkles. This time he only sees a quick flash of her flat white teeth and then she's turning her face into Tieno's neck, cuddling her body into him and avoiding Searin's eyes.

She rests the bag of fruit in her lap and puts both her arms around Tieno, whispering something to him as he wraps his arms around her. Tieno sounds a soothing rumble and then absently rubs the empty scent gland in his cheek against the top of her head.

Feeling rejected, Searing steps away and crosses his arms over his chest. It takes effort to keep from rattling with irritation.

I just want to spar, he tells himself. *I'm annoyed because Tieno is getting soft and not practicing enough. My mood has nothing to do with Mari wanting her master more than me.*

"I've been away, and I want to spend time with Mari," Tieno tells him. "I'm not interested in sparing at the moment. But I've been thinking. There is an old menagerie facility on your property. Why don't you fix it up? Start collecting yourself. You obviously enjoy my collection. Wouldn't it be nice to have one of your own close at hand?"

Searin feels his shoulders go stiff at the suggestion, and his gaze drops to Mari again. Why didn't he think of that? All Talins are expected to have some kind of hobby outside of work and training. Many pursue academic degrees, but building a collection of exotic pets or breeding specific animals is also common.

No one gave it a second thought when Tieno built his enclosures and bought pets. No one sees it as odd that he spends so much time in his menagerie. As long as his work and training are not neglected, not a single Talin would think his time spent at his leisure interest is anything but appropriate and healthy.

"Yes," Searin responds thoughtfully. "I could do that."

Mari gives a little sound of distress, and Tieno hugs her gently. "I'm not going to sell you," he assures her, and she relaxes back against him. "I would never sell you."

Searin wonders how Tieno knew that was her concern, but perhaps that's always the concern for slaves and pets. That begs the question of where Tieno bought his human and if they have another one like her. "Where did you get Mari?"

"It was a private sale," Tieno admits. "Makarian had to sell his menagerie off. He was given a permanent assignment on his clan's battle cruiser and couldn't take any of his humans with him. He didn't trust his family to care for them. I only got to buy Mari after she interacted with me a few times and Makarian was sure she would be happy and I'd take good care of her."

"Master Makie was nice," Mari murmurs, her voice muffled against Tieno's neck. "But he never brought me back the best fruit in the universe."

Tieno sounds another rumble of amusement and pets her back. "Does that mean I'm your most favorite master?"

"You're the master I love," Mari tells him. Love is the human word for scent-bonding or their closest approximation.

Her words make Searin feel an odd sensation. It's a moment before he realizes the feeling is jealousy. He wants a pet human to say the same thing to him.

It's socially acceptable, and even encouraged, for pets to scent-bond to their masters. They're weak and vulnerable. It's only natural that they'd give in to such a base feeling. In fact, Tieno once told him that owners sometimes brag about how strongly scent-bonded their pets are. Some humans even have water fall from their eyes from distress when their owners leave.

What would it be like to have a human shed water from her eyes because she doesn't wish him to go? He'd be very gentle with her, make sure she didn't shed too much water. Maybe even hire a dedicated keeper to look after her if he has to travel. Then, when he comes back, she will rush to him just like Mari rushes to Tieno, eager for attention and touches.

"I didn't know your love could be bought with some fruit," Tieno teases, his words bringing Searin out of his thoughts. Mari looks up at him with serious eyes.

"It can't," she says simply. "It's the only thing from me that can't be bought."

Tieno takes a sharp breath, squeezes her tightly against his chest, and nuzzles his face into her hair. His chestbox rumbles out a sound of affection. Mari refers to several types of rumbles as purring, and this is one of them.

"Sweet little human, my life was cold before you," he murmurs.

Suddenly Searin doesn't want to be here any longer. The pleasant feeling he experienced when holding Mari is long gone, replaced with tension, jealousy, and longing. If he leaves, the tension will still be there, but the jealousy and longing should diminish.

As he's about to go, Tieno calls out.

"Tomorrow, meet me at the North Dock at second mark. We'll go to the auction house on Starn station. I received a ping from one of the auction houses that a human might be there. I wouldn't bother going but…." His sentence trails off as Searin rattles his back plates in agreement.

"Yes," Searin nearly shouts. "Yes, we're going."

"Excellent. We'll find you a human to start your menagerie," Tieno states with a strong, decisive rattle. "You have today to get at least one pen ready. I suggest you hurry."

"Yes." Feeling a little overwhelmed as he thinks of all the things he must get done before the day's end, he fumbles with the gate release. "Yes, of course."

He hears Mari and Tieno talking to each other in muted voices as he leaves, but he's not interested in interacting with either of them any longer. He has an entirely different focus now, and it seems to keep the ever-present tension in his chest from consuming him.

He won't even let himself contemplate the idea that there might not be a soft human female to buy. If he has to, he'll steal one from someone else's collection here on Talin.

After all, he's the Prime Son. Many would willingly give up a human to him, hoping to gain favors from the Prime Family later. He's never thought of sinking so low as to use his status to gain personal use items, but now that the idea's in his head, he'll stop at nothing to gain a human.

There is no scenario where he will not come home with a pet tomorrow.

CHAPTER 3

Searin

Searin sounds a rattle of frustration as he and Tieno walk around the auction house. The place is crowded, and he's already been bumped into several times. Even worse, they've seen every kind of animal and slave but no humans.

They're almost to the end of the second to last row and he's starting to despair. They found the seller that contacted Tieno, but he didn't have a human. It was a many-armed species often used on farms to pick fruits from tall trees. Except for being bipedal, it looked nothing like a human. Searin almost ripped the seller's head off his body out of sheer disappointment. Now they're wandering the auction, hoping to run across a human.

If the items list was accurate, it would be easy to check for humans. But the species is often mislabeled, so now they walk from stall to stall, his hope shrinking each time.

Any human will do, Searin thinks.

He takes a few breaths, trying to get his lungs to expand past the tension in his chest. It feels like his chest plates are all fused together and don't want to move.

It's as if he's slowly suffocating, one shallow breath at a time.

"There!" Tieno exclaims and hurries off so fast Searin almost loses him in the crowd.

Chasing after him, he can't see what caused Tieno to shout until he passes a thick group of Leemrons. At the end of a row of slaves he finds what his friend spotted; a small, scrawny human female tethered to a pole.

He almost rattles his back plates in excitement at the sight and breaks into a lope to catch up to Tieno. Together they reach the human. It's a female and appears to be an adult of breeding age.

The human flinches at their abrupt arrival, and Searin has to check his desire to embrace her before they've even spoken.

He knows from dealing with Mari that the humans like it better when they are invited to touch or be touched instead of being grabbed. Also, this human doesn't know him and might even be a little afraid or intimidated by his size.

He and Tieno tower over most of the species at the auction. Not only are they tall, but full-grown Talin with fully developed plating are fierce and intimidating creatures. He can't fault this little, soft female for being cautious.

"She looks healthy," Tieno declares.

The female gives them a tentative smile, careful not to show any teeth. "Hello."

Tieno nods with satisfaction. "Good, she's got a translator implant. That makes this much easier. I've heard that some wild-caught humans don't have them and it can be an uncomfortable process for the adults."

"My implant has all the most common languages," the human tells them eagerly. "I can read Universal, Dalantee, and a little Nemon. And I even know the silent tapping language of the Norka."

Searin doesn't care about this human's knowledge or skill set, so he brushes off her eager speech with an impatient clatter of his back plates.

The human pales and draws back at the sound, her tether pulling taut and choking her a little. Silently calling himself a fool, he quiets his back plates. He doesn't mean to scare her.

"Searin," Tieno says with censure. The warning is unnecessary. Searin's already switched to a gentle, soothing rumble from his chestbox.

"Hello, human," he says and steps forward, opening his arms to invite her to cling to him. Instead of moving toward him, the human stays frozen in place, watching him with wide eyes.

Searin drops his arms in disappointment. Is this little human defective? She's smaller than even Mari, with a dark brown mane as opposed to Mari's light golden mane. And her skin is slightly darker than Mari's, with eyes much larger than Tieno's human. Although he's not as skilled at reading human facial expressions as his friend, he can tell hers is one of fear instead of interest.

"Remove your covering garments for us," Tieno commands gently and Searin gives his friend a sharp glace.

Tieno looks over to Searin and gives him a annoyed rattle, warning him to be patient. Tieno is the expert on humans, so Searin remains silent and lets his good friend take the lead. Perhaps something might be hidden by her clothes that will tell them if she is defective.

The female is shaking now, but she takes a small step forward to release the pressure on her collar. Then she grasps the hemp of her dress and lifts until the fabric is bunched around her shoulders.

Searin barely keeps from rattling all his armor plates in anger as he sees the state of her body. She's much too thin. Where Mari is round and soft, this human's rib and hip bones jut out.

When Tieno asks her to turn in a circle, he sees old scars on her back. She also has deep bruising around wounds still healing. One wound is so fresh it's still scabbed with blood. She also has old welts on her thighs in the last stages of healing.

No wonder she's fearful. Someone hurt her badly, and her body still bears the marks. He wants to snatch the little female up and guard her, rattling out a loud challenge to everyone around. Instead, he clenches his hands into tight fists and waits for Tieno to speak.

"You can pull your garment back down, female," Tieno tells her gently and draws Searin away. He doesn't want to leave the little female, but Tieno needs to tell him something outside the hearing of both the female and the approaching seller.

"She's been abused," Tieno whispers to him. "She'll be scared and cautious. She won't be like Mari, who grew up loved by her dam and sheltered by her owner. I'll understand if you don't want to buy her. She might never be very affectionate, especially if she was taken from her dam too young. The parents teach the young how to show fondness and adoration. She might have been denied that training."

Searin glances over the human's head to see her price displayed on the pole she's attached to. It's a low number, probably because the seller knows he's got damaged goods.

He turns his worried gaze back to Tieno. "Do you think it's truly that bad? She's underweight, but that's easy to fix. Do you think if she's well-fed, and no longer abused, she might become more trusting and demonstrative?"

"I don't know," Tieno responds with a look back at the female.

Searin follows his gaze and notices her staring at them with both hope and fear. Poor little human. What kind of treatment has she already endured?

"I don't want to hurt her further," Searin confesses as he runs his eyes over her delicate frame, now half-hidden by the ugly gray garment.

"You won't," Tieno assures him. "You are a male of honor, so I know you can be patient with her. But if you decide not to buy her, I will. Mari might like a fellow human, and I can refurbish the cage next to hers for this one. I've been thinking of selling that damn bird anyway. It's too loud and sometimes it disturbs Mari's sleep."

The idea of Tieno buying the female doesn't sit well with Searin and he clatters the armor plates down his spine in a sound of displeasure.

Tieno rumbles out a laugh. "Or you can buy her," he says knowingly. "I just wanted to make sure you're aware that you might be buying a human who won't ever be quite right."

"It doesn't matter. She needs a better home, and I have an enclosure ready. And I've already purchased food and soft bedding. I'll take good care of her."

Tieno gives a satisfied rumble. "You're making a good choice. I know you'll do right by her, even if she isn't exactly what you want. And I'm available to help if you need."

"Maybe eventually I can bring her for a visit to Mari," Searin comments, seeing a future when he could take his new pet out in public for trips.

When Tieno's sister and mother aren't home, he brings Mari into the house to keep him company while he works. Searin wants to do the same thing.

He can already see her, sitting on a soft pad next to his workstation and smiling up at him with sleepy contentment. He could reach down and pet her or pull her into his lap any time he wished. It makes him want to sound a rumble of pleasure.

"Don't expect anything to happen too quickly," Tieno advises, his words bringing Searin out of his pleasant thoughts. "I have a feeling trust will come slowly to this one. Some of those scars look like they're old. She's got a long history of abuse by her previous owner or owners, so she'll be skittish for a while. Perhaps even uncooperative. I wouldn't let her out of her enclosure alone for at least a score of rotations. Maybe not ever."

Searin tensed. "Do you think she'd try to run away?"

"Probably not, but I'd be extra cautious with her at first anyway," Tieno states diplomatically.

Searin nods, accepting Tieno's advice. "Very well. I'll keep her well-contained while she adjusts."

"Honorable ones," the seller says as he sidles up to them. "I see you are looking at the human. She's a well-behaved, friendly slave. Her former master tells me she never gave him any trouble. Unfortunately, she doesn't have any skill sets, but she's clever and can be taught."

Tieno scowls at the Veli seller and gestures to the price with a threatening rattle of his chest plates. "I refuse to pay so much for an unskilled human."

Searin just barely keeps from reacting to Tieno's words. But he trusts no other as much as Tieno, not even his own family, so he remains quiet and listens.

Tieno's strategy becomes clear as his good friend teases out information from the seller about the human's former owner and history. Those things are often kept quiet if there is any question about the legality of the sale.

As Tieno gets the seller to talk, it becomes apparent that the original sale of this human was questionable. She wasn't born a slave but was sold by a family member when she was a child.

How abhorrent.

The more he hears, the more agitated he becomes until it's all he can do to keep from tossing the seller away from him.

While they're talking a Leemron saunters up to the human, licking his lips and showing off sharp teeth. As Searin watches, the Leemron says something that makes her edge away.

The little human says something back to the Leemron and nods her head to where he, Tieno, and the seller are standing. The Leemron looks over, glowers at them, and then grabs the female by her mane. With his grip on her mane, he drags her forward until her collar is choking her.

"No!" Searin roars, his back plating sounding a thunderous war rattle.

Charging forward, he grabs the Leemron around the throat and easily throws the much smaller creature far down the row, mowing down several bystanders in the process. Once the Leemron is out of sight, his entire focus turns to the human.

She's coughing, and her whole body is trembling so badly that Searin snatches her up in his arms, fearful she'll collapse and choke herself further on the tethered collar. She gives a little gasp but doesn't fight his hold. He notes her eyes are tightly shut and her body stiff against him.

"Release her now," he orders as the seller and Tieno move to stand at his side.

"But we haven't reached an accord," the seller protests, and Searin sounds another war rattle loud enough to echo in the room.

"Now!" he roars and regrets it when the fearful human cringes in his arms.

With a whimper of fear, she curls into herself. Drawing her knees to her chest, she wraps her arms over her face as if to protect herself. Now he's holding a tight little ball of frightened human.

He tries to soften his war rattle, but his rage is just too great to contain. "I will lay waste to your family, clan, and species if her collar is not taken off right now!"

"We will pay the asking price," Tieno tells the seller. "But I think moving in haste would be wise right now."

"Yes, of course. Yes, here it is," the seller fumbles on his person until he produces the key to the human's collar. He swipes the small square over the collar and it clicks open, revealing fresh bruising.

Seeing the sorry state of his human's neck, Searin wants to shove the seller out of the nearest airlock. But that would require letting go of his human.

Unless under actual physical attack, he's not going to put her down until he has her safely settled in her enclosure on his property. No place is safe at all for such a delicate creature except under his care.

She's lucky he found her. He vows that even if she is broken and cannot be taught to clutch or lip press as Mari does, he will care for her. She won't go to another who will mistreat her. She doesn't know it yet, but she's safe now.

"According to the auction house rules she needs to wear a collar to leave," the seller tells them as he stumbles back. "And you need to sign the return agreement stipulation and transfer of property agreement."

Searin looks over to Tieno, who gives a small nod and grabs his Identification Cube to complete the transaction on Searin's behalf. More often referred to as Idents, these devices act as a combination of communication device, locator, and identity verifier, recorder, and method of payment, among other things.

As is the custom among Talins, Tieno keeps his clipped to his belt and easily pulls it free to wave it at the greedy merchant.

With Tieno taking care of the details, Searin's free to take a few long strides to a nearby platform and sit down so his human can rest on his lap. Once they're settled, he strokes her head, trying to get her to relax enough to show her face. It's difficult but he stops his war rattle and starts up a soothing rumble.

"You're secure now," he assures her. "I'll keep you protected."

Slowly, she draws her arms away from her face. "I'm sorry I displeased you." Her voice is a tentative whisper.

Why is that the first thing she says? "I'm not displeased with you. But it would make me happy if you would sit up and bare your neck for me."

She hesitates for a moment, glancing over to where Tieno and the seller are talking. "Do you own me now?"

His soothing rumble is interrupted to sound a rumble of agreement. "Yes, I'm your new master. And you're my human."

Still trembling, she sits up. Searin can see she's trying to calm her body. "Thank you, Master. I'm ready for my new collar."

Reaching up, she pulls her shoulder-length dark mane together and holds it piled on top of her head with one hand to give him better access to her neck.

Searin hesitates. He doesn't want to put a new collar on her while her neck is covered in bruises, but he doesn't want to delay leaving the busy auction house either.

He pulls out the delicate jeweled collar he bought at a kiosk that morning while he waited for Tieno at the docks. He secures it loosely around her neck, running a finger between it and her skin to make sure he leaves plenty of room. Once he pulls his hands away, she lets go of her mane and feels the collar at her throat.

She gives him a surprised look. "It's not a disciplinary collar."

"Of course not," he responds with a rattle. "Why would I ever need to shock you?"

She looks at him now, really taking in his appearance. Her gaze roams over the armor plating on his chest and the quills on his forearms. Tentatively she reaches out to touch one, and he moves his forearm a little so she can better examine it.

"Don't touch the tip. It's very sharp," he warns her. "I'll always keep them flat around you, but you must be careful not to catch your skin on the end and hurt yourself."

"I guess you don't have to worry about anyone attacking you. You might be the deadliest sentient species I've ever met."

"We're effective warriors, even without added weapons and armor. Have you ever attacked an owner?" He doesn't care if she has. And if her attack was reprisal for a beating, it might have been warranted.

She shakes her head. "I'm a good slave," she tells him quickly. "I would never attack my master. I promise to be very useful and hardworking for you."

Her words make him hopeful. She doesn't sound broken or unwilling. He wraps his arm loosely around her, letting her get used to the feel of him.

"There is no need to talk of work."

"As you wish, Master," she responds. She sits stiffly in his embrace, but at least she isn't trying to wiggle away. Her words are obedient, but her tone isn't enthusiastic or happy.

She probably doesn't realize she won't be abused. In time, she'll come to understand she's safe and will be well cared for. Eventually, she'll relax and become happy like Mari.

She might be sitting tensely and stiffly in his lap, with her head held high instead of resting on him, but she's still having an effect. The tension he normally carries in his chest is easing a little.

He can breathe! He pulls in a deep breath, enjoying the way it feels to fill his lungs.

Tieno appears at his side, his quills sitting up with agitation. "That seller has no honor," he declares. "He was going to sell her to a meat bordello."

"I wish I could challenge the seller and that Leemron," he grits out, his back plates rattling with irritation.

The female draws a little away from him, so he focuses curbing his temper. It's not like him to be so out of control. For the sake of his new pet, he needs to rein in his emotions.

"You'll find out in time that I'll never strike you," he assures her.

Tieno crouches down so his eyes are level with the human. "Are you in pain, little one? Does anything feel broken? Are you having any problems breathing or swallowing?"

Before answering, she looks to Searin for guidance and he feels pleasure at that look. "You can talk to Tieno. Outside of me, he is one you can utterly trust."

She gives a little nod and turns her attention back to Tieno. "I'm well, Master Tieno. My throat doesn't hurt. I can breathe and swallow without pain."

"I highly doubt that it's without pain, but I can see you're functioning adequately. When was the last time you were seen by a healer?" As he asks, he reaches up to tilt her head a little to better see the side of her neck. The bruising is the worst there, going from the bottom of her neck to her jawline.

"I've never been to a healer."

Tieno looks at him as he lets go of her face. "She needs to see one tomorrow to evaluate her health and to get the proper import paperwork completed."

Searin sounds a rumble of agreement. He's already thinking the same thing. "I'll make it happen."

Tieno stands up and looks around the crowded room with a disgusted expression. "Let's get out of here," he says. "I feel filthy from just having walked these rows."

With a rumble of agreement, Searin stands, keeping his human held protectively against his chest. She gives a little start. He pauses, looking at her inquiringly.

"I can walk, Master," she tells him. "I'll keep one step behind you as is fitting."

Searin manages to keep himself from rattling out a negative sound. He needs to keep his plates silent until she can get accustomed to the noises Talins make. She wouldn't be the first species to find their noises disconcerting.

"I'll carry you. I don't want you to get lost in the crowd or accidentally hurt. It's safer if I hold you."

Keeping her safe is only part of the reason he wants to carry her. He doesn't want to let go of her soft, warm body.

He pulls in her scent as they walk. Her smell is a strange combination of the filth from the auction around them and her human scent. He can't wait to bathe her so she just smells of her clean human scent. Then he thinks about rubbing his scent glands on her. Mixing her scent with his.

It's not something a Talin is supposed to do in public. Rubbing bonding oil from the scent gland in his cheek on his new human should be in the privacy of his new home.

But this isn't Talarian. It's a massive auction house, and he hasn't seen another Talin the entire time he and Tieno have been here. There's no one to see his taboo actions.

Giving in to temptation, he leans his head down and rubs one of his scent glands against the top of her head. She doesn't object or flinch as the oil spreads across her hair.

In fact, after taking a few deep breaths in through her nose, she seems to relax. His pet is already responding positively to him.

With satisfaction, he strides off to follow Tieno, the tension in his chest lighter than it's been all day.

CHAPTER 4

Sora

It's dark by the time they reach her new master's home. She can't see much as he carries her. The ornamental lighting on the winding garden path is more artistic than practical, but she recognizes cages as the path flows into an area sheltered by a high stone wall.

All the cages seem to be empty, including the one he walks her into. He kicks the door closed behind him and then walks into a small hut within the cage. The inside is lit by similar lighting as the path, casting odd shadows all around the room.

A large nest sits in one corner and he gently sets her down on it. It's made of soft warm blankets and strewn with colorful pillows. The thing is large enough to accommodate two Talins and seems overkill for one small human.

The sight of the bed-bed makes Sora wonder if she has been sold for sex as well as labor. She can only hope that Talins' sex organs won't do her damage or be too large. She knows some species have barbs or hooks on their penises. If it's simply large, she can handle that. It can't be any more painful than being whipped. But if he has barbs, she might be seriously injured.

To her relief, instead of getting on top of her or sitting on the nest-bed next to her, he crouches in front of her, much like Master Tieno did at the auction house.

He regards her silently for a few moments. She wishes she knew more about Talins, but today is the first time she's interacted with the species. Their distinct lack of facial expressions is disconcerting. It's a relief when he finally speaks.

"This is your new home. You need to tell me if anything doesn't work or bothers you. And you need to tell me if you lack anything. I'm new to owning a human, but I swear I'll take good care of you."

His speech is another surprising thing to happen to her today. She's lost count of how many times she's been shocked since the two large, half-naked, Talin males rushed up to her at the auction house.

As a slave she didn't expect to be treated so well. They'd fed her repeatedly during the trip back. They'd constantly checked in on her pain levels. She was being cared for like a beloved family member.

It was all too good to be true. She knows something bad is coming. Being a slave means pain. Sometimes the pain is minor discomfort, like missed meals, bruises, or aches from overwork. Sometimes the pain is severe and deliberate.

She's not sure what flavor of pain she will suffer from this large owner, but she's wary and knows better than to voice any complaints or requests. She tries to look content and grateful instead of anxious and worried.

"Thank you, Master. I'll tell you if there is anything wrong," she lies.

He goes silent again, the light in the room casting grotesque shadows on the harsh planes of his face. Her new master isn't ugly, but he is a member of an intimidating species.

"Do you have a name?" he asks. "Or should I give you a name?"

They'd been together for almost an entire day and only now was he curious about her name. She'd find it funny if it wasn't a common experience for her.

"I'm called Sora, but you can rename me if you wish. I know I'll like any name you pick."

She would hate to give up her name. The only thing she still has from her life before slavery is the name her mother gave her. She associates it with a happy childhood before her mother died.

But survival means being willing to even give up the last of her identity, and she's determined to survive.

"Sora is a good name," her new master tells her. "You may call me Searin."

"Yes, Master Searin," she replies and drops her gaze, realizing with a start that she's been looking him in the eyes this entire time. He hasn't reprimanded her for it yet, but she's not sure if he's making allowances because she's new to him, or if he doesn't mind. Better to err on the side of caution and keep her eyes mostly downcast.

"I know this is all new, and Tieno advised me to go slowly with you, but I find I have no patience."

His words make her stiffen. What does he need patience for? He never told her what work she would be doing, and she's suspicious at the lack of slaves in the other pens.

Do his words mean that he's going to hurt her now?

"I want to hold you again. I want you to put your arms around my neck and clutch to me, as humans do," he tells her. "Can you do that without pain?"

Of all the things he might request, that's not what she expects at all. She nods her head. "Yes, Master."

As he stands up, he plucks her from the nest, and sits down in a nearby backless chair. She ends up sitting sideways on his lap.

The smell of cinnamon fills her nose. It takes her a moment to realize the smell is coming from him. She'd caught the whiff of coffee from her master's friend Tieno, but she likes Searin's cinnamon smell better.

Filling her lungs with his scent, she twists her torso a bit, and she eases her arms over his shoulder and around his neck.

She's not sure how hard he wants her to hug, so she keeps her hold light. She braces herself as he wraps his massive, quilled arms around her.

Pain blossoms in her back as his arms put pressure on her welts and wounds irritated from being carried about all day. She's braced for the pain, so she's able to keep herself from reacting.

She's rewarded when she feels him vibrate with a soft continuous purring sound. It's obvious to her, even after a short time among them, that she must learn to read the noises they make. Once she learns all their sounds, she'll be able to judge her new master's moods.

The roaring and deafening rattle at the auction house were clear enough, but this new sound seems to her to be one of contentment.

He strokes a broad hand down her back, and for the first few motions she's able to remain silent, but his hands run the length of one of the fresher wounds and she can't help but flinch at the pain.

He freezes, and she curses her lack of discipline. She couldn't endure the lesser pain, so now she will have to suffer a greater one. She waits for him to roar, toss her aside and strike out at her.

The last shock of the day occurs when he does none of those things. Instead, he pulls his hands away from her back and puts them on her shoulders, tugging her upper body away from his so he can see her face. The rumbling sound he makes changes from a purr to a thumping bass drum being struck slowly from far away.

"I forgot that you're wounded and I hurt you. I'm sorry, I will be better at taking care of you in the future."

Does this mean that the distant bass drum sound was one of worry? Regret? Concern? Maybe it could be all three.

"I'm fine, Master," she rushed to say and held her arms out. "I can hug, uh, cling to you more."

"Not now, little human. Rest tonight and tomorrow I'll make you better."

Then he sets her in the nest and leaves.

CHAPTER 5

Sora

Sora didn't sleep well that night. Despite being exhausted and having access to a bed more comfortable than she's ever known, she couldn't get her mind to calm. The moment dawn brings light into the hut, she rises to explore her new captivity.

The cage encloses a great deal of space, with several trees and a handful of bushes within its fencing. She even finds a small waterfall and pond, surrounded by beds of flowering plants.

She dips a toe in the pond and finds the water cool but not cold. Looking closely, she notices movement under the water and withdraws her foot quickly. She watches carefully and finally sees a small colorful creature swim close to the surface, nibbling on a leaf floating on the water. The moment she moves, the creature darts away, disappearing deeper into the pool.

She can't imagine the thing is dangerous. It looks much too colorful to be anything but another kind of pet or decoration. But then again, Searin himself admitted he's new to humans, so he might have put something in her enclosure that's not harmful to the armor-plated Talins but deadly to her.

Withdrawing from the pond, she explores the limits of her new home. The plants that cover most of the ground are soft and spongy. They feel good on her bare feet and she drags her soles a few times to enjoy the novel sensation.

Everything looks newly planted and she can even see lines where the ground cover must have been dug up in large rectangles and replanted.

It's been so long since she walked on a planet with a natural sky overhead that she feels a little overwhelmed. Master De kept her aboard his ship to see to his whims as he traveled.

When he wasn't on the ship, she worked as a cleaner and helped the maintenance staff. The other workers weren't unkind to her, but none of them were friendly. They saw her very much as Master De saw her, a mostly useless slave to be ignored or given menial tasks.

She saw a lot of slaves over the years while traveling with Master De who suffered much worse fates than hers. Master De's temper was notorious and destructive, but he never broke her bones or deliberately disfigured her.

He made sure everyone knew he was the only one allowed to abuse her, so when he wasn't around, she was safe from beatings.

Every so often, a species that was sexually compatible with humans would visit him on the ship, but he never let them touch her either. She's under no illusions. Her life as a slave could have been so much worse than what she experienced under Master De.

But he sold her and now she's on a new planet, with a new owner, to serve a new role. She just hopes the duties she's assigned are within her abilities, so she won't need to suffer a brutal learning period.

Returning to her hut, she explores some more. Besides the bed, she makes note of the two chairs and a table, all built to accommodate a much larger Talin. Her feet likely won't touch the ground if she sits on one of the chairs.

The few built-in cabinets in the room are empty until she gets to the bathing room, where the cabinets are full of fluffy drying cloths. She finds a decorative bottle of soap and a few small squares of cloth for scrubbing.

She hasn't bathed in days and debates on doing so now. She doesn't want to be undressed and unprepared when her new master shows up, but at the same time, he would probably prefer her clean.

She curses her stupidity; she should have done this first thing instead of walking about her enclosure and staring at water creatures. She pulls out some soap and a towel before fiddling with the bathing chamber's controls until warm water is raining down on her from the ceiling.

It feels luxurious, but she forces herself to hurry instead of indulging in a long bath.

Not seeing any combs, brushes, or any kind of hair tie, she finger-combs her hair as best she can. She only has her shabby dress to wear, so she puts that back on and winkles her nose a little when the smell of the auction house clinging to the fabric hits her.

She'll wash the garment by hand later. She'll have to hang out naked until it's dry, but that doesn't bother her much. She spent a great deal of time denied clothes under Master De when he was feeling petty.

The day is warm and the sun inviting, so she climbs onto one of the ornately carved stone benches in the sunshine near the cage door. She's getting herself situated when Searin shows up.

The sound that comes from him reminds her of the clatter of tools being dropped on the floor. It has to be surprise at seeing her sitting there. She jumps off the bench and hurries to the door.

"Good morning, Master Searin," she greets him with her eyes on his four-toed bare feet and her head slightly bowed with hands clasped in front of her. She forces herself to be still as he opens the cage door and comes to a halt in front of her. She can see his big hand reach out and touch her still-damp hair.

"You bathed," he observes, but she can't tell by his tone if he's pleased or upset. The quills on his arm are lying flat and he isn't rattling. That must be a good sign. Right?

"Yes, Master."

"Don't do that again," he tells her. She risks a quick glance up, confused. He doesn't wish her to bathe? Was she not supposed to use the facilities in the hut? Perhaps this isn't her cage, and she's only here temporarily.

"I won't bathe," she promises.

He starts purring. "Good. Take off your robe and show me your back.".

She has a hard time pulling up the fabric because her hands have started shaking again. She's not sure why she's so nervous; maybe because she's already done something wrong, and it hasn't even been a full day yet.

She turns as she rucks the dress over her shoulders. He gathers her hair and holds it to the side.

"It's even worse than it looked yesterday," he grumbles.

She's quick to assure him. "It's healing. I promise it won't stop me from doing any tasks."

His plates give a rattle that sounds like a hand slapping a thigh. Anger? Disappointment?

"No tasks for you," he announces. The sound must mean no or indicate a negative answer.

"Pull it back down," he orders and lets go of her hair. She lets go of the faded thin fabric and it falls back into place.

Stepping in front of her, Searin takes her hand and leads her to the bench she was sitting on when he arrived. He sits down, sets a small bowl down next to him, and then draws her into his lap, careful not to put pressure on the wounds or bruises.

"We have time for a morning meal before we need to leave," he explains.

He places an arm around her shoulder, careful to keep the touch high on her back where there's no damage. With the other hand, he plucks a bite of food out of the bowl and holds it to her mouth.

Obediently, she parts her lips to accept the morsel, glad to find it bland. She's eaten some truly horrifying food over the years, and bland is much better than rotting. Unfortunately, the food is tough, and it seems to take forever to chew and swallow that first bite.

He waits patiently for her to finish before he talks. "Is that acceptable? It's the human feed the Committee of Pet Welfare recommends."

She keeps her voice and face neutral as she replies. "It's very good."

"Eat up. Tieno said you'll need to consume double what a normal serving would be until you are at a healthier weight. That would be about ten bowls a rotation."

Ten bowls? That sounds inconceivable. The single bite she ate took more effort than food should require. She can't imagine eating ten full bowls of the stuff.

But of course she won't say no to him. For the first time in her life she's worried about disappointing a master because she might not be able to eat enough! Her life has certainly taken a strange turn.

He holds another bite to her mouth. As she chews, he grabs one of the tan balls of food and pops it into his mouth. She casts a quick look at his face and almost laughs when he spits the food out into a nearby bush.

The rumble that came out of him sounded like two pieces of ripe fruit being smashed together. That had to be the sound for disgust!

"This isn't tasty at all and it's much too tough. I'll find you something better. But you need to eat this for today."

He feeds her another bite and once her lips close around it, he puts his palm under her chin and lifts her face to meet his eyes.

"Are you afraid to look at me?"

She experiences a brief moment of panic. He's asked her a question, but her mouth is full of food and she knows some species find it offensive to see food being chewed.

She goes competently still, unsure what to do when his back plates move, making a high pitch clatter very similar to glass-marbles-clicking-together-in-bag.

"My question caused a dilemma, didn't it?" His tone was lighthearted so the wind chime sound must be one of amusement.

"Finish your bite," he instructs. "I'm so eager with you I'm asking you to do two things at once. You can't talk and eat." She nods and tries to hurry her chewing, but the food is difficult and it seems ages before she can swallow it.

"I don't want to displease you," she explains. He looks confused for a moment but then sounds a rumble that sounds like a bunch of people snapping their fingers. His next words clarify in her head that this sound is one of comprehension.

"Your former master must not have let you meet his gaze."

"I wasn't to look anyone in the eyes," she admits. "Not even other slaves."

"That isn't a rule anymore. I'd like to see your pretty eyes on me," he tells her with a stroke of his knuckles down her cheek. "Humans have expressive faces, but I won't be able to see your emotions if you don't look at me."

Keeping her face blank, she murmurs, "Yes, master."

Now that she can stare at his face without fear of reprisal, she examines his features.

He has a prominent brow ridge, and she can see hard plating extending in an overlapping pattern over his forehead toward his crown. These plates are smaller than the larger ones that cover the rest of his body.

He doesn't really have a nose, only the hint of one with two nostril slits. His mouth is a thin slash. His jaw is wide with corded muscles moving when he speaks. A few small plates line his throat and only two narrow strips of smooth unprotected skin lie between his neck plates and the top part of his chest plates on either side of his neck.

She wants to reach up and touch that patch of skin, to feel the difference between that and his armor, but she keeps her hands in her lap and focuses on chewing her "feed."

He's wearing the same style of clothing today as he wore yesterday, pants made of shimmering black fabric gathered at the waist and again a few inches below his knee. The wide belt wrapped around his waist has several items attached to it. They look to be a pouch, Ident, and something that looks like a piece of jewelry.

While the belt is plain, the pouch is embossed with some kind of crest. Tieno wore pants and a belt with no shirt or shoes the other day as well. This must be the fashion for Talin males.

On the opposite hip as the pouch, hanging by a silken cord next to the Ident, is the jewelry item. It's about the size of her fist and resembles the crest embossed on Searin's pouch. She thinks of it as jewelry because it's made of precious metals and encrusted with gems. Tieno didn't have anything like it on his belt.

"We have a few tasks to complete today," he tells her as he feeds her another bite. "First, I'm taking you to a healer. She's a member of Clan Verda. They are considered the elite of the healing clans. Normally I'd have her come here so I don't have to take you into the city, but her schedule was much too tight to accommodate traveling here last minute. Thus we will go to her for this first visit. I don't know her personally, but her references are excellent. Then we will see about getting you better feed and perhaps more supplies."

She swallows the bite as he talks, but she's not sure she can eat another piece without water to wash it down. When she hesitates to open her mouth as he holds another bit to her lips, he frowns.

"There are only three more bites, little one. Please try to eat them."

He's purring again and his tone is so gentle that she takes a risk and puts her small hand over his to keep him from popping the bit of food in her mouth the moment she tries to talk. He doesn't seem upset; instead, he withdraws his hand and waits.

"Could I have some water please?"

He makes the questioning bass-drum-in-the-distance rumble as he tosses the food back into the bowl without even having to look.

"Do humans need to consume liquids when they eat?"

"Usually yes, unless the food is very watery, like soup or stew," she explains. "I can just run into the bathing facility and drink from the tap if you will allow me. I'll be quick."

That water will taste bad because it probably has cleaning microbes in it, but it won't hurt her. And now she's desperately thirsty.

To her relief, he pulls a large flask out from behind his back. He must have had it tucked in his belt.

"No need to drink from the cleansing unit." He unlatches the top and hands it to her.

Greedily, she drinks the entire contents of the flask in one go. The moment she drops the flask away from her mouth, his hand is back, pressing another food bite to her lips. Looks like she isn't getting out of eating, even if she's out of water.

Accepting the bite, she gamely chews until her jaw feels sore. Despite the discomfort, she makes it through the last three morsels and sighs with relief when he praises her for finishing the meal.

Standing up, he sets her back on the ground. "I wish I could carry you, but I worry about your back so you'll need to walk."

He reaches behind him and pulls out a long ornate cord with a clip at one end. He attaches the clip to her decorative collar and holds the other end.

"Don't move away from me suddenly, even if you're frightened by something," he warns her. "I don't want you to hurt yourself."

If you're so worried, you could just leave the leash at home, she thinks, but obediently follows him as he leads her out of the enclosure.

She notices the door swings open when he brushes his hand over the latching mechanism. It must be keyed to him. She hopes not too many people have access to her. She's still not sure of her role and isn't eager to entertain "guests" on that massive nest in her hut.

The trip to the city center takes longer than she expected. Searin's property is extensive and set far away from the bustling metropolis.

Once he parks their ground transport, he tells her to stay. She watches him round the transport and opens her door. He plucks her out and sets her on the walking path between buildings, keeping her leash draped over his arm.

When he turns to fiddle with something in the transport, it gives her time to take in the city around them.

Talins apparently like to use spirals in their architecture because all the buildings have them to varying degrees of size.

They also favor sleek and state-of-the art architecture. She hasn't seen anything that looks less than well-made and maintained. Either the Talins are a rich people or this is their model city.

Searin walks her slowly down a nearby path until they come to a building with prominent emblems carved into a stone obelisk at the entrance.

As he leads her up the short path into the structure, several Talins rush over to him even before they've entered the building. They're all wearing the same light green sleeveless tunics that reach to their knees over matching pants.

"We're so excited to have you use our facility, Prime Son Searin," one of them gushes with an eager rumbles that makes her think of hoofed animals galloping over soft grass.

"Do come in. We wouldn't want anyone to think we weren't prepared for your visit," another comments.

"Oh, yes, everything is ready!" They chatter excitedly as they usher her and Searin inside.

When they enter the building, Sora sees several others wandering the place, all dressed in the same long tunic and pants. The green tunics and pants must be a uniform.

One of the Talins that greeted them is a female. The differences between the sexes are slight but noticeable.

She's just as big as her male counterparts and possesses most of the same armor plating, but she doesn't have the long sharp quills. Instead, she has small nubs with rounded tops running up her forearm.

The female speaks as she leads them across a vast foyer. "Prime Son Searin, I'm Trainee Tamoin." She strikes her fist on her chest. "It's such an honor to have you visit us today. This must be your human. She's a handsome specimen."

Stopping at the far end of the foyer, Tamoin reaches for Sora's leash. "We'll take good care of her."

Searin puts his hand down on Sora's shoulder and draws her back half a step, rattling his back plates in an obvious warning. Unperturbed by the warning rattle, Tamoin drops her hand but doesn't move away.

"I was told I could remain with my human during this appointment."

The male steps forward to get their attention. "Prime Son Searin, I'm Trainee Simal. Of course, you may stay with your pet, but we need to decontaminate her. There's no need for you to be there for the process. We thought you might be more comfortable in the garden while you wait."

"We would be happy to fetch you once the healer is ready to see her," Tamoin assures him, but Searin doesn't let go of her shoulder.

"No," he tells them simply, and both Talins give surprised rattles at his answer, but they recover quickly.

"Right this way, Prime Son Searin," Tamoin says and leads both of them through a series of corridors and finally into a room with several Talin-sized pods standing in a row.

Searin turns to examine the pods, giving Sora's leash plenty of slack to keep from accidentally jerking at her. While his back is turned, Tamoin cuts Sora's dress off with no warning.

Unprepared, Sora jerks against the leash, startled by the trainee's unexpected actions. The dress falls away, and she finds herself standing naked.

Searin turns at the sound of her startlement, rattling out a violent sound that makes both trainees lurch back as he tucks Sora against him. It was the same sound he'd made when the Leemron had nearly strangled her and in the confines of the small room, it was nearly deafening!

"That was uncalled for. Now my human gets to go around naked?" Searin snaps, looking down at the garment pooled at her feet.

Sora pushes her back against him and crosses her arms over her chest, feeling more vulnerable here than she did at the auction house when Tieno asked her to disrobe.

"We'll provide her with a covering," Tamoin assures him. "But this cloth must be disposed of. Normally, all slaves and livestock must come to us directly to be isolated, checked, and decontaminated before being taken home. For obvious reasons, you were given special dispensation."

Searin rattles his back plates threateningly. When he speaks, his voice is commanding. "You will tell us what you are going to do before you do it."

Sora notices Tamoin doesn't seem shocked or even mildly surprised by Searin's harsh words or threat display.

"She's in no danger. We've treated many humans. Your pet is in the best of hands."

Searin's rattling stops, but his shoulders are still tense. "I will be monitoring everything."

"We invite your scrutiny." Tamoin digs something out of the pocket of her tunic and gives it to Searin. "Here is a treat for the human. I can already tell she's underweight, so a few sweet treats won't hurt her."

Searin examines the item and then offers it to Sora, holding it to her mouth in the same way he fed her food earlier. Without hesitation, Sora opens her mouth to accept the food, and when the sweet flavor hits her tongue, she smiles and chews enthusiastically, eyeing Tamoin's pocket for more.

All three of the Talins make amused rumbling sounds deep in their chest. Tamoin hands Searin a few more of the candies before resuming her work.

The rest of the time with the two trainees isn't bad at all. The decontamination process is swift and painless. She just has to stand in one booth for a few minutes with her eyes closed. Then they have her swallow a few vials of tasteless liquids and wash her hair with some kind of acrid smelling soap.

Once that is all done, they escort her and Searin into another room with what looks like an exam table and several chairs. Searin lifts her on the exam table and then pulls out a chair next to her to sit down. She's still naked, but at least the room is warm. Life could be much worse.

Once he's settled in his chair, he reaches over and rests a hand on her naked thigh, absently stroking her skin as they wait. He seems to always want to touch her: putting her in his lap last night and this morning, placing a hand on her shoulder as they stand, combing his fingers through her hair while they listen to the trainees, and now resting his hand on her thigh.

Even as they were in the transport on the way over, he kept reaching over to touch her, as if she might disappear. Or perhaps touching her gives him some kind of pleasure or comfort.

Between what Searin has said and the way the trainees talk, it seems collecting humans is common among the Talin.

It seems she is a pet now instead of a slave. The distinction is important as pets tend to be treated far better and have a higher survival rate than slaves.

She wants to ask Searin questions but can't work up the courage. After ten years of never asking questions and rarely even talking, it's hard to break the habit. She'll just remain quiet and obedient for now; it seems like a wise course of action regardless of her status.

Something else becomes clear to her as she watches the trainees interact with Searin; her new owner is an important male.

He's allowed to flout normal procedure with her. She bets the average Talin would need to leave her at this or a similar facility for several rotations instead of being processed so quickly.

What does that mean for her? Her new master is influential, which might make her safer or put her in greater danger.

She knows some wealthy, important owners will use their slaves as living shields if they're attacked. Searin doesn't seem to be the type to put anything between him and danger, but she could become a target just for being near him.

The door to the room slides open and a female Talin walks in. Her tunic is a darker green than the trainees, and she walks with more confidence. Ignoring Sora, she faces Searin and does the fist-to-chest thing.

"Greetings, Prime Son Searin. I'm Healer Yeshem."

Searin stands and returns the gesture. "Greetings, Healer Yeshem."

Yeshem strides over to Sora, pinning her with a critical eye. "Let us see this new pet."

Sora sits up straighter, trying to look healthy and without pain. She doesn't want this Talin to declare her too scrawny or sickly to keep. The healer's next words aren't comforting.

"This human is much too thin," she declares.

"I know this," Searin acknowledges. "She's been underfed and abused. I purchased human feed, but she seems to have a difficult time chewing it."

The healer makes a rattle noise that sounds troubled. "Did you mix the food with water and crush it up?"

"I didn't know that was necessary," Searin explains.

"The human jaw is weak and their teeth aren't sharp," Yeshem explanes. "The feed you buy needs to be mashed with water. Many of them like it warm. I'm sure she'll be able to eat enough once you do that."

Yeshem leans over and cups Sora's jaw, drawing her face up and to the side, very much like Tieno did at the auction house. Then urges Sora to pivot on the table so the healer can see her back.

She pulls a device from a nearby wall and runs it over Sora, first her back, then her chest, and finally down her arms and legs. The whole time she keeps a running commentary to Searin about Sora's health and body condition.

When the healer runs a flesh knitter over her back to fully heal the old wound, Sora sighs in relief. She hadn't realized how bad the nagging pain was until it was gone.

When she thinks the healer has no more places to poke and prod her, Yeshem urges her to recline on the exam table and spread her legs.

For the first time, she resists a little and looks over to Searin.

"What are you doing, Healer Yeshem?" Searin asks, his warm hand, missing throughout the exam, returns to her thigh.

"I would like to check her reproductive system," the healer explains. "It'll be quick and painless, but I need her on her back and to spread her legs just enough so I can run my scanner over her sex organs and lower abdomen."

Searin gives an unhappy rattle. "Is that necessary? I have no plans to breed her, and she seems concerned at your actions."

Yeshem blinks a few times and makes the clatter-of-metal-tools-dropping rattle of surprise. This must not be the usual response pet owners give. Yeshem drops her gaze to Sora and then looks back to Searin.

"It can wait for now, but I would suggest you have it done at her next appointment. It's good to know if she's healthy in all aspects, even if you have no intention of introducing her to a stud."

"If my intentions with my pet change, I'll bring her back here," Searin informs the healer coolly.

Yeshem isn't fazed. "I'm not sure you realize, but humans can carry Talin babes. They make wonderful surrogates, despite their small size. Our young come out much healthier when humans gestate them. They provide a far superior nurturing environment than an artificial womb."

An impatient rattle sounds from Searin. "That's interesting information, but unnecessary. I haven't formed a marriage contract yet, so children aren't a concern."

"You misunderstand. I'm not telling you this because of a child you might have. I have heard your dear sister, Prime Daughter Halieni, still hasn't produced a child. Once she's at a healthier weight, this human could be a great help in that regard."

"I'm unaware of my sister's breeding requirements. Those are her concerns, not mine," Searin informs Yeshem with stiff formality and another impatient rattle. "Are we done here?"

Yeshem's tone turns just as stiff and formal as his. "As you wish, Prime Son Searin. I will send all pertinent information on keeping humans to your account."

"And clothing? I can't leave here with my human exposed to the elements."

She taps her Ident and then looks back up. "I'll also have a trainee bring a wrap for her, but you'll want to purchase more extensive coverings. Human skin is easily damaged by too much sun or harsh wind. They can grow chilled easily as well, so they must be monitored closely when outside of their kennels or sheltered areas."

"Understood. Is her back healed enough to be touched?"

"Of course. She has a scar, unfortunately. It will fade somewhat with time but won't go away entirely. It won't disfigure her much, and if it bothers you, several healers I know can grow and graft new skin to cover it."

The idea of being "disfigured" doesn't bother Sora, especially considering Searin seems to shrug off Yeshem's advice. "Her skin is fine as it is."

Yeshem turns to Sora, draws something out of her pocket and offers it.

Looking down, she finds the healer holding out several of the same treats Tamoin gave out earlier. Before she can take them, Searin leans over and snatches them away from Yeshem. Sora thinks he's going to deny her the sweets until he holds one to her mouth and waits for her to accept it.

"They can feed themselves," Yeshem points out dryly, and Sora almost chokes on the treat. That's the first time she's heard anyone address Searin with anything less than fawning regard or respectful civility.

"I know," Searin tells her with complete disregard for the tone in the healer's words, "but I want to feed her myself."

Yeshem sounds an amused rumble. "What here until one of my trainees comes with clothing for your pet."

Searin faces her. "Thank you for your gift of time and skill."

That must be a dismissal because Yeshem wishes him a "fruitful rotation" then leaves.

Sora chews her sweets and contemplates how wonderful her life just turned out. Instead of being forced to do difficult physical tasks while fearing the capricious moods of a harsh master, she's being well cared for and fed sweets.

Impulsively, she shifts herself a little closer to Searin and rests her head on one of his chest plates. A rumble comes from his chest and one of his hands strokes down her back.

He leans his head over and rubs his cheek against her hair. The smell of cinnamon fills her nose, making her breathe deeply.

For the first time in a very long time, she looks forward to her future.

CHAPTER 6

Sora

Expecting to be taken back to her cage after the appointment with the healers, Sora's a little dazed when Searin takes her to an outdoor shopping area instead.

The large square open area houses rows of tents and stalls selling all kinds of items. The place is loud, busy, and colorful. After so many years spent in space where almost everything was painted some shade of utilitarian gray, she's dumbfounded by the market before her.

As before, Searin comes around to her side of the transport, but this time he doesn't attach a leash to her collar. Instead, he lifts her out of the transport. Cradling her to his chest, he strides into the melee of color, smells, and sounds.

Everyone around them is quick to jump out of Searin's way, even though he never says to move or rattles loudly. The moment anyone sees him they duck to the side, striking their chest, then move on.

At least they aren't being jostled by the crowd as she struggles to take in everything. Sweet smells hit her nose, and she turns her head, trying to figure out where they're coming from.

"Prime Son Searin, what do you have there?" a booming voice asks, and Searin comes to an abrupt halt. This is the first time anyone's addressed him.

Sora turns her to see a Talin wearing scarlet pants strides up, hitting a fist to his chest in greeting. Searin can't return the gesture because she's in the way, so she expects him to set her down.

He doesn't. Still holding her tightly, he gives a little bow of his head to acknowledge the other Talin. "Greeting, Servant Citizen Gorian. I hope you're having a fruitful rotation."

Gorian isn't paying attention to Searin at all. His eyes are focused on her. "She's so tiny," he breathes out and lowers his head so he's only a few hand-spans from her own.

She wants to draw away from him, but with Searin's solid chest behind her head, there's no room for her to retreat. Unsure if she should talk, she stays silent and keeps a wary eye on this stranger.

"I just bought her," Searin explains. "She's shy. It's going to take her a little time to recover from her last owner."

A powerful rattle that sounds like projections rapidly firing comes from Gorian, making her jump a little. That has to be anger or aggression!

"He's not angry at you," Searin whispers to her as he purrs. It seems she guessed the sound correctly.

"Thank you, master," she whispers back, relaxing into him a little. She watches with interest as Gorian rears his head up to snarl questions at Searin.

"What family owned her? Have they been dealt with? Abuse of a human pet is as severe a crime. As you know, I'm on the Committee for Pet Welfare. No matter how influential the family is, the other members and I will see justice done. No one should treat a precious human so deplorably."

Committee for Pet Welfare? This species has a committee for the welfare of slaves? It even sounds like there are limits to what owners can do to her. This is both startling and important information. Somehow, she needs to learn about these laws. Not that Searin's given any sign he's going to hurt her, but if she's sold or traded to someone less kind, it can only help her to know what's allowed and what isn't.

"Be at ease. She's a former off-world slave. Tieno and I found her at the Starn Station auction house," Searin explains.

She watches Gorian closely as he finds out she's from off-world. Talin faces might not move, but they do have clear body language. Gorian takes in a deep breath of air and rumbles out the many-fingers-snapping sound.

"I see. The poor little thing. That explains her condition," he murmurs. "They're usually in very poor condition when found at auction houses. My committee is drafting a policy regarding the buying of off-world humans."

"To purchase them outright or to inform potential Talin buyers of their location?" Searin asks.

"Purchase. We want government funds to be set aside to buy them. And we also want to offer a 'no questions asked' policy. We won't make the sellers provide proof of a legal sale as long as the human stock arrives in reasonably good condition."

It takes Sora a moment to realize what he means by "no questions asked." Her uncle shouldn't have been allowed to sell her but the buyer looked the other way at the laws he was breaking.

A powerful and influential government like the Talins, specifically seeking humans and willing to forgo paperwork, would have opportunists potentially enslaving entire settlements to make quick credits.

And what did *reasonably good condition mean*? There weren't many humans out in the universe. This could end up finishing them off!

"That could lead to problems," Searin warns him. "They might start capturing free humans to sell to us. There's questionable morality there."

She smiles in approval at his words, surprised he cares, considering he was so eager to buy her.

Searin's words cause Gorian to make a swarm-of-angry-hornets rattle. "It's not gray, Prime Son Searin. It's very black and white. Humans aren't fit to live in this universe without oversight. Even if they're wild-caught and brought to us, it's much better than what happens to all of them outside of our care. Do you know that the average lifespan for a free human is only forty solars? Forty! That's it! It's even worse if they are slaves. An enslaved human rarely lives much into their third decade. Searin, we must do something."

Looking down at her, Gorian softens his tone. "Were you born into slavery, little female? Or were you forced into it?"

Unsure if she's allowed to speak, she looks up to Searin for instruction. "You can answer him. I'm interested as well."

"I was born free," she explains in a quiet voice, unsure if that's what Gorian wants to hear or not. "A few years after my mother died, her brother sold me."

"How many solars did you live before your uncle sold you?"

"Sixteen."

"Just a child. If owned by us, her dam would've lived, and they could've stayed together until she was much older."

"You don't know that," Searin objects. "Even under our vigilant care, the humans sometimes die young."

"I know, but it's rare. Here, we can settle this easily." He looks back down at her. "Do you know what your dam died of?"

"Sickness. I don't know what kind. I don't think any of us knew. We couldn't afford a healer so she just kept getting worse."

Despite the many years separating Sora from the death of her mother, she still feels the sadness fill her. She'd like to think if her mother lived, she never would have been sold, but she can't be sure.

The last few years of her mother's life were full of addiction and pain. If the trend continued, she might have agreed to sell Sora just to get more drugs. When the sickness took her, she begged for the same drugs that probably helped cause her illness to begin with.

A harsh rattle from Gorian interrupts her thoughts. "She probably died of something easily cured or prevented by our healers. Do you understand now? They're not fit to be on their own. If they're to be saved, we must make efforts to bring them here."

"Send me your proposal," Searin murmurs thoughtfully. "I'll look it over and see if the monarch might be interested in weighing in on the matter."

"The monarch has humans also, correct?"

"Yes, but they've had a policy of noninvolvement regarding pet issues, so don't allow yourself too much hope," Searin warns him. "Although I think most free-born humans wouldn't want to be captured and forced here, I believe your reasoning is sound." Searin hugs her a little tighter to his chest. "I have a new appreciation for human frailty. I came across a report recently that estimated only a few hundred thousand humans are left, including the ones already living here."

"I read the same report," Gorian says as he makes a rumbling sound Sora isn't familiar with. "I found it very disturbing. The report concludes that humans could be completely extinct in as few as another two hundred solars. With enough gene manipulation, we can keep our stock from having inbreeding issues, but it'd be so much better if we could just gather more humans here."

It's not a new thing for Sora to hear humans discussed as if they're non-sentient. Her master talked about her all the time while she was present, explaining repeatedly that she was from a dumb species but good for menial work.

She learned to tune out his words and keep her emotions in check. But the last few days have been stressful and strange for her, and she finds her emotions creeping back in.

Part of her likes the idea of all humans being treated like prized pets. So far, she's received plenty of food, a soft bed, and medical care, everything she lacked even before she was sold to Master De. If wearing a jeweled collar, being petted,and hugged is the cost of all this care, it's trivial.

But the other side of the care is the issue of free will. Her uncle might have sold her, but he never thought much of females. She knows for sure he'd never sell a male member of the family.

And if anyone attempted to abduct someone from their settlement, he'd fight to the death to defend them.

She doesn't know much about other human enclaves, but she knows many of the men and women of her community on Staverious station believe freedom is more important than anything else—more important than even living sometimes.

Yet every single one of them stood by and let her be sold. No one fought for her. A strange tangle of emotions—pride, anger, long, and loss—sweeps through her as she thinks of her uncle and community.

None of her emotions are nostalgia.

Gorian's pronouncement that humans are dying out rings true from her insular experience. She attended at least two mourning events every solar, and sometimes many more.

Usually, they were for elders who died, but much too often it would be for a child or adult in their prime. The causes of death are too numerous to list, but all of them would have been preventable if they lived among the Talins. No dying of common diseases or childbirth. No exposure to radiation because the domiciles are made of poor-quality materials. No lack of food.

She's never had the luxury to ponder these concepts before, but now she wonders. What's more important, living as an owned being, or dying as a free one?

"Would you let me hold her?" That question brings her out of her thoughts. Blinking up at Searin in consternation, she waits to find out if she's going to be passed into a stranger's arms.

"She's just finished getting processed and checked with the healers. I think she's had enough new people touching her today," Searin explains gently, but she can feel the tension in him. He doesn't like the idea of others touching her. That's a good thing.

"Of course." Gorian backs away slightly and tucks his hands behind him. "What is your goal at the market today?"

"She needs wraps and supplies," Searin explains, his tone bordering on terse.

"I can help with that," he pronounces eagerly. "My cousin owns a pet supply establishment that specializes in humans. Our whole family is rather dedicated to breeding and raising humans. Come with me." Gorian turns to lead them through the market. Searin doesn't rattle or comment, but somehow she can tell he isn't thrilled with the company.

As they walk, Gorian chats about legislation and human-owning families. Soon they find themselves at a booth crammed full of human-sized wraps, head coverings, shoes, slippers, cleanses, towels, and more.

Sora's never seen so many brand-new human-specific items gathered in one place. It takes a great deal of effort to keep herself still in Searin's arms when all she wants to do is look through the rows of items and touch everything.

The moment she sees the deep yellow wrap, she gives up staying still and wiggles.

"Be still," Searin commands her, and Gorian rumbles out a laugh.

"She wants to touch the clothing," he explains. "Humans are very tactile. You should let her down to explore. Between the two of us, we can make sure she doesn't wander off."

Ignoring Gorian, she looks up to Searin. "Can I be put down, Master Searin? Please?"

Making the rattle of water dripping on metal sound of agreement, Searin sets her down.

"Don't leave the area of this booth," he orders her.

She nods her head vigorously, but she's not even looking at him. The moment she's free of his arms, she grabs up the yellow wrap in both hands. It's so soft it makes her sigh.

It seems all the articles of clothing are in the wrap style. There are long and loose for men and shorter with a more fitted style for women. They all look expensive and well made.

"She can try it on," a female Talin tells them as she comes to stand next to Searin. "That one's made of Dinary cotton. Humans tend to favor clothing made of that fabric the most."

"Greeting's Saterlin," Gorian says with an affectionate rumble. "Cousin, this is Prime Son Searin. He's just acquired his pet and I believe he needs everything for her."

"Greeting, Prime Son Searin, you honor my shop with your visit," Saterlin says as she fishes something out of the pocket of her belt pouch.

Watching with interest, hands still full of the yellow wrap, Sora smiles when Saterlin holds out a hand with more of the candy the healers had. Searin's already snatching the candy from the shopkeeper before Sora can let go of the wrap to take it.

"She was given treats earlier. Is it safe for her to have so many?" he questions, causing all three of them to eye Sora critically.

Huffing out a breath, Sora puts her best pleading look on her face. "I only had a few earlier."

All three Talins rumble out marbles-in-a-bag sound of amusement at her words. Gorian speaks up, his voice indulgent. "If the healers pronounced her healthy, a few extra sweets won't hurt her."

Rumbling out a purr, Searin holds one of the candies to her mouth. "In that case, we will spoil you today."

She accepts it and sighs with pleasure as the sweetness hits her tongue. "Thank you, Master."

Impulsively, she drops the wrap onto a low table and wraps her arms around Searin's waist. He's so broad that her hands can't meet, but she tries to squeeze him anyway. He must like it because his purring gets a little more intense.

"Good human," he pronounces. "You can go explore the shop if you like." Taking that as her cue, she lets go of him and looks around to take in all the items.

"Humans have such a craving for sweets," Saterlin murmurs. "I swear my Bayo would eat a teeki raw if it meant he'd get sweets after."

No longer focused on her, the three Talins delve into a serious discussion about humans and the legislation regarding them. Sora knows she should pay attention, but she's much too distracted by the items in the shop. Soon she's back touching the various wraps and eyeing the soft decorative slippers.

A flash of turquoise catches her eye, and she wanders to the far corner of the shop to run her fingers over a jeweled belt. As she touches it, the jewels change color slightly. It's curled up, and she wants to take it off the shelf and unwind it, but she isn't sure if she's allowed.

As she withdraws her hand, a large Talin appears in her field of vision and plucks it off the shelf. With a little gasp of surprise, she flinches away, even as an unfamiliar purr starts up.

"Don't be afraid," the strange male says in a calm voice, holding out the belt toward her. "Did you want to see this? I know humans like to touch things. You can hold it if you like."

This male is large, just like Searin, and has the same air of strength and command.

When she doesn't take it, he moves a little closer. "I would never hurt a human. You're safe to be near me."

Despite his comforting words, she looks around for Searin. That's when she realizes she's wandered out of his line of sight.

She can hear him and the other two Talins still talking, making her feel more secure. They're so close one cry would bring all three of them to her. But at the same time, she doesn't want to cause problems. For all the years she was a slave, one lesson was drilled into her: slaves who get noticed are more likely to suffer.

Giving the stranger a small apologetic smile, she edges away. He easily steps in front of her, blocking her escape route.

"Be at ease. You're safe. I didn't mean to scare you away from the belt." He holds it out again. "They're Maky stones. When you touch them, they change color, depending on the individual."

He points to the one stone she touched that is now a dark brilliant blue instead of the bright turquoise of the other ones.

"The stones react with body chemistry," he explains and taps one with a finger. It turns a deep blood red, and he sounds a rumble of amusement. "I think you make nicer colors with it than I do."

Remaining stock still, she watches him anxiously. He holds the belt out to her again, shaking it slightly as if to tantalize her into taking it. When she still doesn't move, he lowers his hand and sounds the distant-bass-drum rumble of concern.

"You're acting strangely. Humans shouldn't be this worried about simply taking a belt from me in public. What family owns you?"

Maybe if she takes the belt, he'll leave her alone? Reaching out, she snatches the belt from his loose grip. He rumbles out a purr when she takes it but then stops when she doesn't bother to examine it, instead keeping her eyes focused on him.

"You need to touch the stones if you want to see them change," he reminds her.

When she doesn't move to do as he suggests, he sounds an irritated rattle. When the rattle makes her cringe, he makes a thoughtful sound deep in his chest.

"This isn't normal behavior. You won't talk and you act fearful. You need to take me to your owner right now, female. I need to assess your living situation."

And now she's gotten herself in a dilemma and she's not even sure how she did it. Deciding to talk to him, even if she gets in trouble for it later, she squares her shoulders and meets his intense eyes.

"I'm f-f-fine." She didn't mean to stumble over her words, but after so long being silent, it feels odd to talk. Searin is the first person she's spoken with at any length for many years.

Rarely does anyone engage a slave in conversation, and they certainly aren't asked about their health and comfort. But now these Talins are talking to her and asking questions all over the place. It's disconcerting and bewildering.

The purring starts up again. "You can talk. That's good. You worried me. Now tell me why you're so skittish. Are you being hurt? You need to tell me. I can help."

The sincerity in his statements finally melts Sora's timidness. Willing to risk reprisal, she offers him a smile. "I just got here, to this planet. Yesterday."

Her simple words have a powerful effect. His body relaxes and his voice turns sympathetic.

"You were an off-world slave, you poor thing. That explains so much." He digs into the pouch on his belt, pulling out one of the candies she's rapidly becoming addicted to. "Here's a treat for you. You look like you could use the calories."

Her eyes fix on the candy in his hand, and he rumbles out a laugh. Holding it out to her, he remains still as she plucks it from his hand and shoves it in her mouth.

Does everyone around here carry candy to give to random humans? If so, this is definitely her new favorite species ever!

"Sora?" Searin's voice sounds worried, so she ducks past the stranger and hurries back to her new owner.

"Here!" she says, squeezing between two sets of shelves. The stranger can't fit, so she hears him make his way around. She pops up next to Searin, pressing her shoulder against his side.

"Don't wander out of sight," he orders, and she nods vigorously. Then he taps the belt she forgot she was holding. "What's this?"

"She's entranced by the stones," the stranger explains as he steps up to join the group. "But she was afraid to touch it, so I handed it to her."

"Admiral Ignatias, it's an honor to see you," Gorian says with a happy rumble.

"Greetings Servant Citizen Gorian," Ignatias rumbles out. He turns his attention to Searin. "Prime Son Searin, I take it this is your pet? She's tentative and fearful. What are you doing to mitigate these issues?"

A shocked silence follows Ignatias's terse demand. Sora might not know much about the Talins yet, but she knows her new master is very high ranking. This Admiral Ignatias must not care about Searin's rank to be so bold.

"Greeting Admiral Ignatias," Searin says, his voice tight with suppressed hostility.

Upset by the tension around her, Sora instinctively looks to Searin for comfort. She drops the belt to the floor and wraps both arms around his waist, half hiding behind him.

The Ident Cube on his belt digs into her belly, but his bare torso feels smooth and nice against the side of her face. She feels immensely better now that she's holding him. She hopes she isn't acting badly.

As if to encourage her embrace, he rumbles out a purr, and she relaxes into him. His hand strokes gently down her back and he leans over a little to speak to her. "Be at ease. You're not in trouble."

His calming words make her huff out the breath she was holding. Without moving her head away from where it's resting against Searin's side, she rolls her eyes up to regard Ignatias. He's not standing so stiffly any longer as his gaze bounces between her and Searin.

"This is good," he says, his tone approving. "If she goes to you so quickly for comfort, you've done well in establishing trust." He leans over and picks up the belt she discarded. Rolling it back up, he hands it to Saterlin. "The little female likes this." Without a word, Saterlin quietly adds it to a pile of items.

"Sora has a soft temperament," Searin tells the admiral. "She's easily distressed."

"That's obvious," Ignatias comments. "Most humans that come to us from slave auctions are both physically and emotionally damaged. Count yourself lucky that you found one that looks reasonably fit and appears to have only minor mental issues."

Sora wants to stomp her foot and tell the admiral she doesn't have mental issues. He makes it sound like she's defective. Her brain works perfectly fine, thank you very much!

"I'm lucky indeed to have stumbled across Sora," Searin agrees. "Tell me, what are you doing in this shop? Have the rules changed? Are you allowed to have humans now?" Searin's tone is taunting and Ignatias stiffens.

"As you well know, Prime Son, the laws haven't changed. However, I'll be retiring from military life soon and be allowed to own humans."

"May the ancestors grant you a smooth transition after such a distinguished career," Searin says, although his tone isn't cordial at all. "I wish you luck finding a human of your own to start your collection."

Ignatias concern over her well-being gave Sora the courage to open her mouth to voice an outrageous suggestion. "The human colony on Staverious Station was struggling when I was there. Perhaps you should visit and see if any humans are interested in, um, going with you? The Staverious station orbits Polmic, in the Egorm sector."

All eyes fall on her. Embarrassed, tense, and not a little afraid, she buries her head against Searin's side. Bending his knees, he gathers her up in his arms and lifts, cradling her high against his chest.

"I'll look into it. Thank you, little female," Ignatias says with a gentle purr. "You're an excellent human."

She's not sure if she's an "excellent human" or not for pointing the admiral in the direction of her old colony. But one thing is for sure, if given a choice, at least a few of the people she knew back on Staverious would jump at the chance to live life in this plush captivity. For at least a few of them, being owned will be considered a far better choice than death.

CHAPTER 7

Searin

When Searin first brought the Sora human home from the auction, he didn't have much confidence that she'd ever be as affectionate as Mari.

He knew he expected too much from her the first night. Even so, when she wrapped reluctant arms around his neck and sat so stiffly on his lap, he felt only a disappointing shadow of the pleasure and comfort he received from holding Tieno's human. If anything, he felt worse when he accidentally hurt her with his petting.

He went to bed that night feeling like his lungs didn't want to expand, that his entire chest was nothing but one solid carapace with no room for air. The sensation was so bad he left his bed to first prowl around his silent house and then finally out into the garden to the cages.

Quietly, he made his way into his pet's enclosure, telling himself he needed to make sure she didn't need warmer bedding.

He found her curled up in her nest, sound asleep. She looked so small and fragile and he wanted to draw her into his arms and wrap her in his strength. He kept himself from touching her by reminding himself that she needed rest, and the next day might be difficult for her.

He wasn't sure how long he stood there and stared at her, remembering what it was like to carry her at the auction house.

His chest eased a little, and he found he could draw in a full breath. Stealthily, he leaned over her until his nose was almost buried in her soft mane. He took a few deep breaths, drawing in her scent and savoring it. Straightening back up, he decided that even if the human didn't turn out to be like Mari, this might be enough.

Now, sitting on a stone bench with an empty breakfast bowl next to him, he holds her in his lap while she contentedly cuddles against him. Her affectionate touch seems to loosen his chest plates and make it easy for him to draw in a full breath of air, bringing her scent into his nose. He's never felt fulfilled, not with any part of his job or duties. Not even with soft, sweet Mari. Having this human all to himself makes all the difference.

He squeezes his delicate pet to his chest, delighted when she makes a small sound of contentment that Mari never made for him. Without any urging, she burrows her face into the bare spot on his neck, her breath warm against his exposed skin.

Giving in to the ache, he rubs his scent glands into her hair. She seems to enjoy it because he feels her take in several large breaths and then snuggle even tighter against him.

"Thank you for all the fine clothes, Master," she murmurs to him. "And the belt and the other things."

"It's a small thing," he assures her and pets her back. "And I'm glad we figured out how to feed you properly."

He regrets his mishandling of her food that morning. She admitted her jaw muscles were sore after chewing a full portion of the tough balls of unprepared human feed.

Yet he doesn't like the new form the feed takes when prepared as required. When the pellets are properly made with warm water, he can't feed it to her with his own hand. He makes a mess of trying to hold the bowl to her mouth for her to sip from.

Instead, she feeds herself although he gets to hold her in his lap as she slurps her food. He's disappointed she can't eat from his hand, but he's determined to do more research on what humans can consume and find items he can feed her regularly from his hand that also fulfill her dietary needs.

"I noticed the only thing you asked for was a bag of those treats."

She smiles up at him. "I think I could live on those sweets."

He rumbles in amusement. "Tieno told me not to trust you with them. He said you would gorge if I gave you access to the entire bag and make yourself sick."

She shakes her head against him. "I wouldn't. I'd be good."

"I'd rather not test your fortitude," he tells her, enjoying the banter.

He thinks about all the things he must work on today but can't bring himself to put Sora down. He rubs a scent gland on her head again. She wiggles a little as he does this but doesn't stiffen or pull back. He can smell the wash they used for decontamination at the health center and decides he should bathe and groom her before he starts his workday.

Easily cradling her in his arms, he stands up and ignores her little squawk of surprise. "Master?"

"I'm going to bathe you," he explains as he carries her into the hut. She stiffens a little but doesn't struggle.

Setting her on her feet on the smooth stone floor of the cleansing room, he taps the control panel until water pours out of an ornate bowl set high in the wall. He'd have to duck under it, but Sora fits easily.

Reaching out, he cups some of the water and then pours it on the small strip of skin on his neck, the only place on his upper body that is sensitive enough to tell him if the water will be too hot or cold. It doesn't feel extreme either way, so he turns his attention back to Sora.

He reaches for the ties to her wrap and she brings both her hands up to grasp his. "I can bathe myself, Master," she assures him, and he rumbles out a purr.

"I know you can, but Tieno tells me it's good to bathe you myself." He watches her face carefully, and she doesn't look fearful, just unsure. In the short time he's had her, he's becoming very adept at reading her specific facial expression.

"If that's what you wish," she murmurs and drops her hands away from his. He finishes untying her wrap and pulls it off her body, tossing it casually aside. For the first time since buying her, he takes a careful look at all of her, not just healing wounds or body condition.

Tieno assured him she's a regular size for a human, but as he lets his eyes roam over her, he notices again how tiny she seems. Small and delicate are the words he uses to describe her every time someone asks him about his new pet.

Unlike Mari's wide hips and ample breasts, Sora's body is leaner and more athletic. She'll never be as lush as Mari, but he can hardly wait for her to put on more weight and feel soft and round in his arms. Healer Yeshem assured him it was only a matter of time and food.

Except for the scars on her back, her skin is golden brown and flawless. He runs his hand across her belly, entranced by both the reaction of her skin and the soft flesh under his fingers.

"You're beautiful," he murmurs to her, rumbling out a purr as he reaches for a bathing cloth.

Talins use a harsh abrasive stone to clean their tough hide, but Sora requires a soft gentle cleansing cloth. He read all the literature about pet care and knows exactly how to do this. He just wishes he didn't feel a strange excitement building in his chest.

Ignoring his reactions, he wets the bathing cloth and pours a little of the special soap onto it. He works it in his hands until it lathers before rubbing it over her skin.

He begins at her shoulder, down one arm, and then repeats the process on her other side. She shivers a little, so he reaches out and increases the temperature in the room. Humans are such delicate little creatures. It's a wonder they've survived after they destroyed their planet.

Once he's gone over her arms, he turns his attention to her chest and back. Although Healer Yeshem assured him the scars aren't painful, he still runs the cleansing cloth over her back with an abundance of care. He turns his attention to her chest, running the cloth over her round mammary glands, fascinated by the feel and weight of them. A little sound somewhere between a sigh and a gasp comes out of her, making him stop and pull away.

"Does that hurt?" He watches her face closely as her skin flushes with color.

"No Master, it…." She stops talking and looks away.

"What?"

"It feels good," she whispers, as if she's confessing some crime.

Sounding a rumble of confusion, he starts bathing her again. "I've read athat all your skin is sensitive to pressure, temperature, abrasion, and touch," he tells her. "It's one of the reasons humans need to be held and petted so much. Your species suffers from sensory deprivation if you go without for too long. Bathing should be a pleasurable experience."

He runs his fingers down her side, and she makes a new sound. It takes him several submarks to identify the meaning. "Was that a giggle?"

"Yes, Master," she confirms. "As you said, I'm sensitive to touch, more so in some places than others. I—" Laughter interrupts her speech, and she steps away from him, holding her hands to the side he was just bathing.

"Is that a fear reaction?" he asks with a confused rattle.

"No, it's… I'm… uh, there's this action called tickling, and it makes us laugh."

He reaches out and moves her hand away from her side, revealing the flesh just below her arm on her torso. He sees no discoloration or irritation. When he runs a finger along her skin to feel for unevenness, she laughs and shies away, and that's when he understands.

"There's something in the literature about this," he remembers. "Some humans have an automatic recoil reaction to touch on some parts of their body."

"Yes, ticklish," she repeats with a smile. She's crossed her arms over her chest again, covering her mammary glands, and he finds he doesn't like that.

"Drop your arms," he orders, surprised when she hesitates. He sounds a rumble of concern. "Why aren't you obeying?"

With a little sigh, she drops her arms to her sides. "I'm not used to being, uh, bathed. I feel vulnerable being naked and wet while being touched."

"I'd never hurt you," he objects, taking half a step away from her. Tension fills his chest, and he has to force air into his lungs.

Moving so quickly she slips a little on the wet stone floor, she grabs his wrist, careful not to touch his quills. Her eyes are large and sincere as she speaks.

"I never thought you would," she assures him.

Her little hand can't even reach all the way around his broad wrist, a reminder of how much bigger he is. Feeling foolish, he chastises himself. His little pet is defenseless and was abused by her former owner. Of course, she might feel intimidated by him.

"I'm used to being naked," she continues before he can speak. "But it feels different with you. I don't know why. It just does. And with you touching me," she pauses, and the skin of her face colors again. Her next words are a barely audible mumble. "I guess I just haven't felt like this in a long time, and I'm trying not to do anything stupid."

"What do you feel?" he asks, both worried and curious. She's not in pain, that's obvious, but some kind of discomfort seems to be bothering her.

Shaking her head, she ducks back near the water. "Nothing concerning," she insists. "Would you like me to finish bathing myself?"

She holds her hand out for the cloth, but he pulls it out of her reach and steps close enough to resume bathing her again once she lowers her hand.

"A master bathes his pet," he reminds her.

He focuses on gently grooming her skin with the cloth, noting where she's sensitive to pressure. He notices an obvious change in her skin as he continues the grooming. The heat in the room is high enough that she shouldn't be uncomfortable while wet. His species can handle a large range of temperatures and still be comfortable, unlike humans, so when the tips of her mammary glands change shape and her skin pebbles, he grows concerned.

"Are you chilled?" he asks. She meets his gaze. Her pupils are dilated and her breathing seems to have become more rapid.

"No, I'm not cold," she says, her voice subdued.

A strange, enticing scent hits his nose. He drops to his knees in front of her, uncaring as the water on the stones soaks into his pants. She takes in a sharp breath of air but doesn't move as he puts his head close to the skin of her belly. The scent is stronger there.

He stills his body, letting his mind wrap around the scent. As he parses it out, his own body starts to react strangely. Blood flows to his mating shaft, as if trying to emerge from its protective pouch. His chestbox aches to sound an erogenous rumble. His scent glands overfill to where they're about to leak oil down his face, and his heartbeat speeds up.

He gives in to one of the urges and makes Sora jump a little at his sudden and intense rumble. He's not touching her, only breathing in the scent that's becoming more tantalizing by the moment.

Then it hits him. He's feeling the need to breed.

How could a human be triggering his mating urges? He should move away from her. He should let her finish her bathing and leave the enclosure until he has himself back under control. What he's feeling is wholly inappropriate.

But his legs won't listen. His body refuses to stand, and his head remains near her belly. "Why do you smell this way?" he murmurs to himself, but she answers him.

"I'm sorry," she whispers, her tone scandalized. "I haven't been touched with gentleness in a long time. I'm reacting to… I'm having trouble… I'm sorry," she stammers, and it takes a moment for Searin to finally realize what she's trying to say.

"You're aroused?" She nods and looks away, the color of her face turning from pink to deep red. If he didn't know the color change is common in humans, he'd think something is wrong with her.

"Do I need to find you a male to rut?" he asks and only barely keeps from sounding out a negative rattle. He doesn't like the idea of anyone but him touching her, even if it's another human pet.

"No!" she practically shouts but then continues in a calmer tone. "It's nothing, Master Searin. Ignore my body. Please don't put another male in with me. I don't want anyone else touching me."

Resuming his comforting rumble, Searin wraps his arms around her waist, enjoying the way she folds her body around his head and shoulder. The wonderful smell she was producing is fading now, and even though it makes his body easier to control, he finds he doesn't want it gone.

"You're safe," he assures her, rubbing his scent glands on the skin of her belly. The smell of his scent mixing on her skin fills the air, and she relaxes even more into his embrace.

"I know," she whispers. "You're more than I could have ever hoped for. I won't do anything wrong. I won't mess it up."

CHAPTER 8

Sora

With a last heave, Sora drags a mat right to the edge of her enclosure's pond. She huffs from the exertion and drops the corner of the mat, eyeing it with satisfaction.

Although it's thick and heavy, she wrestled it all the way from the front of the enclosure to her favorite place to lie down outside of the enormous nest she sleeps in. The ground around the pond can become uncomfortable despite the spongy plants covering it so she'd decided to add some padding.

This mat normally sits on one of the stone benches at the front of the enclosure. Searin wanted her to have a comfortable place to sit when she's waiting for him. So far, she's never used it. When she knows he's coming, she stands anxiously at the gate. That's why she has repurposed it.

If Searin wants it back at the front, he'll pick it up and move it back himself. It's what he does when she re-arranges things in her enclosure in a way he doesn't like. There's never a reprimand or order. He just silently moves things around until everything is placed to his satisfaction.

She debated dragging the mat and possibly getting it dirty, but decided Searin probably wouldn't mind. He's amazingly unconcerned about all the expensive things he's purchased for her. When she stained one of the brand new wraps, he wasn't even upset. What a novel experience, having an owner that cares more about her than material goods.

With a little more maneuvering, she gets the mat in the perfect spot. She finds it peaceful to sit or lie there, listening to the water ripple and watching the small colorful creatures appear and disappear. She's lived in her new home for five rotations and hasn't remembered to ask Searin what the creatures are.

Of course, she has yet to ask him anything. She can't get over the years of obedience training to voice any questions or requests. He doesn't volunteer much information either, so she's in the dark about almost all things Talin.

The real mystery is her purpose. He doesn't seem to need much from her, except, well, her.

At least once a day and often several times a day, he comes to her enclosure. He grooms her, or feeds her, or simply cuddles her in his lap.

She's learned he likes it when she hugs his neck and presses her face against that small unprotected area of skin where the hard plating of his neck meets his shoulder plates. It's no hardship for her. She likes how he smells and his touch is always gentle. She doesn't worry about being hit or hurt anymore.

She's not so sure about the chemistry sparking between them, though. When he baths and grooms her, at times she's sure he's aroused, but he never acts on it. Scared of offending him or doing something wrong, she keeps her hands to herself during her baths and keeps her eyes focused anywhere but him.

But she can't ignore how his hands feel on her. Despite his size and strength, he's nothing but tender with her and his touch does things to her she's not sure she wants to think too deeply about.

If they were both human, she might say he's courting her. Even though they bought everything she could need from the shop, Searin brings her gifts on almost every visit.

Sometimes they're small things like a colorful stone or something to use on her hair—or mane as the Talins refer to it. Sometimes it's something expensive, like a wrap made of fabric that shimmers in the sun.

Despite all the gifts, he never touches her improperly. Even when he baths her, his touch feels affectionate but not salacious.

Bathing is rapidly turning into one of her favorite activities. He purchased a basket full of pleasant-smelling soaps and lotions that he uses when he grooms her. He must find great pleasure in it because he seems to draw out the process, especially after she's dry and he rubs pleasant smelling oil or lotion all over her body. Her skin has never felt so soft or looked so healthy.

And she's never felt so sexually frustrated in her life.

She never says anything to him and waits until late in the night to masturbate to images of him. During those times she imagines the bathing takes on a different tone and he starts kissing and touching her. She usually climaxes quickly.

But, goodness, she hasn't felt so horny since she was a fumbling teenager. Memories of heavy petting and awkward coupling make her smile.

As she reminisces, she absently runs her fingers through her hair, soft and shining from the expensive products Searin rubs into it every day.

Not only does her hair and skin look better, her entire body feels amazing. She's spent so much of her life hungry and in pain that it's a novelty to not have either unpleasant sensation plaguing her.

All her bruises are gone. Healthy fat is forming over her ribs and hips, and her breasts are enlarging. However long this new captivity lasts, she's going to enjoy it. Which is why she now lazes in the sun, watching the pond through half-lidded eyes.

Earlier that day Searin fed her a hasty breakfast and left, telling her he's very busy and won't be back until well after dinnertime. He left a handful of covered bowls full of prepared food for her to eat over the course of the day with strict instruction to consume them all before eleventh mark.

She's still not clear on the Talin time-keeping system but assumes it's roughly the time of evening when he normally comes back to feed her dinner. He promised if he wasn't home in time to feed her, one of his staff will. So far, he's the only one to come into the enclosure. She's never met any of his staff.

He also left a small pile of treats with instructions not to eat them all at once. The treats were all gone moments after he was out of sight.

The position of the sun in the sky tells her the day is roughly half over when she hears a noise at the gate of her pen. Excited to see Searin sooner than expected, Sora scrambles to her feet and hurries across her enclosure, only to come to a dead stop when she finds a female Talin she's never met striding into her cage.

"Oh, Searin, got a human!" the Talin exclaims as she shuts and locks the gate. "That explains so much. You seem a little scrawny, but it's hard to find humans for sale. I'm sure Searin had to make do with what was available."

Sora casts her eyes down and stays still, reverting to her old training. The woman's bare feet appear in her field of vision as a hand cups her chin, urging her to look up. She focuses on a point just past the woman's shoulder so she doesn't appear bold or challenging.

"You seem of breeding age," the woman murmurs. "Dinala has several breeding pairs. Have you been bred before, little human? Have you had any offspring?"

"No, Mistress," Sora answers obediently and feels herself quake a little in fear at the question. Is this Searin's wife or mate? Does this woman have power over her? "I've never had a child."

"Have you been examined? Are you able to breed?"

Unsure how to answer that because she doesn't want to invite herself to be examined again, she settles on a more neutral answer. "I don't know, Mistress."

"Of course. How silly of me to ask you something like that. It's not as if the healer would tell you directly. I'll just get the information from Searin." The woman leans a little closer. "Your eyes are a blue color. All of Dinala's stock has darker brown colored eyes. Can you see out of them? Are they inhibited in any way?"

"No, Mistress, I have normal vision."

Letting go of Sora's face, she sounds a happy rumble. "Very good, very good. Follow me," she orders.

She turns on her heels and walks to the nearby bench Searin often sits on when he feeds or cuddles her. Sora follows and stands patiently while the woman sits and shifts her belt a little and moves the pouch more to the side. When she's situated, she looks up expectantly. Sora remains still, unsure what to do.

"Hurry then," she says and taps her lap. Sora blinks, confused.

"I'm sorry, Mistress, I don't know what you want."

"Oh, you must be a little slow, poor human. Hopefully, you won't give that trait to your pups. Come climb on my lap. Let me touch you for a bit."

Of all the things that could have happened when Sora saw this woman enter her enclosure, this is the last thing she expects.

With more speed than grace, she climbs up on the bench and gingerly sits herself down on the woman's lap. The woman wraps her arms around Sora, pulls her tightly against her chest, and nuzzles her face against Sora's cheek.

"You smell strongly of Searin," she declares. "How long has he owned you?"

"I'm not sure, Mistress. Maybe ten or so rotations?"

"Hmmm, you must not be able to judge time well either. It's fine, little human. We don't breed for intelligence. Ten rotations, you say? That isn't long but more than enough time for Searin to have informed me of your purchase." The female makes the pleased rumble again and Sora feels the Talin's chest vibrating against her shoulder. "Now, be good and clutch me as humans do."

It takes Sora a moment to understand that the woman wants a hug. She wraps her arms around the woman's neck and puts her face against the her skin, the same way Searin likes.

This female Talin isn't as massive as Searin, but she has all the same hard plating as a male. Her smell is all wrong, though. Sora takes a deep breath in through her nose and then regrets it as the powerful smell of lavender fills her lungs.

No, not only lavender, but lavender mixed with a harsh cleanser. It's almost like she's gotten lavender infused soap in her mouth, only worse.

The scent makes her head hurt and turns her stomach. Opening her mouth to breathe, she focuses on trying to calm this sudden bout of nausea.

The woman gives a little rumble of happiness deep in her chest, much like Searin does, and squeezes her arms tighter around Sora. This is the first time a female Talin has held her, and she appears to be just as strong as her male counterparts. The tight hug makes Sora squeak with discomfort, and when she wiggles a little, the woman relaxes her hold slightly.

"Sorry," she murmurs, starting up a purring rumble. "I forget how very fragile even adult humans are. I've visited Dinala's humans many times. One of her breeding pairs has a little cub. She's an adorable creature and likes me best of everyone, except for her sire and dam."

The woman continues to talk about how good she is with the cub while holding Sora. She isn't sure how long they sit like this, the woman alternating between hugging her and petting her back or her head as she talks. At one point, she tugs Sora's hair a little and pulls back to look at it with a negative rattle.

"This is much too short. Did Searin shear it?"

"No, Mistress, my former Master liked it this length."

"That won't do. You'll need to grow it out. Humans are far more handsome when their manes are long."

"Yes, Mistress," Sora agrees as she's pulled back into a tight hug.

She might find this situation odd if Searin didn't spend large chunks of time cuddling and petting her each day. This must be a Talin thing, to buy humans for this purpose. At the market, even after they left the place that sold supplies for human pets, she garnered a lot of attention. Most simply watched as they walked by. Some bold individuals asked Searin if they could touch her. If her master wasn't such a high rank many more Talins would've tried to touch her or at least crowded Searin.

While Searin was turned away from her and engaged in a conversation, one female Talin even moved to pick her up without saying a word, just purring so loudly it was echoing off a nearby building. She didn't know Talins could rumble that loudly.

Searin had turned and rattled loudly, making everyone jump and the woman scurry away.

Her grandmother told her about old Earth and how humans kept creatures called dogs. Originally, dogs were kept for protection and to help when hunting, but eventually they became prized as companion animals. They no longer guarded or hunted; instead, they were there for the humans to pet and play with. Not unlike her with Searin.

Being a dog isn't so bad. Well, so far at least.

"I like your soft mane very much. We'll need to breed you to a male with a nice mane to make sure your pups inherit this trait. I'll have to talk to Searin about this today. There's no time to waste. Humans take so long to gestate we shouldn't delay."

Never mind. She takes back all her complimentary thoughts about Talins.

This woman is talking so casually about rape and forced pregnancy it's making her feel a little panicked.

Would they even let her keep the baby or take it away from her? The thought makes tears prick the backs of her eyes. This was never an issue with her former master. His species didn't breed for pleasure, and he wasn't interested in slave children, so Sora was never in any danger of sexual assault.

It appears that in her new situation she's safe from being beaten, but rape and childbearing are on the table.

The woman notices Sora's stiffness and gives her back a little pat. "Don't worry. I'll find you a handsome male with a long mane. I wouldn't let anything brutish or ugly near Searin's pet."

The cage door opening draws the woman's attention. Sora would like to pull away and look, but the woman's arms keep her locked in place.

"Halieni, I didn't know you were visiting," Searin says with the buzz of an annoyed rattle. "You didn't come to the house first to greet me. I wouldn't have known you were here except your husband contacted me looking for you. Your Ident isn't on and he's worried."

Sora feels deep relief at the realization that this woman isn't Searin's wife. Their familiarity with each other makes her think they might be family, perhaps siblings or cousins.

"He worries too much," she states dismissively with a look down at the small display on the Ident hanging off her belt. She lets go of Sora with one arm so she can tap the Ident a few times and then gives a negative rattle as she looks back up to Searin. "Let's not speak of my behavior, but yours! I had to stumble on your pet by accident. You didn't bother to inform me of your purchase." Those words are accompanied by a single, sharp challenging rattle.

"I wanted to let her get settled first," Searin explains, and he sounds much closer now.

Then she feels his powerful hands on her. It's Halieni's turn to make an annoyed rattle as she opens her arms so Searin can pick Sora up.

Once he's got hold of her, he strides to the bench across from Halieni and sits. Arranging her sideways in his lap, he draws her firmly against his chest.

"Hello master," she whispered, eagerly snuggling against him. It's a relief to be away from Halieni's strong smell and even better to have the familiar scent of cinnamon fill her nose.

"This is a venerable hobby for you to pursue," Halieni tells him, her tone cold and formal. "Breeding pets is common in the history of the Prime Family, as Mother likes to point out. Humans are an excellent choice. They are trainable and their appearance is pleasing. I'm confident our mother will be most pleased. Now that you collect, she might even be persuaded to lend you one of her studs."

"I have no plans to breed Sora."

"Oh, but you must." Halieni sounds distressed now. "If you don't want to contact Mother, I know other owners who have studs we can borrow and—"

Searin cuts her off with a loud clacking rattle of his back plates. No need to guess at the emotion behind that sound. He's angry.

His harsh voice reenforces the rattle. "I don't see how this is your concern."

Halieni stiffens at Searin's tone. They all sit in silence for a moment before she speaks again. "I want one of my own."

"A human?" Searin asks in a calmer tone. "You can't use mine as a surrogate. You will need to find another if you want a human to bear your young."

An annoyed rattle sounds from Halieni. "I don't need a human to carry my young. What do I care about that? When it is time for me to have a child, the cresh will grow and raise it. They already have my and my husband's genetic material stored. Let them grow my child in an artificial womb. I don't need a human pet to serve as a womb." Her tone is dismissive as she casually speaks of her yet-to-be-created child. She sounds completely uncaring of her future progeny.

Sora processes this new information. Do all Talins not raise their young or is that the privilege of the wealthy, influential families? Is it because of medical or cultural reasons? How long have they used artificial wombs or surrogates instead of bearing their own young? Do their children ever meet their parents before they are adults?

These ideas are inconceivable to Sora, whose mother was everything kind and nurturing despite living in a place of deprivation.

Again, so many questions and no courage to ask them.

"Then you want one as a pet, for your own use?" Searin asks, his voice inquisitive now instead of harsh.

"Yes, preferably a very young one who needs a great deal of care," Hanlieni's voice is quiet and pleading. "Human pups are helpless. They can't even feed themselves. I want one of them. But ones that young never show up in auctions and even finding young breeding age adults are rare. I've offered to buy a weaned pup from Dinala, but she refuses to sell her humans until they are adults. And then they passed the laws about when pups can be separated from their dams. I can't ask anyone to go against the law and sell me a pup."

"Except me?" Searin questions.

"You wouldn't be selling the pup to me, just entrusting me to care for it. The laws have accommodations if a dam isn't able or fit to raise the pup. If anyone asks, we could claim extenuating circumstances. I'm sure no one would question a member of the Prime Family." Her tone is pleading and just shy of desperate. Sora almost feels sorry for her.

Sora wishes she could ask Halieni why she wants a human child to care for instead of just raising her own young. She's suspicious that perhaps in Talin culture raising a pet is far more socially acceptable than one's own child. This puts her treatment in a whole new light.

The day Searin took her into the city center to see the healer and buy her things, she never saw any Talins touch each other. No one held hands, embraced, or even casually touched another on the back or shoulders.

But there was no reluctance to ask to touch her.

If they aren't interested in touching or showing physical affection with each other, why is every Talin she meets so eager to put hands on her? The only conclusion she can reach is that the Talins have decided to deny themselves affection with each other and now need to find it elsewhere. Humans must be a favorite source.

Suddenly, a deep feeling of pity for the affection-starved Talins fills Sora. Without thinking about it, she does something she's never done before; without permission she reaches a hand up and runs her palm down the back of Searin's plated head. Instead of just passively cuddling or snuggling, she's actively petting him back.

At first, he tenses at her touch, but after she does it a few times, he relaxes and starts purring again.

Halieni's voice reminds both of them that they aren't alone. "I've never requested anything from you before. I wish to ask for this, as your sister and potential future ruler."

Sora's heart breaks for the lonely woman. Still, as bad as she feels, she's glad Searin isn't immediately offering her up as a baby factory.

"I'll think about it, but don't rest your hopes here. If I were you, I would scour the slave markets and auction houses for humans. That's what Tieno does, and that's how we found Sora. There are too few here on Talarian and the demand is too high to rely only on local stock. You should see about investing your time off world to find your own. Or perhaps talk to other owners. Being Prime Daughter means it would be easy to manipulate others. But I wouldn't bother approaching our mother. If she won't let us even see her pets, she'll never consent to letting you take one."

Halieni sounds a soft, unhappy rattle. "I won't stoop to such dishonorable behavior. As Prime Daughter, others might feel obligated to give me their pets, even if they don't want to. And I know you're correct about Mother. I'll think about searching off-world. For now, I can see you won't be sharing your pet anymore today. I wish you a fruitful rotation."

"May you have a fruitful rotation as well, Halieni," Searin responds but doesn't get up or move to follow his sister out of the enclosure. He stays holding Sora and purrs.

CHAPTER 9

Searin

After Halieni's surprise visit, Searing makes sure to visit his pet every few marks throughout the day. That means he's forced to rush his morning work, slapping together data without properly ordering it or assessing it first. It's going to make one of his meetings more difficult later, but if he hurries he gets to visit Sora sooner.

Besides, he argues with himself, after he visits her, he's far more focused and does better work. And being focused during a holo-meeting is more important than drafting a perfectly worded Assembly Law Impact Assessment.

The last fifteen rotations have been the most pleasant he's experienced as long as he can remember. He seldom feels like his chest plates are holding together too tightly to breathe.

Instead, his armor plates feel loose and mobile, and his chestbox is always ready to sound a soothing rumble when his little human clutches him.

"There!" he exclaims with a triumphant rattle. He slaps down a hand on the display at his desk, sending the report to the committees section of the Unibase. Done with that, he stands and rushes out of his home and to Sora.

Entering her enclosure, he searches out the source of his physical relief and mental bliss. He finds her napping by the pond. He's learned to always check there first. It's her favorite place inside the enclosure. Going still, he gives himself a moment to just enjoy the sight of her.

Then he notices she's in full sun with only a single small wrap on, leaving most of her arms and legs bare. A negative rattle sounds from him, waking her up. With a startled gasp, she scrambles away from him.

She's done this before when she wakes, thinking she is still living with her former master. The first time she whimpered and moved away from him with clumsy haste, he was appalled, fearing her mind broken.

It took a panicked call to Tieno to understand that humans have vivid and terrifying memory recall during their sleep cycle they refer to as "nightmares." These memories can seem real and make the human react badly when wakened.

It took some insistence, but finally, Sora admitted suffering from these nightmares, but she assured him she doesn't remember them after she wakes. He's sure she's lying to him, afraid to admit to anything that might displease him. For now, he lets that go. He's in communication with her healer to see about any medication that might ease or rid her of the nightmares.

Patiently, he waits until she's fully awake and realizes she's safe. Once she smiles up at him, he gathers her into his arms and sits on the pad she was lying on.

"You shouldn't sleep in the sun," he admonishes her. "Not without covering yourself. The healer said that humans are especially susceptible to being burned from the UV radiation."

"It's not that bad. A little nap in the sun won't give me sunburns." As she talks, she cuddles into his chest, rubbing her cheek against one of the armor plates on his shoulder.

Although she doesn't have any scent glands, she seems to enjoy rubbing the skin of her face on the smooth texture of his neck, shoulder, and chest. He wonders if she's trying to emulate the way he rubs his cheeks against her to release the oil out of his scent glands when he scent marks her. In reality, it doesn't matter why she does it because the action is voluntary and he finds it enjoyable.

"Perhaps it won't burn as quickly as fire, but it can do similar damage. You'll be more careful or I'll lock you in your hut during the day when I'm not here." She goes still with those words, and he regrets the threat immediately but doesn't retract it. He's loathed to make his pet unhappy, but she needs to keep herself safe and healthy.

"I'll be more careful," she promises, her tone wooden and lacking the bright cadence he's come to relish. He doesn't like it when she speaks like this. It reminds him of the way she talked the day he bought her.

As he thinks of a way to bring back the easy interaction from earlier, he rubs his scent glands on the top of her head, enjoying the way the scent of his bonding oil changes as it soaks into her mane and scalp.

Originally, scent glands were used by a mating pair to mark each other to show affection and create a scent-bond. Now that their society has moved away from primitive methods of reproduction, Talins never release their scent glands on each other.

Sora, with her unique smell, makes his glands almost drip because they're so full. It's a problem he refuses to think about. He's forced to rub a salve on his face before going into the Apogee Assembly meetings to keep others from noticing.

The last thing he needs is to be accused of scent-bonding. Public ridicule for someone found bonding is the least of the bad things that would happen. As the laws are currently written, being discovered as scent bonded is an automatic death sentence.

Pushing those dark thoughts out of his mind, he focuses his attention on lightening the mood with Sora.

"Perhaps I should start wrapping you up in an omnie each morning," he teases her.

The long-sleeved cold-weather wrap reaches all the way to the ground on her slight frame. The thing is lined in a warm synthetic fur full of engineered nanos that produce heat if the ambient temperature drops too low. The cold weather season is far off, but he was eager to provide his pet with everything she might need, so he bought it early.

It doesn't escape his notice that she takes the garment to bed with her, but not to wear. She snuggles with it at night when she sleeps. Tieno explained that humans, especially the females, like to hold or rub soft things against their skin. That's why their wraps must be made of certain kinds of fabrics or risk damaging their delicate skin.

Fragile, frail humans. Even the sun can hurt them.

"It's too warm for an omnie right now," she argues, her posture relaxing a little.

"I'll have them make a wrap for you as long as the omnie and with a hood. Every part of you will be covered," he says. The moment the suggestion is out of his mouth he warms to it. "Yes, that's an excellent idea. An oversized wrap that will keep all your skin safe from the sun. That would be an excellent compromise, yes?"

"I suppose," she says and starts rubbing her fingers on his cheek, right over his scent gland. She isn't doing it consciously, but every time they snuggle, at least one hand finds its way to his face. He tries very hard not to react when she does it, but it feels delicious and forbidden when her delicate fingers play over that very sensitive part of Talin anatomy.

It's not enough for him to rub his scent glands on her hair; she wants his scent on her fingers as well. He's watched her rub her fingers under her nose, probably not even understanding that she's imbuing the skin there with his bonding oil.

She might not understand it, but she's becoming addicted to the smell of him. The scent of other Talin won't appeal to her and could even make her feel ill.

It was the same with scent-bonded Talins back when the practice was still legal. Thankfully it's accepted that weak, needy humans will almost always scent-bond with a Talin owner, but the reverse is never to happen.

"Cinnamon," she murmurs as her hand becomes slick with his oil.

"Cinnamon?" he repeats, having difficulty with the unfamiliar human word.

"Your smell, it's cinnamon," she explains. "I like it."

"I'm glad," he whispers, his comforting rumble drifting towards one of arousal before he can force it back.

The key now is to make sure no one realizes he might be scent-bonding to her as well. It's not supposed to happen. Talins aren't supposed to be able to scent-bond to glandless humans. But he can't deny the truth in front of him. If he's careful, it should remain a secret.

They cuddle for a while before she speaks. "How was work today?"

She often inquires about his tasks, and although she knows nothing of Talin politics or government, she seems to follow his explanations well. He's bought a brilliant human.

"My day was difficult, but it's much improved now," he tells her, reluctant to talk about his frustrations with the Apogee Assembly and the struggle under the current king, his father, who holds a top-ranking chair within that governing organization. He doesn't want his troubles intruding on his time with Sora. "Did you eat the meals I set out for you?"

"I've eaten half of them," she answers. "Thank you, Master." He ignores her use of Master. He's told her repeatedly to call him Searin, but she can't seem to bring herself to use his name, only Master, or if he pushes Master Searin. It's a battle he's not interested in waging at the moment.

Instead, he runs a hand across her thighs and lets it rest on her hip. She's still underweight but is looking much better. He hopes she'll be a heavier weight in his lap soon. He can't wait until her body is lusher with more padding covering her bones.

"Good, just remember to finish them before eleventh mark."

"It feels nice to eat," she admits.

"Is there anything you're missing or need, besides more treats?" he asks, interrupting his rumble of comfort to sound one of amusement.

"I always need more sweets," she says with one of her adorable human smiles. "Otherwise, I'm well, as you can see, Master. I need nothing more."

They lapse into silence, the wind gently rustling the trees around them. The smell of blooming flowers is almost overwhelming, and he looks absently around the garden he had others hastily plan and plant the day before he bought her.

Lying next to the pad is a pile of wilting bright orange flowers. They look to be knotted together to form a kind of circle. He leans over a little to inspect the flowers and Sora shifts her head away from his neck to see what's caught his attention.

"It's a flower crown," she explains, and her face flushes with color. He knows that means she's embarrassed. "My mom, that's my dam, taught me to make them when I was a child."

"And it pleases you to make them now. Is this nesting behavior? Is this a sign that you wish to have a pup of your own?"

He hopes not. He's not ready to have some male rut with his sweet human. He's not sure he'll ever be ready to risk her life with pregnancy and birth. Although with Talin healers ready to monitor pregnancy and assist with the birth, the chances of her being damaged or dying are low, but he can't fathom exposing her to any danger.

He's relieved when she vehemently shakes her head. "No, no, this doesn't mean I want a child. It doesn't mean anything like that." Then she ducks her head and mumbles something he doesn't quite catch.

"Repeat that," he demands, and she gives another little shake of her head.

He doesn't like to be forceful with her, but she said something, and he wants to know what it was. He puts one of his hands on her shoulder and forces her to sit up. When she won't raise her gaze, he rattles in irritation, and she jumps, looking up at him with fearful eyes.

"None of that," he tells her briskly. "Tell me what you said. It can't have been anything particularly bad." She hesitates, and he waits. One doesn't get to his level of politics without the ability to wait out an opponent.

"I'm not interested in having a kid. I'm just a little bored," she finally says in a rush of words and then practically tries to dive her head against his neck to hide her face. She's shaking a little as she speaks again, her voice muffled but audible. "Please don't be mad."

He doesn't pull her away from him; instead, he goes back to holding and petting her. After a moment's hesitation, she brings her arms up and starts petting him back. She learned quickly to avoid the sharp edges of back plates and only run her hand along his head or on his shoulders and neck.

"Bored?" he repeats as he glances around the enclosure.

Her words give him something to think about. It's true he's provided her with a comfortable place to sleep and room to move, but there's little in the way of enrichment in her enclosure. Besides eating and napping, what does she do all day to keep her clever mind occupied?

It's something he'll have to do something about. Perhaps he should contact Tieno. He doesn't want to provide Sora with anything that might distract her from his visits, but he also wants her to be engaged while he's gone.

"Do Talins not touch each other?"

The question is so out of character for the hesitant, fearful Sora that it takes Searin a few moments to register what she's asked. "What do you mean by 'touch each other?'"

"Like we are touching right now," she clarifies. "Do you guys ever hug, or snuggle close?"

"No." He feels uncomfortable with this line of questioning and gives his back plates a quick rattle of irritation. Sora's hands stop moving against his neck, and he almost curses himself. She's just being curious, and he's acting as if she's trying to learn state secrets.

Why is it, he thinks wryly, *when she's finally bold enough to ask questions, it would be on this sensitive topic?*

"I'm sorry, master!" she says quickly and starts petting him with frantic little movements.

"None of that," he says, and starts up a comforting rumble. "What have I told you about being afraid of me?"

"To tell you to stop whatever makes me afraid and that the ancestors would be ashamed of you for scaring me," she repeats.

"So what do you have to say to me?" he asks.

She pulls away a little so she can meet his gaze. "Bad Talin, no ancestors' appreciation for you!"

Her overly dramatic words cause a rumble of amusement to burble out of him.

"Excellently done! As a reward I'll answer your question, but I'm sure you'll find it a dull topic. We Talins aren't encouraged to touch each other with affection," he explains. "Scent-bonding and emotions like it are a weakness. In the distant past, we used to pair up and scent-bond. Scent-bonding was a primitive way to keep a couple together to raise offspring. With our modern technology and the cresh to raise young, there is no need for scent-bonding or anything as weakening as that."

"I never thought of love as making someone weak," she comments softly, her hands moving against his neck again. He wants her to pet the back of his head, where his plates are thin and the sensation is the strongest, but asking her to pet him in a certain way feels almost sexual and he's trying hard not to cross that line.

"When we first became a space-faring species, scent-bonded couples ended up separated by great distances, and both would suffer. If they were apart for too long, they could develop Collapsed Scent disease and often die."

"Die?" Sora gasps. "How awful."

"Not just die, but die a painful lingering death," Searin tells her grimly. "We also call it Ending. It became a problem when couples couldn't travel together. Scent-bonding caused inefficiencies for interspecies trading and in our ability to go to war."

"I can understand why that might lead to outlawing scent-bonding, but why artificial wombs?"

"Our females can't get pregnant without a scent bond," he explained. "Our species was reluctant to give up scent boding until a monarch lost his wife to a ship failure. He almost died about fifty rotations later from Ending. After that, he extolled the virtue of strength and said scent-bonding and affection were traps and a weakness for our entire species. The philosophical essays he wrote about the importance of clan honor, strict moral codes, and clear delineation of duties became almost like laws in our society."

"And that lead to babies being born and raised by a cresh?" Sora clarified.

"Eventually. It took a generation but over time we moved from the old ways to how it's done today. Creshes are excellent places to raise children because everyone who works there is highly trained and dedicated. No child is ever neglected and they're all pushed to achieve the most they're capable of. What more could a child ask for?"

"A mother's love," she whispers. He can tell by her tone that the thought saddens her.

"That is a human need. My mother felt great pride in me," he says. "I was created to honor my clan and my family line, and I've surpassed all expectations. I'm the youngest Apogee Assembly member of my generation, and I'm asked to serve on many committees. Both my father and mother have told me they couldn't have asked for a more accomplished child."

"It seems so cold," she murmurs.

Her words make him hug her a little tighter.

"If you are chilled, I can carry you into your hut for a warmer wrap or an omnie." He's already halfway to his feet when she pats his shoulder and gives a small chuckle.

"I'm sorry. I didn't mean I was chilled."

He settles back down, giving her a tight squeeze and then relaxing again. He doesn't want to continue this conversation any longer. Examining his own culture through Sora's eyes is unnerving and makes his chest tight.

He'd much rather talk of more pleasant things or not talk at all. Simply sitting, being in the moment with his little human warm and soft in his lap, is fulfilling. He starts up a soothing rumble, enjoying the way Sora not only relaxes into him but gives off a quiet little sigh.

"Let's enjoy the quiet," he says, knowing that even with a casual tone, Sora will take his words as an order. Obediently, she shuts her mouth and snuggles, bringing up a hand to pet his head with slow, gentle strokes.

All too soon the Ident clipped to his belt chimes, reminding him that he'll be late to a meeting if he doesn't leave soon. He stands up, her weight so light it doesn't impede him at all, and sets her down on her feet next to him. She gives a little frown, and he hopes it's because she's sad he's leaving.

"I'll be back by eleventh mark," he tells her. He pulls some of her silky mane over her shoulder and rubs it between his fingers. "Perhaps a grooming this evening. Your mane feels dirty." It isn't dirty at all, but it's as good an excuse as any to touch her all over her body without needing to examine his motives too much.

Before he can think too much about her naked body, he turns and leaves without another word.

CHAPTER 10

Sora

Some kind of bugs are in the plants right outside of her hut and because there's nothing better to do, she sits and watches them. They're about the size of her smallest finger with dozens of legs but no discernable head. She can't even figure out what they're doing because it doesn't appear they're eating the plant or harvesting it. They just keep skittering up and down the stems without pause.

The other thing that strikes her as fascinating is that they never run into each other. They move fast and frantically but never pick the same stems to run up and down. Their coloring is very similar to the deep purple of the plant they inhabit, and after a cursory search of her enclosure, she hasn't found them on any of the other plants. When she tries to impede their progress with anything, they turn around instead of trying to go over whatever is in their path.

If she ever gets the courage to ask questions regularly, what these little bugs are doing will be one of the questions on a growing list of hundreds of questions.

The sound of footsteps brings her attention to the path in front of her enclosure. She expects Searin to appear, not a male Talin she's never seen before.

Training tells her to get up and greet the stranger respectfully; instinct tells her to hide. Caught between the two, she sits on the ground next to the purple bushes and watches.

The stranger puts his palm on the gate and it obligingly clicks open. Out of curiosity, she tried the gate several times within the first rotation of her new captivity. It didn't surprise her when the biosignature lock didn't open for her. But whoever this stranger is, his biosignature is programmed into the biolock so he's able to walk right in.

Once inside the enclosure, he locks the gate and looks around. When he finds her, he sounds a short, sharp rattle as he walks. She's not sure, but this rattle sounds anticipatory.

"Human, I'm Favilorn. Come here to me right now."

His tone is authoritative and rough, making her scramble to her feet, but she doesn't hurry to him. Instead, she walks with short, halting steps.

He stops moving the moment she's on her feet and when she gets within arm's reach, he grabs her upper arm and hauls her the rest of the way. His grip is painful, making her gasp.

He gives her a little shake. "I know you can move faster than that. My father told me that humans require discipline and guidance. Your kind can't be trusted to even care for yourselves."

Keeping her eyes on the ground, she rounds her shoulders, trying to look meek and subservient. "I'm sorry. I'll be quicker in the future."

"See that you do. I'm the Prime Son's head of household. It will be my duty to care for you while he's gone. You will obey me and thrive."

It sounds like he's ordering her to be healthy and happy, which is a strange way to go about things.

He glances around the enclosure and makes the dripping-on-metal of an affirmative or approving rattle. "You haven't soiled your living space yet. That's good."

"I know how to use an elimination facility," she mutters to herself but not softly enough.

Sounding the buzzing swarm of wasps rattle, he gives her another shake, his grip more intense. If he squeezes any tighter, he might do more damage to her arm than just some bruising. Considering how gently Searin treats her, as well as all the other Talins she's met so far, she knows this isn't normal. That gives her the courage to speak out in the face of his obvious annoyance.

"You're hurting me."

"I'm not doing permanent damage," he retorts and drags her to a nearby bench. "I've been monitoring Prime Son Searin's schedule closely, and today he won't have time to see to your care himself."

If that's Favilorn's only concern, perhaps she can get him to leave. "He was just here to check on me."

With another shake of her arm, he makes the whooshing-snap of a derisive rattle. "Don't lie, human. Your kind lacks any sense of honor, just as my father warned me. He told me to be extra vigilant with you. You humans have little intelligence and no self-control. Searin has been in meeting all day. He couldn't have visited you."

Dragging her to the bench Searin always uses, he sits down and roughly pulls her into his lap.

He rattles in annoyance as she flails, trying to get herself situated. Losing patience, he grabs with hard hands to steady her. If he keeps this up, she's going to have bruises all up and down her arms.

"I'm going to let you cling to me for a quarter of a mark. I've read that's a basic requirement for your kind every rotation. Don't speak and don't wiggle. You're so clumsy it's amazing you can traverse your enclosure without hurting yourself."

With his arms wrapped around her, he tightens his hold until she can barely breathe.

"Please," she begs. "Too tight, I can't—"

His grasp doesn't ease and his angry rattle interrupts her protest. "Silence! I will diligently do my duty, but I don't need my earholes filled with your prattle."

If she survives this embrace, she's going to tell Searin that humans don't require anything like this suffocating hug. Someone needs to explain to these Talins exactly what humans need and don't need, even if goes against all her slave training.

And this guy needs a lesson on how to properly hug someone. She's starting to get spots in her vision because she can't breathe past this Talin's tight hold.

Closing her eyes, she concentrates on pulling air into her lungs as best she can.

She didn't think the moment could get any worse, but she feels pressure on the top of her head and a strange scent fills her nose. She can't put her finger on what it smells like, but the effect is instant.

Blinding pain shoots through her brain and her stomach rebels. She concentrates on not vomiting for fear of angering him even further.

She's so focused on breathing, she's only vaguely aware of the sound of a gate crashing open and an echoing rattle.

"What do you think you're doing?" Searin's rare fills the air.

She opens her eyes to see him moving toward her, his body nothing but power and purpose.

If she had extra air in her lungs, she'd cry out in relief as he rips her away from Favilorn. He sets her gently on the ground. Her legs don't support her and she crumples to her hands and knees. At least it's a convenient position for vomiting.

Retching violently, she evacuates everything from her stomach. There is the sound of fighting but she can't look up, she's too busy voiding her stomach until nothing is left but bile.

When she can look up, she sees Favilorn on the ground, dazed. The fence above him is dented in the rough shape of his body. Searin must have tossed the servant across the enclosure and into the fence.

As she watches, Searin strides up and grabs the man by his throat to lift him back to his feet.

"What do you think you were doing?"

The armor plating on Talin throats must be tough because Favilorn can breathe and talk while Searin holds him in the air by his neck alone.

"Prime Son Searin, I'm doing my duty to you as head of household."

With little apparent effort, Searin carries the man to where she sits, gasping for breath. She flinches back a little as Searin draws closer, fearful of both men at the moment.

Dropping the man to the ground in front of her, he still maintains his grip on Favilorn's throat. She whimpers and draws away as Favilorn's eyes bore into her.

"Look at her. Does she look like she's being well cared for?"

"She's just a human. We must be strict with them," Favilorn tries to explain but is cut off by Searin's thundering war rattle. It sounds like the pounding of thousands of feet!

"Look at her face. That is the face of a human in distress. You did that to her!" He's roaring again and Favilorn is visibly flinching with each word.

Pulling the man back to his feet, Searin tosses him at the enclosure gate. The gate bends a little under the impact but doesn't break. Favilorn falls to the ground in a heap with the wind knocked out of him. Gasping, he doesn't try to get up.

Searin sounds another war rattle loudly enough that Sora's chest vibrates slightly.

Favilorn cowers and Sora feels no sympathy. Now he knows what it's like to be bullied by someone stronger and bigger!

"You will leave and never come near my pet or my property again."

At Searin's command, Favilorn scrambles to his feet and fumbles with the gate's biolock, leaving it wide open as he runs away.

If Sora didn't feel so horrible, she would have laughed.

Once Favilorn is gone, Searin turns to her and drops to his knees next to her. His quills fold flat against his forearms as his claws retract. He rumbles out a sound of worry.

"Can you talk? How damaged are you?"

She opens her mouth to talk, only to start crying. Frantic now, Searin gathers her in his arms and stands up. "I'll get you to the healers. Please don't expire on me, little Sora. Please hold on."

"I'm fine," she gasps out between sobs. "Not hurt. Just upset."

The whole situation suddenly strikes her as funny. She lived with brutal beatings for years, yet the callous treatment of Favilorn turned her into a weeping mess. Under Searin's tender care, she's gotten soft quickly.

Within a few strides, Searin reaches a stone bench and sits down, carefully cuddling her to him. It doesn't take long for Searin's tender treatment to make her feel better. The strange smell is still there, making her head hurt, but at least she feels safe.

Maneuvering her slightly, he frees an arm so he can reach the Ident clipped on his belt near his hip. Pulling it free, he taps the small square screen on one side. After a brief pause, it beeps, and Searin speaks into it rapidly.

"Topian, get a healer here now for Sora. And make sure Favilorn leaves the property. He's not to come near here again."

"Understood, Prime Son," a voice responds.

With the communication complete, Searin attaches the Ident back to his belt. Then he rubs his face against the top of her head. Unlike Favilorn, this movement feels soothing and when the smell of cinnamon fills her nose, she relaxes against him.

"I can smell his bonding scent on you," Searin mutters, his voice full of anger. "That must be why you were voiding your stomach. Ancestors, what was he thinking?"

"H-he said something about humans needing contact every rotation. But he held me too tight."

"Arrogant and useless. I only took him into my employ because my father requested it. After reading his service report from his last household, I shouldn't have agreed."

He starts to rattle in anger again, but when it makes Sora gasp, he stops and increases the intensity of his purr instead. "I'm going to change the biosignature protocol on your gate, my sweet little Sora. No one but my family, Tieno, and a select servant will get in."

She almost asks if she can have a weapon, but she knows that to be so unlikely as to be laughable. Still, it would've been nice to blast a hole in Favilorn instead of almost being hugged to death by him.

When the healer gets here, the first thing she does is rub something in Sora's hair that makes her scalp tingle. It eliminates the last of Favilorn's scent and makes Sora's stomach calm down.

Then the healer strips Sora down and examines her injuries. She isn't concerned about the bruises that almost send Searin into a rage again when he sees them, but she rumbles with concern when she scans Sora's chest.

"There is damage to a rib and her lung on that side," she informs Searin. The healer gives her a vial of medication to swallow. It quickly mutes the pain and Sora pulls in a lung full of air.

"She's not to do anything strenuous for twenty rotations, and she needs to consume one vial of medication every rotation," the healer explains as she hands Searin several vials. "I'll send the rest of the doses later. Other than that, I can't do much to heal the damage, but it's not life threatening, and the pain is easily managed. Humans might be susceptible to injury, but at least they are easy to treat." The healer rumbles out a laugh at her attempt at humor.

Neither Searin nor Sora find her joke even remotely funny. "I thank you for your gift of time and skill, Healer Yeshem. You are free to go about your day. I wish you a fruitful rotation." With that dismissal, Healer Yeshem gathers up her things and leaves.

Once the healer and her assistant are gone, Sora relaxes against Searin and closes her eyes. She's exhausted and wants nothing more than to fall asleep in his arms.

"Are you afraid of me now, little Sora?" Searin asks in a voice so quiet she almost doesn't hear him.

"Never," she sighs out and knows it's the truth. He's only owned her for a short time, but that short time has been the best days of her adult life.

"I should've seen to Favilorn sooner. I didn't think he would ever come near you. I left instructions with everyone to avoid you."

"He thought he was being an obedient servant."

"He thought he could take advantage," Searin counters. "He rubbed his scent glands on you. He wanted you to scent-bond to him. He'll never have a human and he thought to steal you by forcing you to scent bond to him." His arms tense, but he doesn't tighten them around her. "My servant tried to engineer it so I'd have to give you to him for the sake of your health. I didn't realize how much danger you would face even from a member of my staff. You are just too tempting for others."

"It's hard to predict danger," Sora tells him as she puts her palm on his neck and starts petting him. She leans her head in so she can give that length of exposed skin on his neck a little kiss. "The important thing is that you saved me."

"Always," he promises. "Never doubt it."

CHAPTER 11

Sora

Setting aside the small information square Searin gave her before he left, Sora gazes up at the azure sky and smiles. As she lies there, she lets her mind drift and tries to sort through both the knowledge she just read and her feelings about Talins in general.

Although he canceled every trip he could, the journey to a Clan Assembly meeting turned out to be unavoidable. He left two rotations ago, giving her the information square set up to translate from Talin to Universal. He also gave access to the planet's UniBase so she can read to her heart's content.

Most of the content is dry and difficult for her to understand, but she's slowly learning about Talin law, culture, history, and politics.

As fascinating as she finds it, Searin invades her thoughts constantly. Her mind is always wandering back to her bath times and the way he lingers on her breasts and sex, almost as if he's teasing her. He didn't make any sounds as he bathed her, no purring or rattles, just silence as his broad, powerful hands washed and then applied lotion to her entire body.

She doesn't need the daily bath. She's clean and doesn't do anything to get dirty, so she's not sure what to make of this attention. If it was any other species than the Talin, she'd say Searin is slowly seducing her. But that can't be possible.

After two rotations spent reading, she's much better informed about the Talins, and one thing comes up repeatedly. Talins don't do tender, soft emotions. Marriage and sex—but no love.

And their view on sex isn't much better than their view on love. It's considered a biological function to release hormones and relieve stress only. Intercourse is frowned upon because it can lead to "accidental scent-bonding." Couples who mostly abstain are congratulated for their discipline.

Reproduction happens at a cresh where children are grown in artificial wombs and then raised by skilled staff. Parents only take over the rearing of their children when they reach the adultlette stage, roughly the equivalent of a human at between 17-19 years old. Once they leave the cresh they're expected to learn their jobs and duties within the family and decide on a career.

When she told Searin the Talin way of life seemed cold, she didn't know how correct her statement was. Marriages are about contracts and political liaisons. Children are to carry on family lines.

When she started reading about humans, she laughed herself silly. Most of what Talins believe are fundamental human traits are nothing but exaggerations or utter absurdity.

According to one article, humans can cry themselves into a serious illness. Sure, she's seen depression and sadness take their toll, but no one died of a crying jag.

Another article hypothesized that because humans evolved to be so helpless they were forced to gather in large groups and press into each other for protection back on Old Earth. That theory states this evolutionary trait of huddling for safety is why they need to be held and cuddled all the time.

The one thing that occurs to her after reading dozens of articles about humans is that the Talins have created a culture where touching and cuddling a pet isn't only more acceptable, but the only form of physical affection available to them.

It makes her sad for this species, but she can only be grateful that Searin selected her to be his pet. As silly as all these theories are, those beliefs mean Sora is pampered. She might even go so far as to say she's being spoiled.

Footsteps pull Sora's attention to the front of her enclosure, making anxiety settle in her chest. Searin isn't supposed to be home for several more rotations, and Tieno already checked on her this morning. Her next meal isn't due for at least another mark. No one should be near her enclosure at this time of day.

"Human, I'm here again," Halieni calls out, making Sora relax slightly. She hurries to meet Searin's sister, dutifully casting her eyes down when she gets close.

Halieni doesn't greet her, and Sora doesn't ask why the woman is visiting. She moves to stand in front of her, head bowed slightly, and waits. "I'm in a hurry. Hold out your wrist."

Without hesitation, she holds out her arm, and Halieni wraps a wide black band around it. The band does nothing for a moment but then tightens itself until it's snug but not uncomfortable.

Sora risks a glance up at Halieni, but the woman's focus is entirely on the band. When it gives a few beeps and loosens again, Halieni snatches it off and examines it. Then she gives a happy rumble.

"This is very good," she declares. "The ancestors must be guiding my actions because the timing will work out perfectly. Prepare yourself, human. I'll be back soon, make yourself clean and receptive."

Nonplussed and feeling mildly threatened, Sora watches Halieni leave. Questions flood her mind, so she rushes off to find her information square to do research.

She doesn't find out much because the band Halieni used is a standard health monitor that could check any one of a myriad of items.

Sora wishes Searin were home and Halieni didn't have access to the inside of her enclosure. Those wishes are even more heartfelt when Halieni returns not much later with a human male and two formidable Talins following her. As they all troop into her enclosure, and Sora backs away with a bad feeling growing in her chest.

The two male Talins following Halieni aren't as big as Searin, but they're still large and intimidating. They're wearing matching dark blue pants and both of them have the same emblem on their belts. They must work or serve Halieni.

The human they drag into her enclosure catches her attention. It's obvious he doesn't want to be there as one guard forces him to walk forward with a heavy hand on the leash attached to his collar.

His face is a combination of fear and anger, but he doesn't say anything as he stumbles and tries to grab at the leash attached to him. He must have tried this maneuver before because the Talin casually jerks hard on the leash, making the human stagger and fling his arms out for balance.

The moment he gains his feet again, he tucks his hands behind his back to appease the guard, who grunts and tugs the leash again to move him forward. He walks with small slow steps, risking another yank at his neck.

"Mistress Dinala wouldn't want me here. She doesn't like us leaving the compound," he protests, and Halieni reaches out to give him a little slap. His head whips back and blood appears at the corner of his mouth.

"Be silent," she orders. "I don't need your mistress's permission. I have her husband's instead. While she's gone, he is your caretaker. Now stop this whining and disrobe."

Nothing about this situation is good and she can only think of one reason Halieni would bring a human male here.

Sora tries to speak but can't seem to make the words come out. Dropping to her knees and ducking her head down in submission helps her find her voice.

"Mistress Halieni, Master Searin doesn't wish to breed me." She tries to inject as much subservience into her tone as possible.

I'm not challenging you; she silently tells Halieni. *I'm just trying to remind you that my real owner doesn't want this. Please, please listen.*

"And you need to remain silent as well," Halieni says, her words punctuated by an angry rattle. "I'll make sure you're rutted and with a pup before he gets back. If he decides to get rid of you, I'll buy you. Even if he keeps you, he won't want the pup, so I get it. There is no way I won't get what I want." Her voice is cold, hard, and determined.

"Please, Mistress—" Sora begins but is cut off when Halieni gives a sharp order to one of the guards.

"I can't strike the female. You need to silence her."

He grabs her by the back of the neck and pulls her up on her knees. When she opens her mouth to gasp, he forces something hard and round between her teeth. Straps cinch around the back of her head to secure the thing in her mouth.

When she tries to reach up to touch it, the guard takes both her hands and efficiently cuffs them behind her back. Then he picks her up and carries her into the hut, dropping her unceremoniously face down on the bed. The moment she hits the bed, she tries to wiggle off, but the guard places a hand on her back, keeping her in place.

It all happens so fast Sora doesn't have time to struggle against the guard, not that it would have done her much good. She screams behind the gag, but it comes out like a muffled whimper.

No one speaks during this process. No order from Halieni, no request for information from the guards. This tells Sora they've planned everything out ahead of time. The health band must have had something to do with ovulation. With Searin gone, Halieni has the opportunity to get the child she wants, unconcerned with how it will affect the human pet she's using.

"I can't do this. Please, I just can't," the other human tells Halieni.

Hearing cloth ripping, Sora twists her head around to better see the others in the room. The man is now naked, one guard holding his ruined dark gray wrap. To Sora's relief, the man's penis hangs limply between his legs. He's talking, his expression fearful and his tone imploring.

"Humans don't work this way. I can give you genetic data if you wish to grow a child, but I can't force her. It must be a willing coupling."

"No artificial wombs. I want the baby to be healthy. That means growing within the female herself," Halieni tells him, her voice harsh and her movement violent as she crosses the hut to stand in front of the man. He tries to shrink back, but she grabs his leash and pulls his head forward.

"Make yourself ready for her. You must perform today." She raises her hand again threatening to hit him. The man flinches but keeps shaking his head.

Bitterness chokes Sora. So much for humans being treasured pets. Pet or slave, they're still possessions with little to no independence.

Thankfully, Halieni doesn't slap the reluctant man. Instead, she lowers her hand and gives a rumble.

"I didn't bring two gags. I thought you would be much better behaved. Dinala tells me you're her most favored human, well-trained and smart. You should know better than to refuse any request."

Halieni reaches down and cups the man's flaccid penis. "This needs to be engorged with blood to copulate. Correct? Like a Talin male?" she asks. The male jerks a little but doesn't pull away from her grip. The look in his eyes is pure panic now.

"Yes, Mistress, that's why I can't perform. I just can't get hard, not if she's not receptive." The man is almost in tears, and Sora finds herself feeling for him.

She's suffered all kinds of horrible pain. Would rape be all that bad? Especially if it will save another human from being hurt? She's never been in a position to help another.

The thought gives a strange sort of courage.

She struggles a little, trying to get the guard holding her to look at her face. When he does, he gives a little rattle of warning. "Be still or I'll be forced to put more bindings on you," he warns.

Never has trying to surrender been so difficult. She needs him to take off the gag so she can talk. Then she can assure her fellow human it will be okay. She doesn't want it, but she doesn't want him hurt anymore either.

"Please, Mistress, even if I could make myself hard, I'll hurt her if I try to rut her when she doesn't want it. And if I hurt her, we're unlikely to produce a child," he explains quickly.

After he speaks, he braces for another blow from Halieni. No hit lands. Sounding a frustrated rattle, Halieni steps away and looks first at him, then at Sora, and finally at the guard holding Sora down.

"Do you think the female is truly unwilling?" she asks him. "I've been told mated pairs are lusty creatures."

"She's been trying to scream and struggles despite the bindings," the guard informs Halieni, truthful but unemotional regarding her plight. "If he tries to mount her, I think she'll kick too. From what I've observed, fighting isn't part of their normal mating behavior. Maybe it's because this is an unfamiliar male. If you want this to continue, I'll need to secure her legs to make sure she doesn't hurt the male, but that's not ideal. The best course of action would be to let them get to know each other over the course of several rotations."

"I don't have time for these two to grow familiar. I can't leave them alone together here unattended, even for a few marks. I have too much to do to waste an entire day waiting for two pets to decide they like each other enough to rut." Halieni rattles with annoyance.

Everyone remains still and silent as she looks at all of them. Her irritated rattling stops, and she waves her hands at the guards.

"I'll need to make other plans. Release the female and take the male back to Dinala's compound. I'll contact you when I've thought of something."

The guard holding her takes the restraints and gag off and walks away. She watches the rest of them leave her hut as she remains on the bed, shaking and sweating.

Once she hears the enclosure gate bang shut, she sits up and starts considering the room around her. Halieni will be back, and Searin's not here to protect her. Her next few meals have already been delivered, so she has no chance of gaining the attention of a servant. Tieno won't be back until the following morning at the earliest.

No one to talk to and no way to contact anyone.

She's going to need to come up with a plan before Halieni gets back. She'll have sex with this stranger if she has to, but that's going to be her last resort.

The hiding spot she picked is good enough that she hears them coming, but she can't see them. She forces herself to keep her breathing even. She doesn't want to hold her breath and then gasp because she runs out of air. Even breathing will keep her heartbeat slow. Prey is easily discovered if it moves. She needs to be still and silent.

The sounds of the gate opening and closing. Footsteps.

"Human? Pet? Come out right now!"

She'd laugh if she wasn't so busy keeping herself from succumbing to fear. Halieni doesn't even know her name. That's nothing new. Master De probably didn't know her name. He always called her Slave.

She can just make out some movement as one of them walks around the enclosure. "Why is she being so willful?" Halieni asks with an aggravated rattle.

"Neither human wanted to rut earlier," one guard points out. It's the man who held her down earlier. "It's not surprising that she's being disobedient." His tone is nothing but respectful, but his words feel like he's admonishing Halieni. She doesn't seem to notice.

"Headstrong human," she mutters loudly enough for Sora to hear, even perched high in an ornamental tree. "Fornian, check the enclosure, Remos, strip the male. I'll check in the hut."

The guards don't respond as they go about their tasks. She hears Halieni and Fornian walk away from where she hides. Then she hears clothing rustling and a small sound of pain and a protest from the other human.

"By the gods, be gentle. I'm not fighting you. You don't need to rip anything." The human's voice is strained, probably from whatever the guard is doing to him.

Remos gives off a warning rattle. When he speaks, his voice is threatening. "We brought two gags this time. I don't want to hear any more of your whining."

She hears another rip and a gasp from the human. Remos has no sympathy. "Be quiet, you weak, pathetic thing. You don't even know how privileged you are. You get to have all the female flesh you could ever want with no repercussions and you say no. You can hold them, touch them, rut them, but you refuse. What kind of fool are you?"

"Jealous?" the human taunts Remos. Sora almost gasps at his insolent tone.

She expects to hear the slap of flesh as Remos retaliates. Instead Remos sounds a fast rattle of aggravation, followed by the distinct sounds of a small scuffle. The scuffle ends in the sound of metal clinking and a muffled cry from the human.

Now it's Remos's turn to voice a taunt. "No more walking or talking for you. Act out again and I'll make sure the gag stays on even after we take you back," he growls. "I'll leave your hands bound behind your back and leash you to the top of your enclosure for the rest of the day so all you can do is stand and hope I come back to release you before you grow too tired. Don't test me on this. You know I'll do it."

She shivers at the threat and realizes these guards must work for Dinala, not Halieni, because it sounds like he interacts with this male regularly. Then she's distracted from Remos and the other human as Fornian passes under her.

She took great pains to bathe herself repeatedly, trying to wash all scent from her body. She knows the Talins have an excellent sense of smell, so she used the industrial cleaner she found in a small box of cleaning supplies at the front of the pen. It was probably originally meant to keep the outside of the hut clean. It was harsh on her skin, but if it works, it was worth it.

She also put on the greenest wrap she has to help hide in the tree's foliage. She wrapped her hair up in a piece of cloth normally used as a decorative belt, leaving a long end wrapped loosely around her face.

She climbed the tree with the most flowers and strongest smell, hoping it would cover whatever scent she might produce if she starts sweating from fear.

"She's not in the hut," Halieni declares, startling Sora. She didn't hear the woman walk back. She was too focused on Remos and the human.

"She must be hiding," Remos responds. "Insolent human."

"Indeed, my brother has spoiled her. Leash the male to the bed in the hut," she orders Remos. "Then help us find the female. She can't have gotten out."

She hears Remos lead the male human away as Halieni wanders off. She can just see the woman poking her hand into a bush. Now she just needs to get a little lucky.

"She's on the small side for a human. She could hide in any of the foliage," Remos comments when he returns.

"Sometimes when the humans are reluctant to do something, Councilor Dinala offers them a treat," Fornian volunteers as he searches a bush almost directly under the tree she's hiding in.

Don't look up, she silently pleads. *Please, please, please don't look up.*

But Fornian looks up, and his eyes settle right on her as if he knew she was there the entire time. Her heartbeat races, breaking out in a cold sweat. Their eyes meet and hold for a beat, and then he casually looks away and starts searching another bush.

Fornian might be forced to obey Halieni for the moment, but he doesn't want to. He just showed her, in no uncertain terms, he's on her side.

"What kind of treat?" Halieni asks, then grumbles. "I don't understand why these two are being so difficult. This should be a simple process. I'm not asking them to cut off a body part."

"The male said forced mating brings pain," Fornian explains. "Maybe it's a very intense pain. Most creatures go to great lengths to avoid pain. None of the humans Servant Citizen Dinala owns like to receive or give pain. It might be a human trait. They are very fragile after all."

"You've made your point, Fornian," Remos grunts. "I served Commander Sassion for many solars and he had a breeding pair. The female didn't like the male, but they had pups anyway, so I know for a fact that this human can be bred even if she doesn't want to and it can produce young. Forced breeding isn't pleasant, but it doesn't do permanent damage."

"I'm not sure that's correct," Fornian counters with a challenging rattle.

"Enough," Halieni nearly shouts. "Fornian, what kind of treat does Dinala offer her humans?"

"Depends on the human," Fornian replies. "For Dorn, the male we brought, she offers time with her. He adores her. For Sana, she offers pretty rocks or crystals. For the little ones, it is almost always sweets."

Dorn. She finally knows the male's name and a little more about this situation. It seems both Fornian and Remos work for this mysterious Dinala. The same Dinala that Dorn loves.

Sora's known a few slaves who loved their owners, but they were treated far better than she, and unlike Master De, their owners seemed to feel genuine affection for their slaves. She never understood that until Searin. He's different. He's wonderful, and kind, and gentle, and…

She might already be in love with him. She's going to need to examine that revelation later. Right now, she needs to stay focused on what's going on in her enclosure.

She listens to Remos curse humans under his breath as he beats at the bushes and waits for him to move further away.

The next part of her plan is to slip into a spot they've already searched before they think to search the trees. If she can delay long enough, Halieni will run out of time. With Fornian helping her, she might just make it.

Halieni, Remos, and Fornian comb the bushes under her and then move off to search around the hut. Fornian doesn't look up, and neither of the other two bother.

Once they're on the far side of the hut, she takes that opportunity to slip down from the tree and head to the next spot.

She prepared three other hiding places around the enclosure, hopefully that'll be enough.

She finishes burrowing into the spot next to the hut when she hears footsteps. She can't tell from this angle if it's Fornian or Remos.

Slow, steady breathing, she reminds herself. *Stay calm.*

"I might have a better idea," Remos calls back as he walks by her new hiding place. She hears the gate to her enclosure make a sound as Remos taps on it. Then, to her horror, her collar gives off a sharp chirp.

"She's over here!" Remos shouts as he dives for her. She pops out of the bush and rushes back to the tree, scrambling up into the branches before the Talin can grab her.

Her smaller size serves her well as she climbs up into the smaller branches at the top. Neither Remos nor Fornian can follow her up without the risk of breaking branches and falling.

"Get down here," Halieni shouts. "Bad human! Spoiled, willful pet. Climb down right now. You've wasted enough time with your hiding game."

"This isn't a game to me," Sora retorts, risking Halieni's ire. "Searin wouldn't want this!"

"Get her down," Halieni orders. "I don't care if you hurt her. As long as it's not severe, she can be healed."

New fear spikes through Sora at Halieni's words. She's in danger of injury now.

"No," she protests. "Please–"

Whatever else she was going to say is cut off when Remos steps up to the tree, puts his shoulder to it, and pushes. The entire thing quickly starts listing to the side and Sora gives a little scream as her perch gives way to Remos's strength.

"Newly planted," Remos grunts as he strains. "It hasn't had time to fully take root. Fornian, grab her once the tree falls."

"I don't think this is wise," Fornian objects and moves under the tree. His eyes meet Sora's, and he holds out his arms. "You need to jump, little human. Please. I'll catch you. If you fall with the tree, you might be very hurt."

Sora doesn't have a choice. Remos is making the tree sway violently under her, and she's high enough that she could end up seriously injured if she falls with the tree.

Gathering her courage, she jumps toward Fornian. It feels like he plucks her out of the air and then swiftly moves aside to allow the tree to crash down. He holds her tightly for a moment, the tree between them and the other two.

"I can't stop Halieni," he whispers in her ear. "But I will try to keep them from doing anything extra to hurt you. Don't fight, please. I can't protect you if you fight. Dorn's a good male. He'll try to make it pleasurable for you."

With her plan in ruins, Sora resigns herself to being raped. Tears gather in the back of her eyes.

"I won't fight," she agrees.

"Bring her to the hut," Halieni orders with an inpatient gesture.

Fornian carries her into the hut, and she almost cries out when she sees Dorn. The poor man is gagged and hogtied on the floor next to her nest. When their eyes meet, she tries to give him a reassuring smile.

"It's okay," she mouths to him. "It's going to be okay."

"Hold her still," Halieni orders and steps close to her, blocking her view of Dorn. "If she needs to be willing for him to rut her, then we make her willing. Open your mouth, little human, or I'll cause you pain."

Halieni is terrifying now. This woman wants something, and nothing is going to stop her. Sora opens her mouth, and Halieni shoves what looks like a round, thin, cracker inside.

"Close your mouth, but don't chew or swallow. Let the medication dissolve on your tongue."

Doing as ordered, Sora closes her mouth around the thin object. It breaks apart almost immediately, making her tongue tingle as it absorbs into the lining of her mouth. After a few moments, Halieni taps her cheek.

"Open and let me see." Sora opens her mouth for inspection and Halieni nods her head in satisfaction. "Good. You may place her on the nest. You don't need to bother restraining her any further. She'll be willing soon enough, and then we'll let Dorn go."

Fornian gently sets her down in the soft nest and then locks her collar to a tether one of them must have secured to the wall earlier. She sits on the bed as they all stand, towering over her, staring at her.

She pulls her legs up against her chest, wraps her arms around her shins, and drops her eyes to stare at their feet. She wonders if the medication is supposed to put her to sleep or make her drunk and drowsy so she won't object to Dorn mounting her.

Soon she feels a tingling in her sex and her breasts become heavy and ache. She shifts uncomfortably as wetness gathers between her legs.

With growing horror she realizes what Halieni did.

The medication is an aphrodisiac, probably a hormone of some kind. Right now, she feels mild discomfort, but it's building fast and she has a strong suspicion she's going to really want Dorn in the bed with her sooner rather than later.

Her skin starts to feel hot and sensitive and slick is gathering under her, soaking into the bedding of the nest. It's so hot in the hut, she has an almost irresistible urge to take off her clothes.

All three Talins take deep breaths through their noses. Fornian gives a soft rumbling purr, and Remos rattles with aggression.

"That smell is—" Remos starts to say and then shakes himself and takes a large step back. "The female smells very good. I need to leave this hut, Prime Daughter Halieni. I might be in danger of rutting the little human myself. Her need smells very strong and much too tempting."

Halieni gives a surprised rattle. "Are you telling me you've rutted a human before?"

"I never—" Remos starts and then stops and shakes himself again after taking a step toward the nest without even realizing it. Sora watches him battle himself and finally with a very loud, angry rattle he turns on his heel and leaves, never answering Halieni's question.

Halieni looks at Fornian, "Do you need to leave too?"

Fornian closes his eyes, body tense and hands curled into tight fists. "Her smell is one of the most alluring things I've ever scented."

The purrs vibrating out of Fornian's chest are getting louder and changing a little. The lower tone is doing strange things to Sora.

She uncurls from her defensive position and gets on her hands and knees, crawling to the edge of the nest. She only stops when her leashed collar brings her up short. She doesn't even realize she's reaching out to the purring male until he snaps his eyes open and takes a jerking step back.

"I didn't know humans could smell like this. Dorn will be able to smell her soon and want her despite his dull human senses."

He takes another deep breath through his nose. "She's…
tantalizing."

"Leave. I'll release the male and oversee the rut," Halieni
tells him. She doesn't sound angry or upset, just curious. "Would
you rut this human if I let you?"

"Never," he says sharply. Then he swiftly turns on his heels
and walks stiffly out the hut door.

Halieni makes a sound in her chest. If she was human it
probably would have been a sound of bemusement. "How
interesting."

With both Talin males out of the room, Sora looks down to
where Dorn lies naked and bound on the floor. She would crawl
down to him if she was able. The need building in her belly is
growing unbearable, and she gives a little frustrated whine and
looks up to Halieni.

"Please, Mistress," she begs.

"Are you ready to rut, little female?" she asks and now her
rumble is a purr. "If I let Dorn go, will you willingly spread your
legs for him?"

"Yes, Mistress," she agrees. She would agree to anything if
Halieni would just let a male near her. Any of the males. She'd
even welcome Remos into her bed if it meant this overwhelming
need would stop.

Loud angry voices sound from the front of the enclosure.
Sora registers them in the back of her mind but doesn't pay
attention. Her entire focus is on Dorn as Halieni releases the cuffs
and ankle restraints. When he sits up, she takes the gag out of his
mouth.

"She's more than willing now," Halieni tells him with a
little rumbling purr. "Make sure all your seed goes into her. I won't
get this kind of opportunity again."

"Yes, Mistress Halieni," Dorn murmurs and looks up at
Sora. She can see his face is sad but resigned as he moves to sit in
the nest with her.

She ignores his expression and crawls close, reaching for
his soft penis while at the same time trying to grind her sex against
his leg.

"Please," she begs.

"I know, sweetheart," he murmurs with a forlorn sigh. "I
know you need release. Do you think you can lie on your back for
me? I'll make sure it feels good. I promise."

Sora whimpers but moves off him. Her body doesn't seem to want to work properly, so she ends up gracelessly flopping back on the bed.

She spreads her legs, unconcerned that Halieni is still there, watching them with clinical curiosity. All that matters is that this male is going to take care of her. The bottom half of the wrap pools at her waist, giving everyone in the room a full view of her wet and needy sex.

"Please forgive me," he whispers in a voice so soft she almost doesn't hear him. She wonders why he needs forgiveness but can't focus her mind enough to ask.

In rapid sequence, she hears a war rattle enough to make a bowl vibrate on a nearby table. Sounds of a scuffle. A loud crash. Halieni turns to see what's going on when Searin barrels into the hut.

Inside the close confines of the building, his rattle is so loud the windows shake from the sound. He roars and Dorn scrambles off of her and rushes away, diving into a far corner and making himself small. She cries out and sits up, looking wildly around. She's unsure what to do as Dorn pulls a nearby chair in front of him and Halieni faces off with Searin.

"What do you think you are doing?" Searin roars at Halieni.

"I wanted a pup of my own!" Halieni shouts back at him. "You wouldn't cooperate, so I needed to be clever. I'm doing what is appropriate with pets. You're acting too territorial over this female."

"Dorn!" A female Talin Sora's never seen before rushes into the room with Fornian close at her heels. Sora notices he has a mask over his nose and mouth now.

"Dinala," Dorn cries out joyfully as he pushes the chair out of his way and leaps to her. "I didn't agree. I never would have," he starts to explain, but Dinala just opens up her arms and draws him tightly to her.

"I know this isn't your fault," Dinala says.

Dorn's large enough that he's only a few inches shorter than Dinala, and he's able to wrap his arms around her chest.

He releases a sound that's half sob, half laugh. "I wouldn't have. Never. I promise."

"I have no doubt, my dearest Dorn," Dinala murmurs to him, her purr loud and comforting. Sora watches Dinala hold Dorn, filled with both happiness for the two of them and disappointment for herself.

"They gave her Abinol," Dorn tells Dinala.

Dinala startles and looks from Sora to Halieni. "How could you do that? Abinol is dangerous, too much could stop her heart. And without a male, she'll be in need and pain for at least two marks. What you did is dangerous and cruel."

"Then let Dorn see to her needs," Halieni suggests in a tone that says she's talking to an idiot. When Searin roars again, she ignores him even though it makes everyone else jump. "You've told me what a good human Dorn is. He'll comfort her and get her through the Abinol heat."

"Don't make me," Dorn begs. "Please Dinala, don't make me."

"Calm yourself, Dorn. I'd never force you to rut. You know that." Dinala soothes him and increases her purr. He sighs with relief and nuzzles his head against her neck. Dinala strokes his back and murmurs calming words to him.

Sora wants to scream at them. Is no male going to help her?

"I would never give you permission to use Dorn this way," Dinala accuses Halieni.

"Your husband—" Halieni begins, but Dinala cuts her off with an angry rattle.

"Giloni has no say over my humans," she growls out. "You knew this, but went to him anyway. He's so eager to gain favor that he would grant a member of the Prime Family anything. You deliberately manipulated this situation in a dishonorable way."

Due to the effects of the Abinol, Sora can't follow the conversation going on around her very well. All she can focus on is Searin.

Now that he's here, all the other males pale in comparison. Only he will do. She gives a little whimper as her belly cramps and sends pain knifing through her.

Hearing her distress, Searin moves to kneel next to her, releasing the tether and drawing her into his lap. She sighs with happiness as his smell fills her nose. She always thought he smelled nice before, but now he smells fantastic. She grabs the back of his neck and pulls herself flush against his chest, rubbing her aching breasts against him.

"Why does she smell like this?" Searin demands harshly, even as he wraps his arm around her with the level of gentleness reserved for the most fragile. "And she's shaking and sweating. Is she sick?"

"Halieni gave her Abinol. It's a sexual stimulant," Dinala explains. "By her smell, I can tell she's in full heat. At least she's handling it, so her heart isn't in danger any longer. But the need to rut will stay with her for several marks. The only relief is if she's allowed the pleasures of the rut."

"Let Dorn service her," Halieni starts again. Searin turns his attention to his sister. His roar jolts Sora out of her lust for a moment. She would've fallen off his lap if he hadn't been holding her.

"You will leave!" he booms out, and Halieni takes an involuntary step back, looking intimidated for the first time.

"Brother," she begins, but the increased intensity of his rattling back plates silences her.

"Leave! Now!"

The ferocity of his words makes even Dinala flinch, and she turns to shelter Dorn with her body as if Searin's words are physical blows.

Halieni doesn't protest any further. Instead, she turns and walks out of the hut, her head high and a rattle of frustration sounding pathetic in the midst of the noise Searin is making.

The moment she disappears out the door, his rattling stops. He hugs Sora tightly against him. She doesn't fight it, instead melting into him with a little moan of pleasure. The smell of him is calming her pain to more manageable levels. When he rubs his cheek against her hair, the smell of cinnamon fills her nose.

But the need is still there. She whimpers and attempts to shift in his lap to rub her needy sex against him, but his hold tightens just enough to keep her from moving.

"What do I do, Dinala?" Searin asks, softer now.

"You can't have Dorn," Dinala states firmly. "You'll need to take care of her yourself. There's no time to bring another human to service her."

Sora feels Searin jolt against her. "I should take care of her?"

"Fornian, wait for us at the transport," Dinala orders, and the Talin casts one last glance at Sora and Searin before walking rapidly out the door.

Once the four of them are alone, Dinala turns Dorn around until he's facing Searin and Sora. When she reaches around and gently cups his cock in her hand, he gives a little moan and pushes against her hand.

As she holds him, she rubs her scent glands into his hair and the smell of sweetgrass fills the air. When she's finished, Dorn brings his hands up and vigorously rubs his hair and scalp. The sweetgrass smells seems to change and deepen somehow as it seeps into Dorn's hair and skin.

When he's done rubbing, Dinala pulls him back against her, burying her nose in his hair and breathing in this new scent of the two of them combined with a heartfelt sigh of lust.

"It's the worst kept secret among the Talin. We're sexually compatible with the humans," Dinala explains as she strokes Dorn's stiff manhood. "And they are so free with their affection. It's addicting."

"Love, Dinala. It's love," Dorn chastises her gently, and she rumbles out a little laugh.

"I love you as well," she murmurs to him. A shocked rattle sounds from Searin, and Sora realizes he's more startled by the use of the word love than Dinala's sexual revelation.

Dinala looks back to Searin. "They are very pleasurable to be with in all respects. You can find out what human love feels like. You can feel affection and touch, all the things we deny ourselves for the honor of our species. You can know what it feels like to copulate for joy instead of obligation or basic biological fulfillment. Have faith in your human, Prime Son Searin. Care for your pet now while the Abinol is in her system. When it's gone, woo her, win her love. Nothing else is as valuable as our humans' love freely given."

"It's…" Searin is so stunned he can't get the words out.

"Yes!" Sora moans, and grinds against him.

"It's not…" he starts again but rumbles out a sound similar to the one Fornian made earlier. It's like a purr but deeper and slower. It makes his whole body vibrate a little, making her grind harder against him.

He grabs her hips with his big hands, forcing her to be still. Then he takes a few deep breaths and quiets his sexy rumble.

"Have you ever wondered why the Fading happens?" Dinala asks as she strokes Dorn. She reaches one hand up to his chin and turns his head so she can run her cheek along his, marking him there with her scent glands.

"No one knows why the Fading happens," Searin answers by rote. "Some of us just stop eating, stop talking, and waste away. Death becomes a mercy."

"That's the same thing everyone says. The same thing the Apogee Assembly publishes. The same thing the healers parrot." By the sound of her rumble and tone of voice, it's clear Dinala doesn't agree. "But do we really not know why it happens? In a society that has no place for bonding or affection, are we so clueless why some of us suffer the Fading?" Dinala takes a deep breath. Her purr falters and Dorn reaches up to run his hand along the back of her neck. His touch soothes her, and she continues.

"I stopped eating. Nothing had taste. My body craved no subsistence. I couldn't slumber. I couldn't focus. There was nothing in my world but grayness." Searin sounds a shocked rattle and Dinala nods knowingly. "Yes, I was suffering from the Fading. And then I bought Dorn. He was an impulse purchase; I didn't need any more humans. I had two breeding pairs and several pups already. Why add an odd male to the mix? I thought perhaps I'd purchase him from the slave auction and then make a gift of him to another household. But his scent was too intriguing, and I knew I couldn't part with him. He woke me from the Fading."

She pins Searin with a hard look. "We can't risk scent-bonding with each other, but we can bond with them. Humans are loyal secret keepers. The ones that scent-bond to us would hurt themselves before doing anything to put us in danger. Do you know what that means?"

Wordlessly, Searin stares at her and Sora gets the feeling he's too shocked to respond. "It means you can enjoy your human. You can live a life full of color. Let her fill all the hollow places. Let her be the brightness that keeps the Fading away."

Sora wiggles in his arms, trying to reach between their bodies to stroke his hardening cock. He pulls her hands away and up. The new position lets her pet his face, releasing oil from his scent glands. She lets out a little moan of pleasure as cinnamon permeates the air.

He rolls his eyes until he can see Dinala's face. "I can't," he whispers. His voice is a strange combination of shame, lust, longing, and fear.

"Why do you think collecting humans is so popular? And have you noticed, the individuals and families who own humans rarely suffer the Fading? This is not disgraceful. This is survival."

Dorn turns his head to Dinala and lifts his face, kissing her passionately as if he's putting on a show for Searin. Daring to show his love and adoration for Dinala. Breaking the kiss, Dinala purrs loudly and tucks his head under her chin.

"Fornian told me some of what happened earlier. Your Sora fought against being bred to Dorn. Even now, with a human male in the room, she looks to you for release, not Dorn. She's already picked you, Searin. Right now, she's under the influence of the Abinol, but there is real and true affection there that you can build on after the Abinol is gone."

Dinala hands Dorn the clothing she's been holding the entire time. He gives her a last kiss on the shoulder and dresses quickly. Before the two of them leave, Dinala gives Searin one last look. "Don't listen to our traditions, Prime Son. Listen to your own heart."

With that, she leads Dorn out of the hut without a backward glance. Sora closes her eyes and lets her forehead rest on Searin's shoulder.

"Please," she begs softly. "Rut me."

CHAPTER 12

Sora

"Can you talk to me?" Searin asks once they are alone.

"Yes, Master," she says. "What do you want me to say?"

"No, I meant can you think clearly right now? I know the need to rut is strong, but I want… I need to know if you understand you have a choice."

"I choose you," she answers promptly and tries to tug her hands out of his hold.

He rattles briefly with displeasure. Why is he upset with her? Does her body disgust him? She tries to pull away, but he draws her back and replaces the sound of displeasure with purring. The sound makes her sigh out with relief. She pushes against him again, loving how the smooth armor plates of his upper chest feel against her cheek.

"You can't know what you're saying," he grumbles quietly, as if to himself. That's when she understands he needs reassurance. He thinks he's about to rut with a mindless female who might regret it later. He doesn't know how special he is to her.

"I choose you," she repeats, and before he can protest, she hurries to continue. "It's hard not to touch you when you bathe me. I look forward to those times, but it's torture also. It feels so good when you run your hands over my body, my breasts, between my legs. You rub those lotions into my skin, and I want to do the same to you. Run my hands all over your body. But I want to do more. I want to put my mouth on you, and I want to feel all of you against my naked skin. I don't want you to be disgusted by me, but I've wanted you long before your sister did this to me. Please, Searin, if you want me at all, please touch me as a male touches a female."

When he hesitates, the tears she's held back so far start trickling down her face. "But you don't want me. I repulse you. I'm sorry," she sobs out and tries to curl into herself. Searin's purr intensifies, and his grip is now bruising her wrist.

"You're the perfect female," he assures her. "I've just never heard you say so much at once. Getting you to talk is like trying to drag a moon into a higher orbit. Yet here you are, suffering the effects of a powerful drug and able to give a speech that leaves me without words."

Sniffing, she tries to blink away the tears. "Does that mean you want me the way I want you?"

"More than you're probably prepared for," he vows. He sets her on the bed and stands up. She watches with interest as he strips out of his belt and pants. Once he stands naked in front of her, he pauses, letting her take in the differences between him and a human male.

He has a kind of pouch that his erection is emerging from. As she watches, he tugs the pouch down and out of the way. A thick cock emerges, gorgeous enough to be the envy of any male.

"My mating shaft is engorged," he tells her, his voice a little unsteady. He's rumbling, but it isn't a purr. It's a little deeper and slightly irregular.

It's a rumble of desire.

"You're beautiful," she murmurs, reaching out a hand to run it gently along his length. "Teach me how to please you." He rattles his back plates, making a sound she's never heard before, like the low rattle of an engine.

He grabs her hands but doesn't draw her away. Instead, he holds them tightly around him, showing her how much pressure he wants. She follows his lead but also leans forward so she can draw the tip of him into her mouth as he presses her hands to the root of his shaft. His sharp taste fills her mouth as a few drops leak from the head. Then more.

It takes her foggy brain a moment to figure out that he isn't producing pre-cum, like a human male would. He's producing lubricate. And it tastes amazing. It's almost like he's infused with cinnamon.

She wants to rub and lick him until he climaxes and she can swallow him down, but at the same time, her own need is making her skin feverish and her belly burn with pain.

Drawing her mouth away, she keeps her hand on him, even though his hand has since fallen away. She looks up at him as she moves her palms up and down his length, trying to appear subservient as she voices her demand. "You need to be inside me."

She's not a virgin. Before her uncle sold her, she had a boyfriend. As teenagers are wont to do, they performed awkward and mostly unsatisfying sex in uncomfortable hidden places. She knows the basics but suspects that what Searin will do to her will feel a whole lot better than her teenage dalliances.

Searin pushes her back and rips at the ties holding her wrap closed, spreading it open and revealing her body to his gaze. She shouldn't be shy. He's bathed her almost every day since he bought her, but for some reason she's apprehensive. The Talins are built much bigger and stronger than humans. She worries he will find her too small and weak to be desirable.

Nudging her legs apart, he settles himself down in the space between them. His nostrils flare and the deep coral color of his eyes brighten. "Your smell does things to me," he tells her, his purr so loud now it echoes slightly in the room. "I wanted you before. I fought my desire for you when I thought it was improper. I told myself you couldn't possibly want me. All you could feel for me is affection, not lust."

"You're wrong," she assures him.

Lowering his head until his nose is just above her sex, his purring is replaced by the low buzzing rattle. "I know this smell. You have it sometimes when I bathe you or hold you. It was a faint smell then. A perfume that teases me and then disappears. Now it's so strong it feels like I'm wrapped in your scent. Drowning in it."

He nudges the lips of her sex apart with his face. "I wonder, pretty little human, do you taste as good as you smell?"

She makes a mewling sound of need and pushes her hips up a little, wanting his mouth on her. He takes a long lick, running his tongue the length of her sex, making her squirm as he laves her clit but then passes over it.

"Your taste is exquisite," he murmurs and licks her again.

"More, please!" she moans.

"You want more?" he asks her, raising his head a little and replacing his tongue with his fingers. He gently pushes one digit, and then a second into her, careful to keep his claws retracted so he doesn't hurt her. The thickness of his finger penetrating her feels good but still isn't enough. She sobs with need and blindly grabs his other hand, gripping her thigh. She draws it to her clit, pushing the tip of one of his broad fingers against the nub of flesh.

"This little thing?" he murmurs as he pushes her hand out of his way and rubs his fingers over it. The sensation is almost too much yet not enough. She gives a little cry and grabs handfuls of bedding on either side of her to keep her hands from grabbing him.

"I didn't know this about humans," he says as he draws his hand away. Her eyes fly open to beg him to keep touching her, but the power of speech is taken away from her when he draws the nub into his mouth. He rubs his fingers inside of her, making her convulse under him.

The strongest orgasm of her life makes her bow up and scream so violently he jolts from surprise but doesn't stop. He keeps his mouth and fingers on her as mumbled words pour out of her. She's not even sure what she's saying, but finally, the orgasm fades and she's left much too sensitive and pushes him away from her.

Obligingly, he follows her tugging hands, pulls his face away from her sex, and brings his hands to rest on either side of her. Her breathing is ragged and her skin is covered in sweat.

She opens her eyes to see him watching her not rumbling or rattling. He's silent, and she's not sure what he's feeling or thinking.

"Was that pleasurable?" he finally asks, his voice uncharacteristically hesitant and with a hint of apprehension.

His question makes her giggle and she grasps his shoulders and draws him down on top of her, wrapping her legs around him. He brings both his arms down to brace his weight on his forearms so he isn't crushing her. She kisses at his mouth until he opens it and she gently traces her tongue inside. He hesitantly matches her movements, and then he grasps her head, deepening the kiss.

He moves his hips forward and she can feel the tip of his erection probing her. Even though she has only ever seen two males to compare him to, her teenage lover and her brief examination of Dorn, she knows he's big and feels a moment of fear that he might not fit.

But need builds in her again and she throws caution to the wind. She breaks off the kiss and wiggles her hand between them, taking his length in her fingers and guiding him into her heat.

"Slowly," she requests. "At first, go slowly." He grunts and starts easing himself forward.

Backplates start softly rattling as he fills her. He's almost too big and his intrusion borders on painful. But once he's fully inside, he feels glorious. He withdraws and starts the slow push in again.

"More," she demands, tightening her legs around him and pulling him hard into her—or at least trying to. He pauses for a moment, showing he can easily hold against her movement, but then he follows her lead, letting her set a faster pace.

Every time his length slides into her, his pelvis rubs her inflamed clit. She's not sure if that would be enough normally, but between the previous climax and the Abinol in her system, she's rapidly building to another orgasm.

"Nothing has ever felt like this before," he groans and then rears up. He gathers his knees under him, pulls her hips up, and starts thrusting into her with something close to brutal force. This new position scrunches her under him and puts more pressure on her sensitive flesh. It only takes a few more thrusts before she's clutching at him and crying out.

His plates rattle faster as he thrusts. Then he strains against her, roaring. She feels him filling her with so much hot liquid that it's seeping around him and out of her. Gasping, he pulls her up until she's sitting on his folded legs, her legs still wrapped around him. More accurately she's resting on him because she's too relaxed to cling to him very well.

They stay like that as he shudders through his long orgasm. His gasps, rumbles, vibrates, and rattles, filling the room with his sound.

Finally she feels his body calm. The rattle stops, the rubbles go from the deep sexual to the lighter faster purring.

He maneuvers their bodies until he's lying on his back and she's draped over him, his hard male flesh still embedded inside her. Letting his head thump back on her pillows, he presses her down against his chest, rumbling out a soft purr as she wiggles herself into a comfortable position.

"Rest," he murmurs as he strokes a gentle hand down her back. "Rest until the need builds again."

"Again?" Raising her head, her expression aghast, she looks at him. "Again?" She feels his chest rumble with amusement.

"It will take several marks to work the Abinol out of your system," he reminds her. She feels so sated she can't imagine having any sexual need ever again! But if it happens, she's sure she can make Searin do all the work.

"Thank you, Master," she murmurs and rests her cheek back down on his breastplate.

"Searin," he corrects her. "You need to call me Searin."

"Thank you, Searin," she complies, feeling happiness coil around her heart.

"From now on, no matter where we are or what we're doing, it's Searin," he tells her. She nods her head against him.

"Yes, Searin," she agrees and lets her eyes droop closed.

"Rest for now," he rumbles. "My beautiful Sora. I'll take care of you. I'll always take care of you."

CHAPTER 13

Searin

"What's the Fading?"

The question is so unexpected that Searin almost drops the bottle of cleanser he's holding. His back plates rattle from startlement. He quiets them because he knows most of his rattles make Sora uncomfortable. He concentrates on the simple task of opening the bottle, keeping his face averted.

"Is it a secret?" she asks.

"It's not a secret, but I find I don't want to explain," he says as he pours some of the soap into his big hand. Without meeting her gaze, he sets the bottle down and starts working the cleanser into her wet hair. She closes her eyes and makes a sound of pleasure, probably unaware of the impact it has on him.

When the effects of the Abinol finally wore off, his poor little Sora was exhausted. She fell into a deep sleep, not even rousing when he softly called her name. Unwilling to leave her, he carried her into his house and settled her on his bed. If any of his servants thought it was odd that he held a naked human reeking of his scent and sex in his arms, they were all far too circumspect to say anything. It made him even more aware of what he learned from Dinala.

If Talins are taking humans as lovers regularly, how could he be so woefully unaware? He remembers Mari's declaration of love to Tieno. Were the two of them lovers also? He's seeing Mari and Tieno's relationship in a whole new light.

He's seeing Sora in a whole new light as well.

"Searin?"

Rumbling out a purr, he rinses the soap out of her hair. "The simple answer is that the Fading is when one of my species stops eating or working. We only need to eat once a rotation, but those suffering the Fading don't even do that. They eventually become unresponsive. We call it Fading because they fade away into death."

Her voice is full of shock. "They stop eating and let themselves die?"

Searin fights to keep from rattling his back plates in frustration. He doesn't want to tell her any of this. He doesn't want her to know how weak Talins can be.

"Yes, most die," he confirms. "When the Fading starts, very few recover."

"What causes it? Is there a cure?" Abruptly she snatches up one of his hands in both her diminutive ones. "Are you Fading? Are you dying?" Her voice is high-pitched and frantic. He increases the volume of his rumble to soothe her.

"I'm not in danger," he promises her. "I ate just yesterday, and the food tasted delicious. If I was Fading, food wouldn't taste good. It wouldn't taste at all." She gives him a relieved smile and leans over to wrap her wet arms around his torso, clutching him with her little weak human limbs.

"That's good," she sighs. "That's very good." She must have thought of something else worrisome because she pulls back and tugs him down. He drops to his knees next to her. The bench she's sitting on puts their faces at an even height now.

"What causes it? How can we keep you safe? If you get it, can it be cured?" Her rapid-fire questions make him rumble in amusement. The concerned expression on her face turns to mild annoyance. "Stop laughing at me. I don't want anything bad to happen to you."

Her care makes a very particular feeling rise in his chest and causes the purr to start up again. "According to official documents, no one knows why some Talins suffer the Fading," he states vaguely.

"But?" she prods. She's gotten very skilled at picking up on Talin nonverbal cues, and she can be quite stubborn. She wants answers, and unless he's willing to flat out tell her no, the questions will continue until she's satisfied.

"To understand the disease, I think I should give you a brief history," he says finally. "Let me finish here and take you to my room."

She nods and closes her eyes to let him finish washing her. When he rubs lotion into her delicate skin, she makes a pleased sound and he smells her arousal. He wants to rut with her again but worries about hurting her. He needs to take her back to the healers to make sure there aren't any lingering effects from the Abinol and their repeated energetic rutting. But that can wait for another day. For now, he'll lavish her with care and allow her to rest.

Once he's satisfied her skin is well coated, he picks her up and carries her back into his bedroom. When he sits down on his bed, she doesn't try to get off his lap. Instead, she snuggles close to him, wrapping one arm around him and nuzzling her nose into the strip of bare skin at his neck.

He rumbles in contentment at the feel of her warm breath washing across his vulnerable flesh. Giving in to instinct, he rubs his scent glands on her hair. She takes a deep breath as their scents combine and snuggles even closer to him.

"Several millennia ago, we were different," he explains. "Marriages weren't contracts. They were made because a pair of Talins scent-bonded."

"Is bonding like being in love?" she asks, using the very human term.

"No, It's a biological drive," he argues, although the difference seems shallow. "Once your scent bonded the smell of another bonding oil is abhorrent. Only the scent of our bonded partner can satisfy us. "

Sora sounds a soft sigh. "That's so romantic."

"It's dangerous," he counters. "Problems started to arise because scent-bonded pairs can't spend too much time apart or they become ill."

"Wait, I got sick when Favilorn rubbed his bonding oil me, that means we're scent bonded!" she announces with wide eyes. "Did you know humans could scent-bond with Talins?"

"Yes. It's in all the literature that human pets can become addicted to their owner's scent. But every article points out it's a one-sided bonding. The pet bonds to the owner, but the owner doesn't bond to the pet. That the bond can easily be broken with some medication. Every article on the topic stresses that it's impossible for a Talin to scent-bond with a human." Searin takes a deep breath and rattles with irritation because he's reluctant to tell her the next part. But his little human is too clever for him.

"I'm guessing that's not true," she murmurs, unperturbed by his rattles. "You've scent-bonded with me, haven't you?"

"To my shame, yes," he admits, his back plates quieting.

"Is it shameful to love, I mean, scent-bond with a human?" He can hear the hurt in her voice, and he tightens his hold around her, rumbling out a purr to soothe her injured feelings.

"It's a shame to scent-bond at all," he clarifies quickly. "As I mentioned before, when we became a space-faring species and found our place among the other civilizations in the stars, scent-bonded pairs suffered. It was difficult, and often impossible, to keep the bonded pairs together as we developed trade routes, started colonies, and went to war, so it was common for bonded pairs to get sick and die from being separated. When that happens, we call it Ending." He pauses, thinking about how painful it would be to die from a broken scent-bond. Unlike Fading, Ending is not a peaceful way to die.

"It sounds bad," Sora murmurs.

"It was. We struggled and came close to defeat several times. In an attempt to save us by example, after Monarch Revelon survived the death of his wife, he refused to scent-bond again. Our technology was growing by leaps and bounds at the time, and he demanded the scientists develop a way for us to reproduce that didn't require a bonded pair. Our females can't get pregnant outside of scent-bonding, so he was determined to find a way to have children without the burden of bonding."

"It all makes sense now," Sora murmured. "The artificial wombs, creshes, and the way you treat each other. You're all starving for affection."

"Extreme measures needed to be taken." Searin feels obligated to defend his long-dead ancestor. "We were losing wars and in danger of becoming either enslaved or extinct. He grew his two children in artificial wombs and then assigned others to raise them. He designed the protocols and curriculum himself."

"I bet you guys are still using his protocols, even so many generations later," she challenges, and Searin rumbles out a sigh.

"We've made modifications, but yes, most of what Monarch Revelon implemented is still in practice, if more formalized. It's not as bad as you think."

She raised an eyebrow. "It isn't?"

"The children are raised together in a cresh, making lifelong friends and learning to cooperate. All the staff are specially trained and dedicated. They instill in us the most important aspects of being Talin: honor our species, then our clan, and our last concern should be our family. We are never expected to think of ourselves. We learn to live for the advancement of all of us. That's why we are such a powerful empire."

"Must be easy to train kids to care about their entire species before their parents when you barely know them," Sora observes. "So, no scent-bonding for any Talin, but humans scent-bonding to Talin owners is acceptable?"

"It's not just acceptable. It's expected because you humans have such delicate and needy temperaments," Searin explains. Sora's snort stops him before he can continue.

"Sure, we're the needy ones," she teases, with a roll of her eyes. "Before you bought me, the only touch I received for ten solars was when Master De beat me. I don't think the lack of cuddling and stroking was the worst thing I faced."

Searin's back plates rattle loudly from anger at her words. "I'm going to find your old master and gut him."

A small smile plays on her lips at his words and violent rattle. He's glad to know she no longer flinches at his aggressive rattles. His little human has no fear of him at all. It's a gratifying feeling.

"That's not particularly logical," she points out. "Besides, I heard a rumor that he's rotting in debtor prison right now. Let him stay there. It's much worse than a fast death."

Her words calm Searin, and he goes back to purring. "You had no one to hold you for ten solars?" How did his little human survive both the abuse and neglect?

"Yup. Yet here I am, alive," she points out. "I think some of your theories on humans are a little skewed. We can be affectionate, sure. My mom was incredibly loving and kind before disease took her from me. We're not fond of being alone and without affection, but most of us won't die from it."

"You might be wrong," Searin argues. "I believe you're an exceptional example of your kind, far superior to all others. We Talins have been collecting and raising your people as pets for hundreds of years. Our accumulation of data on human care is quite extensive. The way humans rapidly scent-bond to Talins is just more proof of how needy your species is."

"It's not need," Sora tells him softly. "It's willingness. We aren't scent-bonding to you guys because we need love to survive. We're doing it because there's no reason for us not to. There's no stigma among humans against love."

Searin stiffens at her words, feeling vaguely insulted. "Your species destroyed your homeworld before you were even truly adapted to space travel. Humans survive as indentured labor, pets, or slaves not as sovereign entities. It appears your belief in love hasn't served you very well. Has it, pet?" He emphasizes the last word, expecting her to become irritated at his deliberate cruelty.

But she shrugs, unconcerned, and keeps her body snuggled against him.

"Humans aren't good at seeing long-term consequences," she admits. "I read that we were too disorganized and busy fighting each other to bother trying to preserve Earth. If it's true, then it's sad but not surprising."

He gives a little rattle of triumph. "So you have no place to judge a successful species like the Talins."

She doesn't appear hurt or angered by his mild taunt. She smiles with that deep serenity he's become familiar with.

"One thing you can say about us humans is that we're survivors. We're not all indentured servants, pets, or slaves. There are pockets of free communities anywhere other species have let us settle."

"Surviving but not thriving," he points out, suddenly feeling glum. How could he be so cruel as to point out the deficits in his pet's ancestors? She had no control over them.

"But it's not extinction either," she answers, seeming unconcerned. "I'm alive right now. That's more than I expected."

Shame hits him. "You're correct. Your survival proves that humans can be stronger than we think. I shouldn't denigrate your species like that."

Her lips twist into a wry smile. "Considering most of the humans I grew up with weren't very nice, I'm not sure I care if we all die out."

Those words make him tighten his hug. She wiggles and taps his chest.

"Humans need to breathe, Searin," she teases.

Lessening his hold, he sounds a rumble of amusement. "Sorry, but a universe without you would be atrocious."

She gives the patch of skin on his neck a little kiss. "I don't think anyone has cared so much about me since my mom died. I'm glad you're alive too."

They fall silent, and Searin allows himself to just enjoy the feel of Sora in his arms. He'll worry about meetings, politics, and consequences later.

She's still for so long, he thinks she's fallen asleep, but then she asks a question that tells him not only isn't she asleep, but her mind is still puzzling things out.

"What do creshes and scent-bonding have to do with the Fading?"

His Sora is tenacious. "According to official reports, no one knows why the Fading happens."

Sora shakes her head minutely at his words. "You've said that. But what about unofficially?"

"Many of us are weak," he admits in a rush and waits for his sweet human to pull away from him in disgust. "Some of us are so weak we can't live without affection or scent-bonding. Our minds take us to a place of solitude where we no longer wish to live."

Instead of pulling away from him, Sora makes a thoughtful sound.

"Sounds like you guys might suffer from a kind of depression. If scent-bonding with humans helps, why not just start bonding with each other again? It seems like the simplest answer."

Giving in to the overwhelming urge to empty his scent glands into her hair, he rubs his cheek against her in an almost frantic need. Not only isn't she rejecting him, but her naïveté means she's willing to overlook his weakness.

When he's done marking her, she rubs her fingers into her hair so the oil from his glands reaches her scalp. His scented bonding oil mixes with her hair and skin to create a slightly different scent, unique to the two of them.

That mixed smell makes them both sigh with satisfaction.

"Simple but impossible," he counters as she takes a deep breath, pulling their scent into her lungs and showing that she's just as affected as he is. "Scent-bonding is a sign of weakness. If it's found out I bonded to you, I'd be stripped of my duties and probably exiled from my clan. The same would happen if they found out I was Fading before I bought you. Both are seen as severe deficiencies."

Sora pulls back just enough so she can meet his gaze. "You guys have made both the sickness and the cure disgraceful. You know that's dumb. Right?"

"I don't think I can argue against your point," he concedes with a comforting rumble. "But no matter how I feel personally, the laws and taboos are set and have been in place for a very long time."

"But it's not just you," she points out. "Dinala basically said lots of you guys scent-bond with us humans. Didn't she call it the Talins' worst kept secret? If everyone's doing it, how is it still a crime?"

Searin draws in a deep breath, glad to note his plates feel loose enough to pull in air. He half expected this conversation to cause his chest to constrict. But with Sora's soft body in his arms, he feels perfectly content.

"I won't risk losing you to challenge an antiquated law," he explains. "If I make too much noise about scent-bonding and Fading, it might draw too much scrutiny. If I'm found out, not only will I be dishonored and outcast, but you will be taken away. I refuse to put you at risk." His back plates start rattling with agitation at the thought of losing Sora.

Petting the back of his neck, she kisses his skin again. "Shhh," she soothes. "It's okay. I'm not going anywhere."

He focuses on the feel and smell of her to help calm his reaction.

"I love you, big guy," she tells him. "If I have to be your pet to stay with you, it's no hardship. I'll keep your secret safe."

"Our secret," he prompts, and she nods against him.

"Our secret."

CHAPTER 14

Sora

Shifting a little on her kneeling pad, Sora taps her information square and watches as the diagram changes to show the full seating chart of the Apogee Assembly. It's a lot of names to memorize, but she only needs to start with the half-dozen individuals who sit close to Searin during meetings.

"What are you mumbling about, sweet Sora?" Searin asks, making her look up. Her kneeling pad is placed right next to his chair so he can reach down and touch her any time he needs.

She tries not to distract him as he works. Unfortunately, if she moves even a little or makes a slight noise, he automatically reaches down to check on her, even if he's in the middle of a holo-meeting.

"Sorry, Searin." She turns her information square to show him the seating chart. "I'm just trying to remember names."

He takes the information square from her and sets it on his desk. She goes up on her knees and puts her hands on her hips.

"Hey, I was using that."

"Learning those names is an unnecessary burden," he tells her. "Most won't even talk directly to you. They'll ask me about you instead."

"I know that. I know I'm a pet," she replies quickly. "But if they decide to talk to me, I want to be prepared. I want to be an asset to you."

He starts purring as he pulls her into his lap. "You're already more of an asset than you could ever know."

She twines her arms around him and nestles her face against the patch of exposed skin on his neck. She feels him rub his cheek on her hair and the familiar and comforting scent of cinnamon fills the room. She waits until he's done and then sits up a little so she can carefully rub his scent oils into her scalp. This is a familiar ritual between them now.

It's been several dozen rotations since Halieni dosed her with the Abinol, yet she hasn't spent a night in her enclosure since. To keep up appearances, Searin had one of the many rooms in his home fitted with barred windows and a heavy locking door.

He refers to it as her "indoor enclosure" and explained to the staff that she was much too delicate to be kept outside. Not a single member of the staff questioned his decision or even made a rattle of surprise or questioning rumble.

The men contracted to work on the room commented that it was becoming the style to keep human pets indoors now. New research has come that finds humans don't react to the Talarian climate well and need more sheltered housing indoors.

Amused, Sora didn't comment on anything the workers said. She saw through the Talin artifice.

Neither the servants nor the workers pointed out that her indoor enclosure is right next to Searin's room. Of course, she's sure if asked, the men who outfitted the indoor enclosure would say most of the humans being moved indoors are kept close to their masters. Scent-bonded humans are so needy, after all!

When she voiced her suspicions to Searin, he agreed with her. The new popularity of indoor enclosures probably means that Talins secretly scent-bonding to their human pets is becoming more common.

Understanding the dire consequences of being found out, Sora can't blame the Talins for their secrets. Even here, among servants who would do anything to please the Prime Son, she and Searin carry on the charade.

Every night Searin makes a show of locking her in her room. The servants do their last checks of the evening, making sure she is settling in for the night. Once they leave, he collects her and carries her off to his bed. Then he returns her early in the morning before the servants arrive for the day.

With great delight she finds out by the second night that while the Abinol might have made her mad with lust, being without it doesn't diminish sex with Searin. If anything, it feels even better without the drug because she doesn't feel the driving need to sprint toward an orgasm. She can spend more time enjoying herself and learning what Searin likes also.

Every morning, he reluctantly wakes her up and returns her to her cage to wait for his staff to "wake" her with her first meal. Then she's led to his office where she spends the bulk of each day sitting on her pillow, using the information square he gave her or napping.

One thing the literature on humans has right is the fact that she requires a lot more sleep than Searin. Talin rest periods only last half the time a human would need, so she welcomes the midday naps to make up for the enjoyable but sleep-deprived nights.

"I have bad news," Searin tells her as she snuggles against him. She stiffens and tries to pull away so she can see his face, but he holds her tightly against his chest. She doesn't struggle and instead just waits. Her trust in this Talin is absolute.

"There's a Clan Assembly meeting I need to attend. It's on the other side of the planet, so I'll be gone for several rotations," he explains. "It would be too difficult to return home each evening."

"Then take me with you," she suggests easily.

The Talin government is made of Clan Assemblies, with each sending one representative to the empire-wide main governing body, the Apogee Assembly, in the capital city, Moravi.

Searin serves on the Apogee Assembly, but because he represents the Prime Family, he often receives requests to arbitrate at lower-level Clan Assemblies when the issues are fractious.

"You planned to take me to the next Apogee Assembly meeting," she points out when he hesitates. "A smaller Clan Assembly meeting shouldn't be any harder."

"Clan Assemblies tend to be more raucous," he explains, and his purring stops. It's replaced with a soft, anxious rattle.

"Do you guys get violent at these Assembly meetings? Do fights break out?" she asks, horrified.

"No, nothing like that," he tells her with an amused rumble. She relaxes and goes back to rubbing the overlapping back plates on the back of his neck. He leans his neck forward, separating the plates and silently asking her to rub the skin and muscle under them. She slides her small fingers between the hard plates, careful not to cut herself on the sharp edges, and massages the tense muscles there. He lets out a rumble of pleasure.

"Then it should be safe for me to go with you," she points out as she kneads. "We can just do what you planned to do here in the capital. Put a kneeling pad down next to you, and I'll stay nice and quiet while you argue politics."

"We don't argue. We arbitrate," Searin corrects without opening his eyes, making her huff out a laugh.

"I've watched some vids of your arbitration," she counters. "I saw some pretty loud arbitration. But yelling, rattling Talins don't scare me anymore. I know you won't let anything happen to me."

"I'd never knowingly put you in danger," he agrees. "Which is why I don't think you should go."

She remains quiet, letting Searin think over his words. She learned quickly that if there's something he's not telling her, remaining silent will get her an answer much faster than badgering.

"They'll want to touch you," he finally admits. "The area we're going to doesn't have a single human. Not one. It's the only territory on the entire planet where not a single clan, family, or individual owns a human. You'll be rare, and everyone will want to touch and interact with you. I don't think I'll be able to handle it."

"I don't think I'd like that much either," she admits. He starts purring again as they just enjoy touching each other for several minutes. As much as Searin needs her touch and the bonding scent on her skin to keep himself sane, she has become addicted to the feel of him holding her. Even going a few days without him sounds painful, and she worries about what effect it will have on him.

She's sure, given some time, she'll think of a way she can go and still remain safe. Maybe she could simply stay in his room while he's at the assembly meeting. It might get a little boring, but as long as she has an information square, it won't be too bad.

With her on his lap, he goes back to work, shifting her a little so he can reach the display in front of him even as he keeps one protective arm wrapped around her.

She's drifting off when a servant hurries in, his back plates rattling anxiously. "Prime Daughter Halieni is here requesting an audience with you, Prime Son Searin."

Sora jerks to a sitting position, almost hitting Searin's face with the top of her head. Anxiety swamps her at the sound of his sister's name.

"My sister?" Searin repeats, accompanied by an angry rattle.

"I know you told me to refuse her entrance and deny any request, but she's threatening legal actions and even saying she'll contact the monarch over this."

"I doubt she'd bother either of our parents over a sibling dispute," Searin comments with an annoyed rattle. He looks down and Sora gives a small smile and mouths, *I'm not scared*. He nods and turns his attention back to the agitated servant.

"Show her in," he orders, and the servant disappears. Sora debates climbing out of his lap so she can hide behind the desk, but before she can decide on an action Halieni walks in.

"Greetings, Brother," she says stiffly. Then her gaze drops to Sora, and she rumbles out a purr. "You look very nice today, little human. The color of that wrap complements your mane nicely."

Part of her wants to slink off Searin's lap and huddle at his feet, out of sight of the woman who terrorized her. Another part wants to call Halieni bad names and demand she leave. Again, Searin keeps her from having to make any decisions.

"Don't talk to her," Searin barks with a threatening rattle.

"I was merely voicing a compliment," Halieni states with a little jump of startled surprise and a rattle of annoyance. "There's no need to react so aggressively, brother."

"You scared her, gave her a drug that could've killed her, and tried to force her to rut a human she didn't know. These things were done without my knowledge or permission. Now please explain to me, dear sibling, why I shouldn't be upset."

"I acted without honor," Halieni admits, sinking into one of the backless chairs in the room. "I wasn't thinking clearly, and I've come to beg forgiveness, from you and your pet."

"Really?" Sora's question draws the attention of both Talins to her. She didn't mean to talk, but the word slipped out before she could think.

"I acted without thought, and I've caused irreparable damage to several relationships," Halieni answers, looking Sora in the eye. "Dinala refuses to communicate with me and has banned me from her property. She has a bonded pair that just had a pup. I used to visit them almost every rotation, and they'd let me hold their young, but now I can't visit them anymore." A rumble that Sora's not familiar with issues out of Halieni's chest.

"Stop trying to gain my sympathy," Searin orders. His words might be harsh, but Sora's pretty sure the purr coming from his chest is partially for his distressed sibling.

"Do you regret your actions because of the consequences or because you hurt me and Dorn?" Sora asks. Having Searin's brawny arms around her makes her feel bold.

"I believe it's both," Halieni admits. "When I tried to apologize to Dinala, she asked me how I'd feel if I was drugged and forced to mate with an unknown male. I told her it wasn't the same thing but…" Her voice trails off and she looks down at the floor.

"But it is the same thing," Sora finishes for her. The sobbing rumble coming from Halieni's chest gets louder, and Searin shifts a little, clearly agitated.

"Stop your wailing," he commands. Halieni nods her head, but the sound only softens. It doesn't stop.

"I was desperate," she explains. "I didn't think of the consequences. I didn't think about how I might adversely affect others. All I was focused on was getting a pup in my arms."

"Even if you got Sora with young, I wouldn't have given you the pup," Searin tells her, his words blunt but his tone gentle. "I know Sora would have wanted to keep the young, and I'd never make her part with her pup."

"That didn't occur to me," Halieni murmurs, her gaze still focused on the floor in front of her. "I was so sure you wouldn't want to share her attention with a wailing offspring."

"Why do you want a human baby so badly?" Sora already knows the answer, but she wants Halieni to say the words.

"It will need me," she says simply. "I'll feed it, hold it, and care for it. The pup will need me as no other needs me. No one will demand a human child be sent to a cresh. The pup would be mine."

"Have you been eating?" Sora asks gently. Searin sounds a startled rattle at her question, his gaze focused on his quietly sobbing sister.

"No," Halieni confesses.

"For how long?" Searin demands.

"Too long," Halieni admits. The rumbling sobs coming from the distressed woman get louder.

Acting on instinct, Sora slides off Searin's lap and makes her way to the distraught sister.

"Easy," she whispers as she eases behind the chair Halieni is sitting in and wraps her arms around the woman from behind.

"Take some deep breaths with me." She exaggerates her breathing and Halieni, sitting stiffly in her embrace, mirrors her.

In a strange twist, Halieni drops her head back to rest it on Sora's shoulder, making herself subservient and vulnerable to a human pet. This is a clear sign of how far gone the woman is.

"Thank you," Halieni whispers as her rumbling sobs get quieter and her breathing evens out.

Acting on impulse, Sora lets go of the woman, straightens up, and walks around the chair to stand in front of Halieni.

Taking the woman's unresisting hand in hers, she pulls the woman to her feet and leads her around the desk to stand next to Searin. Reaching out, she takes his hand and tugs him to his feet. Once the two are standing and facing each other, Sora grabs them both in a fierce hug, drawing them closer to her and each other.

Neither of them resists her, and with a little maneuvering, she gets them to hold each other as well as her. Both Talins are stiff at first, but as Sora keeps them all locked together, the two slowly start to relax.

"There now," she murmurs happily. "Isn't this nice?"

The three-way hug goes on until Sora feels her shoulders start to ache from having to raise them so high to rest on the much taller shoulders of Searin and Halieni. She wiggles a little, and both Talins step back so she can lower her arms and roll her sore shoulders.

"I forgive you," she tells Halieni. "You weren't thinking clearly, and I know you won't ever do anything like that again."

"Thank you," Halieni whispers. "Gaining the forgiveness of my brother and you were the last things I needed to do. I'll accept my fate and I won't fight the Fading anymore."

Shaking her head, Sora grabs the woman's hands to draw her attention. She doesn't talk until Halieni meets her gaze.

"The fight isn't over," she insists. "You didn't see it, but Dorn comforts Dinala. We could find you a human to comfort you.

Searin said males are easier to get than females. We can't find you a baby, but you could have someone like Dorn."

Halieni stares at her silently for so long Sora wonders if she's shocked the woman. But then Halieni gives a slow, thoughtful nod.

"I'll search," she states, then abruptly turns and starts to leave. She stops at the door when Searin calls out to her.

"I haven't forgiven you yet," he tells her, but she stands tall and meets his gaze without flinching.

She doesn't turn around. "I understand, brother. In your place, I wouldn't be charitable either."

Searin sounds a loud purr. "I might not forgive you, but Sora has, so you're welcome to visit if you wish. And I wouldn't ever refuse Sora anything, so if she forces us to touch, I won't resist."

Sora hugs Searin tightly, realizing this is a way for him to tell his sister he wants to help her and he's already halfway to forgiving her.

Talins need to work on their emotional communication skills, Sora thinks.

"Thank you, brother," Halieni murmurs as she leaves. "I'll seek you out for a meal when I'm ready."

Those words fill Sora with the hope that both siblings can be rescued from Fading, not just her Searin. The door closes behind Halieni, and Sora looks up at Searin.

"Well, my work here is done," she declares with a cheeky grin as she grabs her information square off his desk and sinks onto her kneeling pad. Searin watches her get comfortable and then sits heavily in his chair.

"As far as I'm concerned," he tells her as he leans over and runs his scent glands over her hair. "Your work will never be finished."

"That's excellent news," she says as the scent of cinnamon fills her nose.

CHAPTER 15

Searin

A quiet mumbling makes Searin look down at his feet where he finds Sora curled up and asleep on her kneeling pad. Considering how much sleep humans need, he's amazed their species stayed awake long enough to overpopulate their planet!

She breathes out another indecipherable word and twitches out a hand. He leans over and puts his fingers close so her grasping hand finds them. When her fist closes around his fingers, she settles. His touch seems to soothe her when she's having a disturbing dream. Although this time she doesn't seem too agitated.

He checks the information square on his desk and notes how late in the day it is.

"Little one," he calls out softly as he pushes the chair away so he can kneel next to her. He wiggles his fingers in her grip and leans over to brush his lips across hers. She likes it when he uses lip presses on her.

"Sweet human, wake up for me. It's time for you to be fed."

Wide, expressive eyes blink open, and he watches with fascination as she smiles at him even before she's fully awake. It's one of the things that he adores about her, the fact that just the sight of him makes her happy.

"Searin," she murmurs and lifts her face for another lip press. It's such a human thing, to press lips together as a sign of affection. It might be foreign to Talins, but it's a pleasant activity and one he's glad Sora introduced him to.

Breaking off the lip press, he urges her to sit up. "You need to be fed," he insists.

"I'd rather do other things," she comments, blatantly eyeing his lap. Searin keeps himself from letting out a lusty rumble but barely. He refuses to let her distract him.

"Perhaps later," he concedes. "But for now, food." She gives a disappointed sigh and an adorable human pout.

"I think I might be eating too much," she comments as she stands up. "I'm getting fat."

"What is fat?" Searin asks with a concerned rumble.

"Right, you guys don't have that issue," she mutters. "Fat is when humans eat too much and the food is converted to fat in our bodies to be stored for times of famine." She pokes despondently at her rounded stomach. "I know too little fat is bad, but I'm not sure about too much." She points to her belly. "This is the roundest I've ever been. Of course I'm getting more food than I've ever had before too."

Eyeing her stomach, Searin blinks thoughtfully, "But I like how you feel." He wants her to be healthy, but he likes how soft she feels in his arms. Over the last month, rutting with his human has become a bit of an obsession, and as her frame has filled out, he's only become more enamored.

"We'll talk to the healer," he decides. "We'll abide by what she says about how much you should eat." Surely Sora's healthy as she is. Searin can't imagine the healer saying differently.

"Do we have to see the healer?" Sora whines, making him rumble out a laugh.

"Absolutely," he tells her firmly as they amble out of the office toward her indoor enclosure. A meal is waiting for her on the small, low table specifically made for her height. Two chairs sit at the table, one small for Sora to sit at when she's by herself, and a much larger one to accommodate Searin's bulk. Sitting down in his chair, he pulls her into his lap and hands her the bowl of food. She makes a small face after the first sip and hands it back to him.

"What's wrong?"

"It doesn't taste right," she admits. "But I'm not hungry anyway. Maybe we could cut out some of the meals? I'm not underweight anymore."

Worried, Searin sips at her bowl, tasting nothing but the same bland food she normally eats. Making a mental note to speak with the servants about her food, he sets the bowl back down and lets her snuggle into him.

"One meal," he allows. "You can skip this one meal, but you have to eat all the other scheduled meals until we meet with the healer."

"Fine," she replies, flashing him the little wicked smile he's become so fond of. "I guess we have a little time on our hands. You usually allocate at least half a mark for feeding me. What would you like to do with the remaining time?"

"I should perform my own examination of your person," he suggests, enjoying the way she wiggles against him in anticipation.

Much more than half a mark later, Searin sets his flushed and sweaty pet on her kneeling pillow back in his office. He needs to attend several holo-meetings, so she settles down with her information square, content to entertain herself. He starts up a holo-meeting with a Clan Assembly member who's apprising him of current trade issues.

He and the Assembly member are in the middle of a polite argument when he glances down to check on Sora. He's expecting to see her asleep and twitching. Instead, wide eyes meet his gaze. Her face pales and she slaps a hand over her mouth.

"Searin?"

Looking up, he sees the Assembly member staring at him over the holo feed. "I apologize, Assembly Citizen Yoviana. What were you saying?"

Yoviana begins droning on about a quality issue when Sora scrambles off her pad, hand still clasped over her mouth. Searin watches her disappear out of the room and sounds a worried rattle.

"Is there a problem, Prime Son Searin?" Yoviana asks.

"Sora," he starts to say as he gets up and then shakes himself. "My pet just ran out of the room. She's normally very well-behaved."

"Don't stand on ceremony," Yoviana says quickly, and Searin notices a small human face pop up into view. A little voice asks a question he can't quite hear, and Yoviana looks down and starts making a comforting rumble.

"Yes, he has a pet too, but she can't possibly be as wonderful as you. Now go off and play," Yoviana says.

Searin glimpses a human pup skipping off. Yoviana meets his eyes and stops purring. "Go see to your pet. We'll return to this discussion at a later time."

With that, she cuts the feed and disappears. Searin sits stunned. Yoviana is head of one of the most powerful clans, known for stringently adhering to traditional Talin values. Her clan motto declares *strength, honor, and loyalty above all else.*

Yet this titan of traditional values, this absolutist, not only owns pets but has a human child running around her office while she's working. A child she didn't reprimand. A child she purred for. This same woman who demanded a holo meeting take place even after she suffered from a grievous injury received during a battle ended a meeting simply because of concern for another Talin's pet?

Sora!

Cursing himself for getting distracted, Searin hurries out of his office and to Sora's indoor enclosure. Hearing noises from her cleansing unit, he pauses at the open door to find her kneeling before a trash receptacle vomiting violently. Nothing is coming out of her except bile, but her body doesn't seem to want to stop.

Dropping to his knees next to her, he puts his arms around her, attempting to help support her as her belly tries to force out contents that don't exist. Finally, she stops retching and slumps back against him with a small moan.

"What happened?" Searin asks with a frantic rattle. "What's wrong with you?"

"I don't know," Sora admits, looking up at him with watery eyes. "One minute I was sitting on the pad studying Talin law. Then next thing I knew, I needed to throw up." She takes a few deep breaths and rubs her knuckles over her eyes. "I feel fine now," she says as she tries to get up from the floor.

Rumbling out a purr, Searin holds her to his chest. "Don't stand," he tells her. "I'm going to put you on your bed and then call the healer."

"I want to wash my mouth out," she insists, and Searin nods, standing up and setting her carefully on her feet. He keeps a hold of her as she washes her mouth with oral refreshing microbes. Once she's done, he picks her up and deposits her on the bed.

"Don't move," he commands and strides back to his office. One of his servants is in the hall, back plates rattling with concern.

"Is the human ill?"

"I don't know," Searin says curtly. "I'm going to call Healer Yeshem."

"I'll fetch the chef. He can come back to fix some soup," the servant says. "Fornian gave me a recipe that their chef uses for Dinala's humans. He says they find it comforting when they don't feel well."

Searin regards his servant. "What's your name?"

"Monian," he says with a little bow. "Tieno sent me to replace the dishonorable Favilorn."

No wonder he didn't recognize the man. "Did Fornian contact you to volunteer this information?"

"No, Prime Son Searin. I engaged him in a holo meeting to learn how to care for humans. He's the staff member that works with Dinala's humans the most. Especially now that she no longer employs Remos. Fornian was kind enough to give me a list of Talin food that humans can safely eat. He also included a list of items they like."

Surprised at Monian's diligence, Searin rumbles with appreciation. "You've done well. Did you purchase the extra soft bedding?"

"Yes, sir," Monian answers eagerly. "Does she like it? I can get more for her kneeling pillow in your office. Sora is a very talkative and sweet human. I could take her for walks when you're busy. She likes the garden and might miss the flowers outside now that she lives indoors."

"I'll think on it," Searin replies. "Stay with her while I contact the Healer. See if she's interested in your soup."

"Yes, sir!" Monian bustles away, and Searin turns back to his office.

It doesn't take him long to arrange Healer Yeshem's visit. Most of the time he curses being Prime Son, but at this moment he doesn't mind because Healer Yeshem can't assure him quickly enough that she'll arrive within the next mark.

When he gets back to Sora's room, he finds her pale but talking animatedly with Monian. The servant's sitting in a chair next to the bed, purring for Sora but not touching her. The moment he sees Searin, he jumps up and offers the chair.

"She says she's just a little fatigued," he informs Searin. "Chef is here and preparing soup now. I'll make sure he makes enough for several days. And I had one of the chef's assistants check the human feed. He says the contents appear fine, but he's going to order some fresh bags just in case."

"Very good," Searin says as he takes the seat Monian vacated.

"Thanks, Monian," Sora calls out to him as the servant moves to leave the room. "You're just wonderful. I can't wait to try the soup."

"It's my pleasure," Monian says with an eager rumble and then disappears out the door.

"It seems you charm everyone," Searin teases her. The skin of her face flushes, making Searin rumble out a laugh. He adores it when she changes color like that. Leaning over, he rubs his scent glands on her skin, cheek to cheek. When their combined scent fills the air, she makes a joyful sound, and the worry that was causing his chest to tighten eases.

They stay like that until Monian dashes back into the room to announce Healer Yeshem. Searin stands as Healer Yeshem strides into the room. He hurries through the greeting, uncaring if he appears rude, and ushers her to Sora's side.

"I hear you don't feel well," Yeshem comments and rumbles out a soothing sound as she unties Sora's wrap and then pulls a small scanner from the pouch on her belt. Yeshem uses the scanner and then asks Sora a few questions. Finally, she puts the scanner away and hands Sora a treat before standing up and facing Searin.

"Sora is well within healthy human ranges," she informs Searin. "I'll have some medication sent over for the nausea and I'll make sure you have all the information you need to properly care for a breeding human, but sudden bouts of stomach voiding are unfortunately common at this stage and not indicative of any serious issues. I wish you had brought her in for a check before deciding to breed her, but it looks like everything went well with whatever stud she rutted with."

"Breeding?" Searin rattles in confusion.

"Why, yes," the healer says, glancing back at Sora and then at Searin. "It can often take quite a few visits from a stud to get them pregnant, but it seems you've been successful. I'm assuming she's not part of a bonded pair since I see no male around?" The healer rumbles out a laugh. "It's just about impossible to separate bonded human males from their females. I've been hit a few times when trying to deal with distressed bonded pairs."

"No, I don't own a male," he says as he tries to comprehend the implication of the healer's words.

"It's better if the females are in a bonded pair when breeding, but you have enough resources to make sure she's well cared for. Humans are robust breeders despite how delicate they are. I'll make sure she's on the schedule for regular checkups. I couldn't find any medical history on her, so I'm assuming this is her first breeding. It can be an anxious time for them. You might want to ask around and see if anyone has an older single female who could act as a companion to her in the later stages of her pregnancy. Many of the elder human females are very good at calming the younger ones. I'm sure plenty of families or clans out there would lend you a human for the last third of her pregnancy."

"Yes, I'll look into it," Searin says, his mind in chaos.

"Prime Son Searin?" Yeshem touches his forearm to get his full attention. She rumbles out a small, soothing sound. "Your pet is young and healthy. There's no reason to foresee any troublesome issues arising. Although I should warn you, breeding females can become rather irritable as the young mature. Try to be patient with her. Soon you will have a lovely human pup. They're quite adorable. I promise you."

"Of course," Searin mumbles. "Your advice is heard and will be abided by. Thank you for your gift of time and skill."

After a few more words of encouragement, the healer leaves and Searin looks at Sora. Her expressive human face shows shock and fear.

They stare at each other for several silent moments. Then Searin turns on his heels and leaves. He doesn't even notice the door slamming and locking behind him, or Sora's small cry of distress. He's much too lost in his troubled thoughts.

He's one of two Prime Citizens in line for the monarchy. He's expected to be the epitome of Talin values. How can he reconcile what he's supposed to be with what he's done?

CHAPTER 16

"I've brought more soup," Monian calls out softly through the bars of her inside enclosure door. She looks up from her spot on the bed and sniffs. She's been crying inconsolably for the last mark, and the sight of Monian standing there holding a steaming bowl of soup makes her realize she needs to get herself back under control.

"I'm not very hungry," she tells the kind servant. "But if you have time, I'd enjoy some company."

Eager to please, Monian unlocks the door and steps in, carefully latching it behind him.

Although she normally has the run of the entire house during the day, Searin slammed the door shut and engaged the locks. This made the servants assume he wants her to remain locked in her enclosure until he returns. Considering the loud distressed rattling he was making when he left, she's pretty sure he didn't even realize what he was doing when he departed so abruptly.

"Prime Son Searin will no doubt be home soon," Monian assures her with a purr. She sits up in the bed and crosses her legs. Resting one elbow on a knee, she plops her chin down on her palm and regards Monian with a sad little smile.

"I hope so. I want to talk to him." She needs reassurance that she and the baby are safe. His baby. Their baby.

If he can't give her that assurance, she needs to start seriously considering a plan. She rarely thought about escape as a slave, even under her brutal former master. She lived on a ship with little to no avenue of escape. Besides, as a human with no skills, her life under Master De seemed better than any unknown fate she might encounter out in the universe.

But now she's got much more to consider besides her own life. Her child deserves to live, but for that to happen, she might need to take extreme measures.

First, she needs more information.

"You seem to know so much. How many other humans have you cared for in the past? It must've been dozens." Her compliment finds its mark when she hears a pleasurable rumble briefly interrupt Monian's purr.

"You're the first human I've ever actually met in person," he admits. "But I've diligently studied the literature. I was told you've scent-bonded to Prime Son Searin, so I'll be careful not to let my scent glands open or touch you with them. What did the healer say? Are you sick? Is that why Prime Son Searin was so upset when he left?"

It's a relief to know outside of her, Searin, and the healer, no one knows she's pregnant. And for now, only she and Searin know it's a hybrid child.

"I don't think I'm sick," she says vaguely, retreating into the role of clueless pet to keep from having to answer any more questions.

"I'm sure you're going to be fine," Monian affirms quickly, increasing the volume of his purr. "The healer didn't seem worried at all."

"What does it mean to be a Prime Citizen?" she asks, both to gather information and change the subject. So far, she's only studied the role of Clan Assemblies and the Apogee Assembly. She hasn't bothered learning anything else about Talin government or culture because she found Assembly law complex enough to keep her attention. Now would be a good time to understand Searin's place in Talin society.

"Our monarch has ruled down an unbroken line for over three millennia. The family of the monarch is called the Prime Family," Monian explains with a proud rattle. "Each generation of monarch takes a spouse from a different family, so no one family or clan can gain too much royal favor. Whoever marries the monarch gives up all former affiliations to become part of the Prime Family. Then the monarch and spouse produce two heirs, a male and a female. Those two heirs are the Prime Son and Prime Daughter."

Sora's eyes go wide. She was bought by a prince! Of course, then she was terrorized by a princess, so half the story is romantic and the other half is the bad chapter of an adventure tale. "So Prime Son Searin will become the next monarch?"

"Not necessarily," Monian says. "Either heir could be chosen. They're both required to prove themselves worthy of the crown by engaging in politics and the military. Both heirs served their military terms on the battleship Gozer. Now Prime Son Searin works as the mediator between the Clan Assemblies and the Apogee Assembly. Prime Daughter Halieni is diligent in her work with diplomatic clans. She also works to support our scientific clans. Because of her, we now have a triple yield mazo."

"Impressive," she murmurs, despite having no clue what a mazo is. It seems there's hope for her yet. Perhaps she and Searin can sneak off to live a life in solitude if his sister is picked to be the next monarch. "Both siblings seem so accomplished. How will the monarch decide between them?"

"I'm sure Prime Son Searin will be chosen," Monian says with a delighted rumble. "But not for many more solars. Our current monarch is far from retiring."

Not a single thing he's telling her is comforting her. The heir to a throne or a monarch would live in the public eye, making it impossible to keep a mixed-species baby a secret. Some of her sorrow is for herself and her child. But also for Searin. If she's forced to run away, she knows he'll suffer. He's already admitted that he'd be stripped of everything if it's found out that he scent-bonded with her. Even worse, if she's no longer there, he'll suffer from the Scent Collapse disease he mentioned.

If they're found out, she might be taken away from him anyway. Would they kill her and the child? Erase any evidence of a Prime Citizen scent-bonding with a human?

Fear washes through her, making the tears she thought had run out start rolling down her cheeks again.

"What's this?" Monian rattles with agitation. "You're shedding water again. Do you hurt? Should I call the healer back?"

"It's called crying," she explains. "And it's nothing. Some humans do it more than others. I…I just miss Master Searin. That's all."

A distressed rattle sounds and Monian stands up. He takes a step toward the door, stops, turns back to her, and tries to rumble out a purr. The purr competes with his anxious rattling, creating a discordant cacophony that makes Sora wince.

"Please sit," she implores. Monian drops so fast into the chair next to her bed he almost knocks it over. "Are you not allowed to contact Master Searin?"

"I've tried to contact him, but he's not responding," Monian admits. "It's not an emergency, so I can't request a location from the Ident tracking system, but if he knew you needed him, I'm sure he would return."

"Of course," she murmurs. Suddenly all she wants is to be alone. Through force of will, she blinks away her tears and summons up a smile. "I'm calm now, thanks to you. Could I please be alone to rest?"

"Oh yes, humans require long sleep periods," Monian says with a purr. "I'll leave you now. Rest might be just what you need."

Sora watches Monian leave, the door automatically locking behind him. Slumping back, she stares up at the light pattern on the ceiling over the bed. Absently, she rests a hand over her belly, wondering what the child inside will look like.

"I already love you," she whispers. "And I'll do anything to protect you."

CHAPTER 17

Searin

It takes almost a full mark to track down his father, but when Searin finally barrels into the room where the man is lounging in a low ornate, backless chair reading something on an information square, he finds himself suddenly reluctant to speak. He was so focused on finding Mavianin, wishing to seek advice, that he hadn't thought of what to say.

"Greetings, Searin," his father states formally, and sets the information square aside. "I received excellent reports from your last Clan Assembly arbitration. I'll make sure your mother reads the same report. Perhaps we should put them on the UniBase so anyone can access them. Everyone should know about your accomplishments."

"Thank you, Father," Searin mumbles. His back plates rattle anxiously. "But that's not why I'm here."

Mavianin sounds a surprised rattle. "What is this? You're agitated. Do you come to me with a problem, my son?" His father doesn't rumble out an affectionate sound or even a soothing one. He never does, no matter how aggravated Searin might be. His father has never treated him as anything else but a colleague to be groomed for a high political position.

Searin pauses, taking a good look at his father. Although his mother came to visit him regularly at the cresh where he and his sister were raised, he only remembers seeing his father a handful of times, all of them brief and formal.

At least his mother would spend time talking to the two of them. She would ask questions and reward them with verbal praise for their diligent studiousness. But this male had little patience or interest in either of his offspring.

Even after Searin began his political career, his father took no notice until Searin was an accomplished politician.

Was this the man he should be confiding in?

"You're usually more eloquent than this," his father admonishes impatiently after a protracted silence. "Stop thinking and begin speaking, my son."

"Do you ever regret that I was raised in the cresh?" He didn't expect that question to come out of his mouth and by the sound of his father's rattle, he's not the only one.

His father quiets his confused rattle. "Where else would you be raised except a cresh?"

"At home with my parents," Searin states quietly, dropping his eyes to the floor.

"At home?" his father nearly bellows the question. "What are you asking me? Did I ever want to break with our laws and customs and ruin my son's mental health by raising him myself? What kind of question is that?"

"It's a simple one." Searin suddenly feels a strange calm go through him. "If you could do it without social or political repercussions, would you have wanted to raise me yourself?"

"Of course I wouldn't," his father states coldly, no longer rattling. "I'm not trained in child care."

When Searin finally understood that the healer was saying Sora was pregnant with their child, his first thought was for himself. Discovery would not only mean the end of his career and chance at being the monarch, but also his death if they were separated.

On the heels of that thought was a greater fear for Sora. Even more important than his own life is finding a way for Sora to keep her child and both of them to be safe, happy, and healthy.

Begging his father for help seemed like a sensible idea, but now he understands that's not what he wants from his father. He needs something else.

"Searin, did you barge in here to ask me pointless questions about traditional Talin laws and customs?" his father asks aggressively, probably because Searin's silence has stretched too long.

In a soft voice that belies the intense emotions ricocheting through him, he asks his father what he wants to know.

"If our laws weren't as they are and you could raise me as well as trained cresh staff, would you have wanted to raise me yourself? Would you have wanted to have me by your side as a child? Do you feel anything for me except vague pride?"

His father stands up to confront him. "This is ridiculous. Where are these questions coming from? Are you questioning my competence as king? I would never risk doing anything that might damage our people."

"Of course, you wouldn't," Searin murmurs. "I didn't mean to impugn your honor or dedication to the Talin species."

A voice from the doorway interrupts their tense discussion. "What is this all about?"

Turning, Searin sees his mother stride into the room. Although into her sixth decade of life, she stands tall, her eyes vibrant and her voice strong. Searin doubts his mother has suffered a weak moment her entire life.

"My husband, you're being loud enough to be heard in the far wing of the palace. What is so disturbing?"

"I'm sorry, my wife," he apologizes. His aggressive rattle quiets, but it doesn't stop.

She looks to Searin and sounds a questioning rumble. "Searin?"

"Greetings, Mother," Searin says, tapping his chest with his fist. "I'm afraid I've upset Father with my questions."

"He should be reprimanded for his questions," his father states aggressively. "I've been told repeatedly that Halieni is too sensitive and weak-willed to be the next monarch. I wouldn't have thought that of my son as well."

"Quiet, King Mavianin. I'll deal with our son since you seem emotionally compromised."

Her words make him rattle with anger. No Talin likes to be accused of being out of control. But his very anger points to the truth of her words. Without saying anything further, he turns on his heels and strides out of the room. His angry rattle echoing down the hall as he goes.

Turning his attention to his mother, Searin tries to sound an apologetic rumble but falls short as his chest tightens and his chestbox starts to feel frozen.

"I'm sorry for disturbing the peace," he says, his voice strained.

Sounding a soft rumble of comfort, she steps forward and places a hand on his arm. "Speak to me, my son," she requests. "You've always been one to fulfill your duties with no complaints or demands. Tell me what troubles you. King Mavianin can be stubborn and too focused. I promise to hear what you say without anger."

Feeling defeated by his very birth, Searin's shoulders slump. "I don't think you can help me, my mother. This might be beyond even your power."

"We won't know that until you confide in me," she responds and leads him to sit on the very chair his father vacated earlier.

Settling across from him on a slightly taller chair, she quiets her rumble and waits. Even though his mother played a distant role in his childhood, he still feels closer to her than his father. The only reason he came to his father instead of her was a strange belief that, as a male, he should seek his father's council first.

"If you had a choice," he starts to ask slowly, fearing a second angry encounter, "would you have wanted to raise me yourself instead of the cresh?"

She doesn't answer right away, and Searin finds himself holding his breath as she considers his question.

Finally, she gives a little rumbling sigh and nods, "I would have."

"You would?" Searin asks incredulously. "Despite millennia of tradition and current laws, you would want to raise me yourself?"

"Not just you, but your sister also," she says. "You probably don't know this, but I visited you more than was appropriate. I always had good excuses, but I know there was gossip that I spent too much time at the cresh checking on you."

"I remember you visited often, but I thought it was because we were one of your duties, heirs to the throne."

She sounded a negative rattle. "You and Halieni were always so much more! I wanted to fight against all the traditions and laws that made it taboo for me to even hug my child. Do you remember when you were very clumsy? You fell down as often as you walked?"

Searin sounds an affirmative rumble, remembering a time period when he was very young and seemed to have a difficult time coordinating his feet. Thinking back, it only takes him a moment to realize why she's mentioned it.

"You were always picking me up and checking me for injuries. I remember the cresh workers telling you I was fine, and it was normal for children to go through a clumsy phase, but you wouldn't listen to them. You always picked me up and ran your fingers over my arms and legs before putting me down."

"That was the best part of your childhood for me," she admits. "I had an excuse to touch you at least a dozen times a visit. I regret that Halieni didn't go through the same clumsiness. But you, my precious boy, were clumsy for almost a whole solar. I mourned the day you found your feet and no longer tripped yourself to the ground."

Despite the tension in his chest regarding the dire situation facing him and Sora, a rumble of humor sounds from his chestbox.

"If I'd known, I would have pretended to fall more. Much of my memories of the cresh have all blended together, but not the times with you. I remember your hands holding me. I remember the smell of you when you held me close. And I remember the sound of your voice when you told me I was handsome and brave."

"You still are, my dear son. Now tell me what has prompted these questions."

Her honest and revealing answers give Searin the courage to tell his mother the truth. "My human pet is breeding."

A rumble of delight sounds from her chest. "That's excellent. Human pups are messy but charming. I have several human pairs and many pups here at the palace. I'm here if you need advice."

Searin holds up a hand to silence his mother and tries to quiet his anxious rattle. "She wasn't rutted by another human."

With a confused rumble, his mother leans forward. "Did you buy her, and she turned out to be pregnant? Do you know what species the baby is mixed with? That could be important to know."

"It's mine." The silence that follows his words is deafening.

"I didn't expect this," she murmurs and grows silent again. He waits for her outrage. Waits for her to declare him unfit. Waits for her to cast aside her only son.

But she does none of those things. She straightens up and asks one simple question. "Are you scent-bonded to her?"

The tension in his torso is so bad it feels like his chest and back plates all fuse together, making it impossible to draw a full breath of air. If he loses Sora and the baby, he's already lost everything, so why not be honest with his mother.

"Yes."

"Were you Fading? Before you acquired the human, were you suffering from the Fading?"

It's logical, he supposes, for her to guess that. "Yes."

Standing, she walks over to a nearby wall display and taps it. A familiar voice answers the summons. "I'm available. What would you have of me?"

It's Revalian, one of his mother's longest-serving ladies-in-waiting. He can't remember a time when the elegant Talin wasn't his mother's constant companion.

"I'm in the east resting room. Come find me and bring little Lela," his mother orders and then walks back to the chair and gracefully seats herself.

"My mother," he begins, but now it's her turn to hold up a hand to silence him.

"Be patient," she orders. Soon Revalian comes striding in, holding the hand of a little human child. The pup is skipping next to her, happily chatting away. When she sees him, she ducks behind Revalian's leg and peeks out shyly.

Searin is shocked. This is the first time he's met any of his mother's humans.

"Worry not," his mother calls out. "This is my son, Searin. Come here and greet him."

The little girl hesitantly steps out from behind Revalian, stands for a second staring at him, and then scampers to his mother. Without a word, the dignified woman lets the human child climb onto her lap, leaving dirty fingerprints all over her pants and plating.

"My name's Lela," the little girl announces.

Revalian comes to stand next to his mother and places a proprietary hand on her shoulder. Searin takes in the scene before him but his mind blanks because this can't possibly mean what he thinks it does.

"Tell Searin who your mother is," Revalian orders the little girl. Both women rumble out comforting sounds, and the little girl smiles at Searin.

"This is my mommy," she declares and places her tiny, grungy fingers on the hand Revalian is resting on his mother's shoulder. "And this is my other mommy," she explains proudly and moves her hand to pat his mother on the cheek. "I'm not supposed to tell anyone, but I guess you're special so I can tell you."

Searin feels his body go weak. If a chair wasn't right next to him, he would've dropped to the floor. For once his back plates are silent and his chestbox isn't rumbling, not because he's too tense to breathe but because he's too shocked to make a sound. His eyes jump from his mother, to Revalian, to the little girl, and then back to his mother.

"My mother?" he croaks out.

"You're not weak, Searin," she tells him softly. "As our laws and customs become stricter, we become a weaker species. Most of us scent-bond where we can. I couldn't raise you, so I raised Lela's mother, Lamica. My human, Lamica, fell in love with one of the studs I presented her with, and Lela is their youngest child. All of us raise her. We are all her mothers, Lamica, Revalian, and me."

"Revalian?" Even that one word is difficult for Searin to get out.

"Revalian and I have been close to each other our entire lives. Important to each other," his mother explains. "I scent-bonded with Revalian long before I married your father. She agreed to forgo marriage to another and stay with me as a lady-in-waiting, even though I had to share your father's bed occasionally."

"It was no hardship," Revalian points out with a little laughing rumble. "He might require you occasionally, but I get you every night and it's my name you whisper in your sleep."

The strong attachment between the two is obvious now.

"All this time," Searin says with wonder. "If anyone knew, if anyone suspected…."

"And that's why almost no one knows," his mother responds. "And that's why you're going to go collect your human and move into the palace. You're going to move into my wing under the pretext that I need your expertise close at hand at all times. You'll continue with your work in the Assemblies, and your human and child will be kept safe with us. We've filled the south wing with those loyal to us. We've created protective barriers between us and the rest of Talarian."

For the first time since the healers startling news, Searin has true hope for the future. "We can stay together?"

"Yes," Revalian says. "I have a safe place for you, my son, to live and bond with your human. A safe place for your child to be born and raised."

Searin opens his mouth to speak, but nothing comes out. His mother stands up and strides toward him, carrying Lela in her arms. Pulling him to his feet, she embraces him, putting the child between them. Lela doesn't protest. She wraps one arm around his mother's neck and one around his neck.

"You've given me everything," he whispers as he hugs her back with awkward enthusiasm.

"Thank me by helping to change Talin culture and law," she challenges. "It'll take time, but we didn't become this way overnight. We must work to undo the damage our ancestors wrought."

"I promise," Searin pledges fervently. "Whatever it takes, I promise to do it."

"Come with me," she urges. "Come to the south wing and meet the rest of your real family."

CHAPTER 18

Sora

Exhaustion finally pulls Sora into a restless sleep, but the sound of several sets of footsteps in the hall pulls her right back into wakefulness. Sitting up, she hopes to see Searin but expects to see Monian. Instead of either, several strangers are standing at the closed and locked gate of her indoor enclosure.

"Stand up," one of them barks, and Sora scrambles to her feet as he sounds an angry rattle. "Do you know who I am?"

"No, sir," she says, casting her eyes down, fear building in her chest.

"I'm King Mavianin, Searin's father," he tells her. "And I came to see the human who's trying to destroy him."

Sora gasps at those words and looks up to meet Mavianin's eyes. "No, King Mavianin, I swear I want only the best for Searin. I love him."

"Love? Humans, weak and biddable," he scoffs. "So easy with their emotions. It's no wonder your kind is almost extinct. Your entire species is too busy fucking and feeling to bother surviving."

Dropping her gaze, she tries to think of what to say to placate this powerful male. "I'm a good slave," she offers. "I do as Master Searin commands."

"Did he command you to get pregnant?" Mavianin hisses out with a rattle loud enough to shake the chair next to her. She flinches so violently she almost falls backward on the bed. Sinking to her knees, Sora leans forward and puts her forehead to the ground, fighting the sobs that want to break out of her chest.

Before she can beg him for forgiveness, Monian appears. "King Mavianin, what may I do for you? Prime Son Searin isn't here, but I'm sure he will be back any time now. Sora hasn't been well all day, so perhaps we should leave her to rest. Can I offer you refreshments in the garden?"

Mavianin turns to Monian and shoves him at the locked gate. "Open it."

"My King—" Monian protests, but Mavianin's enraged rattle echoes through the corridor. "Open it or I'll have you jailed for treason."

With shaking hands, Monian reaches out and unlocks the door. The barred barrier silently slides open and the two men with Mavianin push past Monian.

With a small cry of fear, Sora scrambles away from the two men. Helpless, Monian stands in the doorway and watches.

She crawls under a table, but it takes no effort for the two Talins to topple over the pieces of furniture with a loud crash and grab her arms. They lift her to her feet and half drag, half carry her to Mavianin.

Behind him, Monian disappears down the corridor. She can't blame him for running away. If she could follow the servant, she'd be running too.

Mavianin brings a hand up. She tries to move her face away, but he easily grabs her jaw in a bruising grip and forces her head up.

"You're a fine looking human. I'll grant you that," he declares as he examines first her face and then the rest of her. "If he could have just kept you as a pet, this wouldn't be necessary." Letting go of her jaw, he looks at one man holding her.

"You're sure you heard correctly? She doesn't look large enough to be breeding right now," he questions the man.

"There is no mistake. I was right outside in the hall as they spoke," he confirms. "This human is carrying his young. Half-breed bastard. He said he had feelings for her, plain as day. Scent-bonded," he spits out the term like it's a foul taste in his mouth. "He's not fit to rule."

"Silence!" Mavianin roars. "Don't question the fitness of my son. He will rule, not a daughter who lets emotions cloud her judgment. She gave food to the Illona Colony. If a colony can't feed itself, especially a colony of outcasts, they should be allowed to die off. Searin would never make that mistake."

"He's fallible. The evidence is right here," the guard argues, shaking Sora a little. She whimpers at the pain caused by the guard's brutal grip on her arm but doesn't struggle. She needs to save her struggles for a more opportune time.

"This is not my son's fault," Mavianin denies. "This wretched human has exploited him. His sister probably did this. She knows she's no match for him. I'm sure she's trying to sabotage Searin's chance at the throne."

"Please," Sora begs softly. "If you let me go, I'll disappear. I'll find a place far away from the Talin Empire. I'll never contact Searin or come back. I swear."

With an aggressive rattle, Mavianin looks down at her. "Don't worry. I'm going to make sure you disappear."

The moment Searin leaves the safe confines of the south wing, his Ident pings urgently. The communication suppressor net in the palace has kept messages from getting through.

Plucking it off his belt, he sees dozens of messages from Monian. Activating a com link on his Ident makes a small holo of Monian's face appear.

"Prime Son Searin! I've been trying to reach you. He took her. He took her, and I couldn't find you." The servant's anxious rumble and frantic rattle are so loud they almost drown out his words.

Feeling his blood run cold, Searin fights to stay calm. Yelling at Monian won't help him to find out what's happened.

"Who's taken whom?"

"Sora! King Mavianin was here. And he had guards. And he made me open the gate and no one else was here because you sent us all away. But I stayed because I was worried about Sora. She kept crying after you left. She was so sad and her pretty little human face was red and splotchy, and I thought I might need to call the healer back—"

"Monian!" Searin barks. The servant stops his frantic talking with a rattle of fear. "I need you to calm down. Are you telling me my father was there? He took Sora?"

"Yes! Yes, he did. He had two guards with him, and they said she was breeding, and it was yours. Of course, that's not possible. It must be a rumor started by someone with no honor. But your father believes it and took her away. Is he going to hurt Sora? Please, Prime Son Searin, you need to get her back. She never ate her soup, and she was sobbing and begging them not to hurt her when they took her. She—"

"Did he say where they were taking her?" Searin asks, interrupting his frantic servant.

"No—" is all he gets out before Searin ends the comm link.

He knows there's no point in going back to his own home. No clues will be there. The king won't kill her. His father is too practical for that. A human pet is a currency he could use to curry favor by gifting her to someone. But he'd want her off-planet.

His child, though, evidence of weakness, is something his father will be eager to destroy.

Tapping the Ident, he sends a comm request to Tieno. His good friend answers with surprise. "Searin, I didn't—"

"My father took Sora," Searin interjects hastily. "I'll explain later, but we need to find her. I'm going back into the palace to speak to my mother, but I need you to scour the space port for any trace of human cargo. Contact my servant Monian. He can help you search."

"I'll contact you if I find anything," Tieno responds without asking time-wasting questions. "I'll contact the palace general comm to request you."

Searin grunts, shuts off the Ident's comm, and turns to storm back into the palace. First, he needs to tell his mother. Then he needs to find his father.

CHAPTER 19

Sora

Sora has no idea where she is. The cage they stuffed her into has solid sides with tiny slits to allow air in. Even with the slits, the inside of the cage rapidly becomes unbearably warm. Sora's already sweated through her light wrap.

She hasn't heard anyone for some time, she could be on a ship or sitting in an empty basement somewhere.

Do they mean to leave her in the box until she dies of dehydration? The thought is horrifying. Sora fights to keep panic from overwhelming her. Thrashing won't help her, especially if there is a plan to let her out.

If they meant to kill me, I wouldn't be in a box with slits, she reasons.

She hears voices outside the box and holds her breath, listening intently. She can't make out much of what they're saying but hears the word *human* several times. Then the unmistakable sound of worried rumbles and footsteps hurrying toward her.

The latches on the box are released, and the lid opens, revealing three Talin faces peering down at her—two females and a male, all wearing the light green tunics of healer trainees.

"What was he thinking, putting her in this kind of transport box? It's not fit for human cargo," the male asks with an outraged rattle.

"He's the king. I'm sure he's not used to thinking about such details. Poor little thing. Let's get her out of there," one female says with a purr.

Several sets of hands reach in and lift her out. They put her on her feet, but she's too shaky to stand on her own. So the male scoops her up and carries her to a nearby chair. Sitting down, he keeps her in his lap as another green tunic trainee holds a canister of water to her mouth.

"Don't be scared," she soothes as she slowly tilts the canister. "Drink slowly. There's plenty."

The second female is consulting an information square. "Her name is Sora, but it says here that the king demands her name be changed. Why would he want that?"

The male keeps up the soothing rumble as he talks to his fellow trainee. "Probably so it's harder to trace where she came from. The king might not want anyone to find out he's giving away a gift given to him."

"You might be speaking the truth. It says here that she being sent as a gift to Commandant Holian. She's to have a full health check before she leaves Talarian. Also, she's breeding."

"Oh, do you have a little one in you?" the male asks as he sounds a happy rumble. He looks up at the woman reading off the information square. "I find it enjoyable when the human young get to be big enough to walk and talk. They're so lively and entertaining. We had a pup in here just yesterday who wanted to hold the scanner. She was so cute when she tried scanning her owner and then her dam."

Shaking her head and sounding an angry rattle, the woman looks up from the information square, meeting the eyes of the man holding her. "We're supposed to terminate the gestation and then put her on the next transport to Commandant Holian's property on Kalor Colony."

Sora's reaction is swift. With a cry of fear, she launches herself away from the male holding her, knocking the water canister away in the process. Water splashes all over the trainees as both Talins sound startled rattles.

Fueled by desperation instead of any plan, she grabs at the door, but before she can get it open, powerful arms go around her and lift.

"Don't struggle," the male orders her, easily holding her off the ground. "None of us want to hurt you."

"Should we drug her?" one woman asks, but the other speaks up quickly.

"No, we need to assess her first. We don't want to give her anything that might hurt her."

"Then we'll need to physically restrain her," the other female announces grimly.

With that Sora redoubles her efforts to get out of the man's hold. He grunts when one of her flailing hands catches him on the hard plating of his chest. She cries out in pain and the male rumbles out a soothing sound.

"Calm yourself, Sora," he says, tightening his hold on her and making it hard for her to breathe. "You're going to hurt yourself. Stop struggling."

Going limp from lack of oxygen, Sora pants in his arms, but his hold doesn't relax. He carries her over to the exam table in the room and lays her out. He helps hold her down as the women make quick work of securing her.

Desperately trying to keep herself from hyperventilating from fear, Sora catches the eyes of one of the women.

"Please don't hurt my baby," she begs. The woman freezes at her words. A distressed rumble sounds from the woman's chest, which gives Sora a sliver of hope.

"My mother had my same eyes, and her mother too," she tells the woman. "My little girl will have my eye color. Please don't take her away from me."

"You can't know it's a female child," the male objects, but his voice isn't as sure as his words. "We have no record that you've been examined since being fertilized, so you can't know what gender the child is."

Looking over at the male, she sobs out a little breath. "I know it's a girl. I can't explain how, but I know." Focusing her pleading eyes on the second female in the room, she keeps talking. "My mother was an amazing woman. She loved me so much. I want to be like her. I want to hold my daughter. I want to tell her I love her and watch her grow."

All three of the Talins are purring, trying to soothe her as she begs through her tears. One of them reaches for a scanner while another unties her sweat-soaked wrap.

"We're not going to do anything yet," she promises as the other holds the scanner over Sora's naked belly.

The one holding the scanner looks over at the male. "While I do a health check would you do a fluid analysis?"

He nods and walks out of Sora's field of vision to fetch something.

"I'll see if I can find her a clean wrap," the other woman murmurs, and Sora hears her open drawers and rustle through items. "We never asked King Mavianin for proof of ownership," she muses.

"It didn't occur to any of us to question the king," she agrees. The male appears next to her and presses a device against her arm, making Sora jump with fear.

"Easy, little human," the male soothes her, increasing the volume of his rumble. "This is just going to take some samples."

He addresses the woman with the scanner. "I don't like the idea of terminating the gestation," he states flatly and gives a little frustrated rattle.

"I don't like it either," she agrees, giving Sora a little reassuring pat on the shoulder, "but we can't go against a direct order of the king."

"It's so hard to find humans. Why would he want to terminate the gestation of a perfectly healthy female?" the second female asks as she steps into view holding a wrap in the same light green as their tunics. "My clan owns a bonded pair, and the families fight constantly over who gets to host them for the year. We're hopeful they'll have a pup soon. It's such a delight when humans breed. The young are so sweet and affectionate. How could anyone, even King Mavianin, want to do this?"

"He's a hard one," the male mutters, and Sora can tell by his rattle that he isn't a fan of the king. "He's too narrow-minded and rigid. Even if he doesn't want her young, he shouldn't deny someone else."

"Perhaps the sire is genetically damaged," one of the females suggests. "King Mavianin might not want to continue a weak bloodline, especially if she's going to be a gift."

"The father of my daughter is perfect," Sora volunteers, feeling the three Talins in the room starting to be swayed to her side. "I didn't want to be parted with him, but King Mavianin took me away. I love the father, and I'm scared I'll never see him again."

"Are you bonded with another human?" one female asks with a shocked rattle. "It's illegal to separate a bonded pair."

Before Sora can answer, the male rattles with anger. "It's illegal unless you're King Mavianin. He oversteps all the time. My sister works with him and tells me a lot of stories of his harsh and oppressive treatment of those around him."

The two women both rumble with anger at the man's words. Their disgust and anger give Sora hope.

"I've been taken away from my male," Sora repeats, skirting the species of her "male." "Please don't take my daughter away from me too."

Her words have a powerful effect on the three Talins. They freeze and regard her intensely. Then they all start conversing rapidly.

"We can't do this. If she's bonded, having a child might be the only thing that keeps her healthy now that she's separated from her male. It could kill her if we deny her the child also. Separation Sickness is a dire threat to her health."

"You're correct. Humans don't handle grief well. Taking her away from her bonded male along with ending the gestation will almost certainly cause a fatal case of Separation Sickness."

"King Mavianin doesn't need to know if we let the pregnancy remain. She's being shipped off world. If she's put in with a stud right away, they'll just assume the child is a product of the stud. She's not very far into her gestation. Human gestation timeframes are never perfectly accurate, so a few weeks won't raise any suspicions."

"That could work. Commandant Holian is known for his breeding pairs. I'm sure he'll start introducing her to studs right away."

"We could include a notation with her transport papers that she's currently fertile. That would guarantee she's put in with a male immediately upon arrival without the mandatory isolation period."

The three of them stop talking and exchange looks that Sora can't interpret. The lack of Talin facial expressions is severely hampering her right now because none of them are making any sounds, so she can't tell what they're feeling or thinking.

Finally, the male breaks the silence. "We could lose our positions if anyone finds out."

"I think the question we need to ask ourselves is what's more important, obeying our king or honoring our vows as healers?" one woman states with a rumble of conviction. The other two nod at her words, and she looks down at Sora.

"We're going to help you keep your young, little human," she says. "But you need to keep it a secret. Can we trust you?"

"Yes," she cries out quickly. "I'll do anything. I'll never tell a soul. No one will ever know. I promise." The tears that stopped flowing while the healers were talking start up again, and all three start purring again.

"Try to cease your weeping," the male says. "You'll make yourself sick."

"We need you to pick a new name for the transfer documents," the woman holding the information square tells her.

"Hope," Sora answers quickly. "I want to be Hope."

"That's a good name, little human," the other female tells her with an approving rumble.

"Is the pet ready yet?" a familiar voice calls out from the doorway. Sora lets out a little fearful sound. It's one of the guards who was with King Mavianin.

"Not yet," the male calls out. "We're almost done, but you need to find a better transport cage. She won't survive the trip to Kalor Colony in that thing." The male kicks the cage disdainfully.

"I don't have time to find a new crate. The next transport leaves soon and she needs to be on it," the man states with an irritated rattle.

"We can't sign off on her health documents until we know she'll be transported in a cage certified for human use," the female states boldly, not at all intimidated by the much larger Talin. With a curse, the guard disappears, and Sora breathes a little sigh of relief.

"Don't worry, Hope," the woman who challenged the guard tells her. "Kalor isn't far. You won't be stuck in the transport cage for more than a few marks."

"I'm going to give you a sedative," the male tells her. "That will make the trip more bearable."

"My child," Sora whispers fearfully, and the male rumbles out a soothing purr.

"It's safe for breeding humans," he assures her as he holds a vial to her lips. "We're going to do our best for you." She opens her mouth and lets him pour a small amount of liquid in.

"Thank you," she murmurs as the drugs hit her system. Her eyes feel too heavy to keep open, so she lets them slide shut. "Thank you for my daughter."

"Humans might be weak and fragile," the male comments as the drug drags her into sleep. "But there's nothing as fierce as a dam protecting her pup. I think I might be envious." She's asleep before she hears the others reply.

CHAPTER 20

Sora

"I think she's waking up," a male voice says.

A female voice responds. "It's about time, poor thing. Do you have water ready? Those sedation drugs might make her thirsty."

"I've got it right here," the male answers.

Sora opens her eyes, but everything seems much too bright to keep them open for long. Her throat feels dry. Her head hurts, and her mind feels foggy. Neither voice sounds familiar, but they do sound human, so she isn't fearful yet, just uncomfortable.

"I'm going to help you sit up," the male voice tells her as his hands work their way under her back. "Don't open your eyes yet."

Human hands pull her into a sitting position, and then pillows are piled behind her. When she leans back, her upper body is elevated and her head isn't throbbing as badly.

"I'm going to hold a canister of water to your mouth. Sip slowly," he tells her, and then the cool metal of a canister is being pressed against her lips.

She sips awkwardly, feeling water dribble down her chin. But soon her muscles start working properly, and she can't drink the water fast enough. It's soothing against her parched throat, and she makes a small sound of distress when the canister is pulled away.

"You can have more later," he assures her. "Can you try opening your eyes?"

She complies, blinking rapidly as her eyes slowly focus on the face in front of her. Her assessment of him as human from the voice appears to be accurate. He looks to be a bit older than she, with long straight gleaming jet-black hair, dark brown skin, and large dark eyes.

It's been so long since she's seen another human face that she finds herself smiling at him. He smiles back, showing a mouthful of beautiful even white teeth.

"Your head probably hurts. Doesn't it?" he comments. She tries to nod but winces instead. He gives her a sympathetic smile. Without moving her head she rolls her eyes to take in the area around her. She's lying in a nest within a three-sided stone shelter. The small glowing stripe running the length of the top of the shelter tells her the openside has an deployable energy field. When turned on it would make the small stone structure a true shelter. There's a narrow door on one side of the shelter and she bets that leads to a small cleansing and elimination room.

It's not as big or nice as her outside enclosure at Searin's house, but if Mavianin can't get to her here, then it could be the size of a shoe box and she wouldn't care!

"What's your name?" the female voice asks, and she rolls her head to see who's talking.

About a foot beyond the bars of her enclosure is another set of bars. Looking through both enclosure barriers is a woman sitting on a fluffy, bright colored kneeling pad. She appears to be about Sora's age with large, coral eyes and long light brown hair falling around her shoulders in curly waves. watching her with interest.

The woman's brow furrows as she frowns at Sora. "Do you remember your name?"

"Her name is Hope," a new voice calls out, drawing all their attention to the front of the cage. A Talin stands there holding a tray in one hand and opening the enclosure door with the other.

"She's a gift from King Mavianin to Commandant Holian," he explains, and the events that led her to be surrounded by strangers come rushing back to her. Reaching up, she finds the jeweled collar Searin put on her is gone and a plain utilitarian collar in its place.

"Hello, Keeper Eranan," the man greets the Talin with no evident fear. "She says her head hurts. Could she have some medication please?"

Eranan rumbles out a purr, "Is that correct, Hope? Does your head hurt?"

"Yes," she says in a quiet voice. "Just a little." It takes her a moment to understand why they're calling her Hope, but then the memories of her time with the healer trainees come back to her.

"It hurts her more than a little. She was moaning from pain a moment ago," the human male states, and she casts him a worried glance. Eranan notices it and increases his soothing rumble.

"Don't be afraid, Hope," he tells her as he sets the tray down on the enclosure floor near the nest she's lying on. "No one's going to mistreat you here."

"Keeper Eranan is really nice, and when Master Holian visits, he always brings treats," the woman calls out cheerfully.

"Nol, see if you can get her to eat. I'll be right back with something for the pain," Eranan orders as he strides back out of the enclosure.

Nol plucks a small bowl from the tray and holds it to her lips. "Try a little sip. It's good. I promise. Master Holian has a chef dedicated to feeding all of us humans so we don't have to put up with that nasty human feed."

After the first sip, Sora takes the bowl from Nol's hand and drinks it herself. It's a flavorful broth that slides down her throat and warms her belly.

"Thanks," she mumbles between sips, some of it dripping down her chin.

"That human feed stuff is the worst," the woman calls out. "I'm Henni. I'm glad you're here. I've been all alone!" She gives a dramatic sigh, making Nol laugh.

"Hey, you have me!" Nol argues with a grin.

"But you live over with the other studs," Henni replies. "When Master Holian moved Kell and Sulli into the house, that left the rest of the women's enclosures empty except for me."

Nol rolls his eyes. "You know you could ask to be moved inside but you like getting more attention from Eranan. I see him sneaking you treats all the time."

Henni pretends to gasp with outrage. "If anyone here is desperate for Eranan's attention, it's you!"

Sipping the second bowl of broth slower, Sora listens to Nol and Henni banter.

From what she can see, both of them appear happy and healthy. The enclosures aren't very large, about the size of a ship's cabin. All of the ones in their row look empty except for Henni. She can hear what sounds like human men talking, but they seem much farther away, that must be the "stud" enclosures.

"I wish they hadn't moved Suli into the house," Henni complains, looking over her shoulder, presumably in the direction of the house. "Or Mai. I miss Mai. She's good at braiding hair."

"Once the baby was born, there was no way he was going to let her stay out here with us," Nol points out gently.

"But I could have helped," Henni whines.

"Once the baby is through the dangerous first year, he'll let her come back out if she wants to," Nol assures Henni. "Then you'll get to play with the baby all you want."

Henni looks excited, "You think? They're always telling me I hog the babies, but I can't help it. They're so darn adorable!"

"Is the baby all human?" Sora asks, interrupting the two. She's not sure why she asked that but blames the fact that her brain is still a little muddled from the drugs.

"Of course," Henni says with a giggle. "What else would it be?" Sora isn't sure, but it almost sounds like Henni is nervous about something. A touch on her arm brings her attention back to Nol.

Nol gives her a curious look. "Are you new to being a Talin pet? Were you bought at a slave auction?"

Sora nods, wondering how much she should tell these two. Before she can think about that any further, Eranan returns. Leaving the enclosure door open, he strides up and sinks to a kneeling position next to her. He's a large male, and she flinches away from him without thinking. He rumbles out a purr and freezes. Moving much slower, he extends his hand toward her face.

"Let this dissolve in your mouth. It'll make your head feel better," he tells her.

Remembering the Abinol, Sora keeps her mouth shut and shuffles her body away from him until she's brought up short by the stone of her shelter. Fearful of reprisal, she braces herself.

Instead of getting angry, Eranan sits back and holds the wafer-like thing up to Nol's mouth. "Would you mind consuming this so she sees it's safe?"

With a careless shrug, Nol opens his mouth so Eranan can pop the medication in. Nol keeps his mouth closed for a moment, moves his jaw a little, then opens his empty mouth to show Sora that the medication has dissolved.

"It's just a pain med," Nol assures her. "It's mild, and they give it to us all the time."

"It's not Abinol?" she questions.

Eranan sounds out an angry rattle. "You were given Abinol? That's not safe. It's good you're here. I'd never let anyone feed a pet Abinol."

"What is it?" Henni asks boldly.

Eranan looks up and quiets his rattle before he resumes purring. "It's used to force pets to rut if they don't want to," he explains. "But it can cause heart issues and even death. Commandant Holian is petitioning the Apogee Assembly to make it illegal."

Henni regards her with pity, "Were you forced to rut?" she asks gently. "That'd never happen here. We get to pick the studs we rut. If we don't like any of them, no one forces us."

Tears gather in Sora's eyes, and Nol reaches out a comforting hand and grasps hers. "If you were a slave, you know how bad it can be out there, but it's not like that here."

"I won't force any medication on you," Eranan assures her as he pulls a second wafer from the pouch on his belt and sets it on the tray next to the pallet. "If you feel brave enough to take it, I'll leave it here."

He stands up and takes several steps away, giving her space. "I can move Henni in here tonight so you two can cling together."

Sora grabs Nol. "Can he stay with me? Please!"

Eranan sounds a rumble of affirmation. "If that would make you feel better, of course." He looks at Nol. "Do you mind spending the night with Hope? I can bring in extra bedding so you can expand the nest."

Nol gives her a curious look as he nods his head. "I don't mind staying. Between having me in here and Henni next to us, Hope wouldn't feel alone."

Eranan looks at Sora. "I read in the healers report that you're fertile right now. If you want to rut with Nol you don't need to worry. I can give you a reproductive limiter if you like. You don't have to have a child until your ready."

"I, um, I don't…" Why was it so hard for her to talk? Her baby's life depended on it!

"She's uncomfortable, in pain, and scared," Nol says to Eranan. "Rutting a stranger is probably the last thing on her mind."

"Excellent point, Nol," Eranan says. "I've gotten ahead of myself."

Henni makes an excited sound. "But babies are sooooo cute! When the healer finally clears me to get pregnant I plan to have a dozen!" She gives Sora a mischievous grin. "If you don't like Nol because he isn't very tall, Morig is a sweetheart. He's got pretty dark eyes like Nol, but his skin is a little lighter. Hal isn't as tall as Morig, but he's really handsome. Oh, and Jas is so funny he'll have you laughing all the time."

"Hey," Nol objects with a laugh. "Let her settle in before you start trying to match her with one of the guys!"

"After she's settled, we can take her around and introduce her to the studs," Eranan agrees. "Now is probably too early for her to meet to many new faces at one time."

"I don't need a stud. I'm…" She almost tells them she's already pregnant but comes to her senses and shuts her mouth.

"Don't distress yourself," Eranan says as he steps out of the cage. "You have plenty of time. No one will pressure or force you here."

"Maybe a little too much time," Henni grumbles. "I think Healer Vormian likes telling me no! I've been an adult forever and she still won't take me off the limiters."

"It's to keep you safe, Henni," Eranan reminds her gently. "Growing offspring is dangerous for even healthy humans. None of us are willing to put you in danger."

Henni pouts at Eranan. "I think I'll need extra sweets to make me feel better."

Eranan sounds a rumble of amusement as he gets up and explains that he'll be back later.

Sora's shocked at the level of camaraderie, not just between the two humans, but with Eranan also. She watches Eranan disappear past the cages and then looks down at the wafer.

Nol pushes the tray toward her a little and points to the wafer. "I promise. It's what we say it is."

She can tell he's genuinely worried about her. When she still doesn't take the medication, he takes one of her hands in his.

"I don't know where you came from, but I get the feeling it was pretty bad. I want you to know, it's different here than the rest of the empire. Really different."

Grasping Nol's hand, she whispers urgently, "I need to get out of here."

With a stricken expression, Nol leans forward. "No, Hope, that's a bad idea. It's dangerous for us out there. It's safe here. Other owners might not be as wonderful, but Master Holian and Keeper Eranan are dedicated to us. This colony is full of kind Talins who adore humans. They'd never hurt you and probably die to keep you safe."

The tears start to fall as she shakes her head. She wishes she could believe him. "Trust me, it'll be better if I leave."

With a sigh, Nol nudges the tray closer to her. "Take the wafer and drink some water for now. I'll tell you about this place. Maybe that'll help you feel more comfortable."

The promise of information pushes her to grab the wafer and shove it in her mouth. As with the Abinol it has no taste and dissolves quickly on her tongue. Nol lifts an eyebrow at her and frowns.

"I get the feeling that wasn't a show of trust," he mutters.

She knuckles away the last of her tears and sits up, relieved to find the wafer is acting fast and her headache is already subsiding.

"Talk to me," she demands. "Tell me everything you know."

CHAPTER 21

Sora

Nol and Henni can't seem to say enough nice things about their owner and the other Talins who live on Kalor Colony. She wishes she could confide in them but knows it's wiser to keep her own council. She listens to everything they tell her, asks questions that aren't too suspicious but might be helpful for escape, and keeps a wary eye out for the king or one of his servants.

To her relief, she finds out that the security around the human enclosures is strong but mostly focused on keeping other Talins out rather than keeping the humans in.

"Last solar, a group of Talins broke in and tried to steal a few of the women," Nol explains, his face twisted in disgust.

"That was so scary," Henni admits, rubbing a hand across her mouth. "They put a big gag in my mouth so I couldn't scream and tied me up."

"You're safe now," Nol reminds her, stretching his arm out between their enclosures. Henni reaches out and grabs his hand in hers, holding it for a few seconds before letting it go.

"I still dream about it sometimes," Henni admits.

"What happened?" Sora asks.

"It was in the middle of the night. After they tied us up, they put me and three other women in bags and started carrying us. I didn't see where they took us, but Master Holian himself came after us. I heard fighting and weapons fire, and then Eranan was there, pulling me out of the bag and untying me."

"They were at the port," Nol elaborates. "They were about to load the women on a ship. Master Holian, Keeper Eranan, and some of the men who live in the woods killed them."

In the slave world where she came from, kidnapping was common, but it was usually a crime of convenience. Drug someone at a bar or catch them coming home alone and then sell them off for a quick credit. It sounded to her like the Talins who tried to steal the human women were organized and probably well-funded. What Nol and Henni are describing seems like a lot of trouble to go through just to steal a few humans.

"Who were they?" Sora asks, fascinated.

"We never found out," Nol admits. "They all died in the fight, so Master Holian couldn't question them. He thinks they were mercenaries, hired by one of the wealthier clans, probably from the Sky Province. None of the clans in that province have humans and are always trying to buy them. No one will sell because the Sky Province clans have a reputation for cruelty."

"How do you know all this?" Sora asks.

Nol shrugs. "If you ask them they'll tell you."

Sora is skeptical. It couldn't possibly be that easy. Whenever she gained knowledge it was by being in the right place at the right time and overhearing something.

Nol notices her doubt. "Ask Eranan anything. He'll answer or have a good reason why he can't."

"Oh, tell her about the fini cubs!" Henni says. "When we're lucky the warriors living in the wild will bring them for us to meet and play with."

"They are really cute," Nol agrees and launches into a description of fini cubs.

They've been talking for several marks now, and Sora has a basic escape plan. Nol seems mildly suspicious of her, but as long as he doesn't warn Eranan, she doesn't care what he thinks. She'll need to do one thing before she escapes, though.

She needs to have sex with Nol.

The thought twists her stomach, but it has to be done. If she's caught and put into isolation, she needs them to think the child is Nol's. As she gets larger with the pregnancy, she might be able to escape again, but only if they think the father is one of their studs.

The sun is low in the sky by the time a Talin she hasn't seen before shows up carrying a tray of food.

"You're back!" Henni shouts, clearly familiar with this Talin and excited to see him.

He unlocks her enclosure, walks in, and makes himself comfortable on the stone bench. The moment he sets the tray next to him, she crawls into his lap, snuggling up against him and whispering in his ear.

"That's Ianino, Holian's son. His mother died a few solars ago, but she lived on Talarian. None of us ever saw her but he was brought here the moment he was an adultlette and could leave the cresh. He spends most of his time offworld but visits every chance he gets."

Sora watches Ianino and Henni cuddle. "Henni likes him."

"Henni is his favorite. Holian told him if he achieves his next rank, Henni will be his reward."

"It looks like Henni would like that," Sora murmurs. The sight of Henni nestled in the Talin's lap makes her long for Searin.

"Henni might talk a big game about liking to be with a lot of males," Nol says in a voice too quiet to carry beyond the two of them, "but I think the reason she hasn't fallen in love with any of the human guys is because she loves Master Ianino."

The smell of rosemary hits Sora's nose as she watches Ianino rub his cheeks against the top of Henni's head. Nol makes a soft, disapproving sound.

"He's not supposed to do that," Nol murmurs, his tone indignant. "But Keeper Eranan never says anything. I think Ianino's worried Henni will pick someone else, so he rubs his bonding oil on her whenever he visits."

"Would he get in trouble with Holian?"

Nol grins at her. "Unlikely. Holian knows everything that goes on around here. I'm sure Holian knows those two are set on each other. The only reason Holian is making Ianino wait is because he's worried about Ianino having to travel without Henni."

Nol's expression turns conspiratorial. "Between you and me, I don't think there's anything wrong with Henni's health. It's just an excuse to keep Henni waiting for a child until Ianino takes possession of her."

She's not sure what to think about all this new information. "I guess it's a good match."

"It's an excellent match. Ianino's next rank will keep him here on the Colony, so he'll have time to care for Henni. She's a little high-strung and needs a lot of reassurance."

Sora looks over at Nol and raises an eyebrow. "High-strung? Tell me you don't mean that."

Nol gives a little shrug and grins. "I know, I know. The Talins think we're so weak and needy, but in this case, there's a little truth to it."

"They need us to keep them from the Fading," Sora states boldly and then holds her breath, waiting for Nol's reaction.

Instead of acting scandalized, Nol doesn't even blink, and his tone is bland. "It's something we don't talk about much. But, yes, it's true."

His unconcerned attitude is a surprise. Maybe things are different on this colony. "Have you always been here on Kalor?"

"I've only lived here a few years. Before that, I was on Talarian, the Talin home world. My dam was owned by one of the rare families that will sell their humans the moment it's legal, and they bred my dam almost every year."

Sora sucks in a breath. She knows from her experience back when she was growing up that pregnancy and childbirth are some of the most dangerous things a woman can do. "A kid per year? That's extreme."

Nol's smile vanishes. "They did that to all the women. I thought it was normal. Then I was bought as a gift to Holian by a man who wanted a political favor. I was a little shocked at how kindly I was treated once I got here. It took a while, but eventually, I told Keeper Eranan about my life growing up. Holian tried to buy dam, but she was already dead."

Sympathy wells up in Sora. "My mom died when I was young too. I'm sorry you lost her."

Nol looks confused for a moment, but then nods with understanding. "Mother, right. I forget that word. Talins call our mothers dams and fathers sires. After Commandant Holian found out about my dam, he brought the families' breeding practices to the attention of their Clan Assembly and the Committee for Pet Welfare. They were found guilty of abuse and all their humans were taken away. They also had to pay a hefty fine and a lot of other families won't do business with them now."

"Breeding your mother too often was a crime?" Sora asks, shocked.

Nodding emphatically, Nol gives her a small, sad smile. "We aren't meant to have so many children so often. I think my dam had almost twenty children before she died. They started breeding her when she was only fourteen. They broke a lot of laws regarding the care of female humans."

"But we're slaves," Sora murmurs.

"No, Hope, we're pets. You've already mentioned the Fading, so I'll just say it again. They need us to survive. We are the only acceptable place to receive affection among Talins. I can tell you must have either read some of the literature about us humans or heard Talins talking. Most of it is wishful thinking because they need us to be so weak and pathetic. They've created a concept of humans that doesn't exist because they refuse to change their culture. That means without us, they die. Everyone knows it, but no one talks about it. The clans in the Sky Province are dying out, and it's not a coincidence that they're having issues with so many succumbing to the Fading and a total lack of human pets."

"You know so much." It's both a statement of fact and a question. "Everything really is different here."

Her statement is punctuated by a loud giggle from Henni.

"It is," Nol agrees. "Being sent to Commandant Holian is the best thing that ever happened to me. They treat us well. The laws and customs are strict here, unlike other places in the Talin Empire."

Everything Nol is telling her is good information but still doesn't answer her most important question. Is the "worst kept secret" known and practiced here?

The sound of footsteps stops their discussion. Soon Eranan appears, carrying a large tray of food. Easily holding the tray in one broad hand, he unlocks the gate and walks in. Coming to a stop next to the pallet, he lowers himself down to a sitting position on the ground. Setting the full tray next to the first one he delivered earlier, he rumbles with approval when he notices the wafer is gone.

"I knew I could count on you to make her feel comfortable," he tells Nol as he rumbles out a purr and then turns his attention to Sora. "Does your head feel better now, Hope?"

"Very much," she assures him, casting her gaze to the ground between them. She and Nol are sitting in the nest, and the two trays are between them and Eranan.

Rattling in displeasure, Eranan reaches out and cups her chin with his hand, forcing her to look up and meet his gaze.

"We don't do that here," he tells her gently. "Humans show emotions with their faces, so I need to see what you're feeling when you talk. Don't ever look down. Understand?"

"Yes, Keeper Eranan," Sora says quickly, feeling a little bolt of fear go through her.

"And now you're frightened. I'm sorry. I didn't mean to cause that," Eranan says as he releases her face. "I can see we have our work cut out for us. But you'll learn in time. No one's going to hurt you here." He reaches out and tugs a lock of Nol's long hair. "Has Nol been anything but pleasant to you?"

"Nol's very nice," Sora assures him.

To her shock, Nol bats Eranan's hand away from his hair. "Either hold me properly or don't touch," he scolds the Talin.

Instead of reprimanding Nol, Eranan just rumbles out a laugh and holds his arms out. Without further prompting, Nol crawls over and situates himself into Eranan's lap. Nol sits facing forward and grabs the Talin's arms, drawing them around his smaller human chest and clasping them with his own.

Eranan goes back to purring. Lowering his head, he rests his chin on the top of Nol's head. He doesn't rub his scent glands into Nol's hair, but Sora gets the feeling he wants to.

"You might be my favorite," Eranan murmurs, and Sora feels like he might have forgotten she's there.

"I know I'm your favorite. You should ask Holian for me," Nol murmurs back.

He gives off an anxious rattle. "I would if I was able."

Looking over, Sora sees Ianino feeding Henni, and between that and the interaction right next to her, a deep feeling of loss hits her.

Even if she's able to escape, could she go back to Searin? Does he even want her back? And if he wants her, what's to keep his father from just taking her away again?

A small sob bubbles up, and she jams a hand into her mouth to keep it inside. Suddenly, both Nol and Eranan are on either side of her in the nest.

"Easy now, Hope," Eranan murmurs as he tugs her hand from her mouth and draws her against his chest. His purr sounds in her ears.

Nol eases up to her, placing his solid warmth on her other side. Another sob presses up her chest, but she can't stop this one.

"I know this is a new place and you're scared, but I promise it'll get better," Nol says.

Both males hold her as she weeps. It feels good to let go, allow the tears to pour out of her as she mourns Searin and the perfect life she had with him for much too short a time.

When the tears finally stop, overwhelming fatigue makes her slump against Nol.

"You'll feel better tomorrow," Eranan promises. He eases her off Nol and settles her down in the nest.

They both murmur gentle words as they cover her in soft blankets. She hears them move away but doesn't open her eyes.

I'm just going to rest for a little while, she promises herself. *And then I'll figure out what my next move should be.*

It's dark when Sora wakes up. Soft snoring across from her makes her look around to find a small pile of pillows and blankets next to her nest. Nol is laid out, one arm flung over his head, one leg sprawled off his makeshift bed. His long, silky black hair is splayed across the pillow, his handsome face relaxed in sleep.

Easing herself out of her nest, she kneels next to him. He's an attractive human, and he's been nothing but kind and patient with her. Before Searin, she wouldn't have minded bedding him. Now the thought of being with anyone else turns her stomach. But she doesn't have a choice.

When she starts to lie down he comes awake with a little grunt. Rubbing knuckles over his eyes and yawning, he finally focuses on her.

"Hope?"

"Can I share your bed?" she asks.

"Let's both move to your nest, he'll be more comfortable," Nol whispers and urges her back. Her nest is bigger than his bed but barely. The two of them fit, but it's tight.

"Did you have a bad dream?" he asks.

"No, but I can't sleep." She's lying on her side, facing him. She tucks her head against his chest and tries not to think of Searin.

He rubs a hand up and down her back. "I'm here for as long as you need," he promises. "Tomorrow we can ask for a couple's nest. Don't worry. I won't take advantage."

"This is fine," she assures him. "I trust you."

They fall into a brief silence before she speaks again. "I think I want to have sex," she states hesitantly.

The hand petting her back goes still. "You think?"

"I mean, I know," she amends hastily.

Nol shakes his head. "You want to rut with me about as much as a Talin wants to suffer the Fading."

His words make her stiffen with worry. "That's not true. I want to rut with you. I really do." But even she can hear the insincerity in her voice.

With a sigh, Nol resumes petting her back. "If you still feel that way tomorrow, we'll talk about it then. But I'm not going to take advantage of you because you're scared. Slaves trade sex for comfort, but not pets. You get to be comforted no matter what."

More determined than ever, Sora reaches down to touch Nol through the thin fabric of his wrap. She can feel that he's semihard. It probably wouldn't take much to make him interested in her.

"Please," she begs. "I'll put my mouth on you to help you get ready."

A little shudder goes through Nol before he reaches down with his hand and pulls hers away. "You're hard on my self-control." He tucks her even more tightly against him, keeping her one hand trapped against his chest. "Tomorrow," he repeats. "I've never raped a female and I refuse to do it now."

"But I'm willing," Sora protests.

Nol makes a sound of disbelief. "You don't want to do this. You feel like you have no choice. That's rape, Hope. I might not have any say in who owns me, but I have control over this. I've rutted other humans, and one of my children is living in the house now. I see her every other day when they bring her out to the run to play. She's a beautiful child, and her dam and I had a joyful time creating her. I'll never let any young be conceived in any other way."

Sidetracked, Sora asks a question she wouldn't have had the courage to ask before being bought by Searin. "Do you love her mother?"

"Yes," Nol says simply. "Not an all-consuming love, like bonding, but I do love her. If they ever moved her out into my enclosure, I'd take good care of her and our daughter. I love Henni too, and Mai, and most of the other humans housed here. We're a big family. Things are done differently here. We're given a lot more freedom and concessions. We even…" His voice trails off as if catching himself before blurting out a secret.

She waits for him to continue his thought, but when he doesn't, she prompts him. "What were you going to say?"

With a small sigh, he shakes his head. "Just trust me. Outside of the incident last solar, we're more safeguarded here than anywhere else in the galaxy."

"I want to believe you," Sora mumbles, dispirited.

"Just give it a little time," Nol encourages her. "There's lots of wonderful humans living here. People who can be your new family too."

Nol paints a perfect picture that Sora briefly wishes was true. How much better would her life have been if she'd been sold directly to Holian at sixteen?

But she can't go back in time and change things. Life is what it is, and she's got to figure out how to survive it.

"Try to go back to sleep. Everything will be better tomorrow." Nol runs his fingers through her hair. His strong fingers massage her scalp, and she can see why Holian liked him to rub between his neck plates. Nol has a skillful touch.

"Are you two awake?" Eranan asks in a quiet voice. She hadn't heard him walk up.

"We are, Keeper Eranan," Nol answers, sitting up. "Is everything well?"

"I didn't do anything!" Sora promises, sitting up and pressing her back to the soft edge of her nest.

"You're not in trouble, Hope." With a soft rattle of irritation, Eranan enters and approaches them. "I'm afraid I need to take you back to your enclosure, Nol. You've done nothing wrong, but I have orders from Commandant Holian to isolate Hope."

Panicking, Sora grabs onto Nol. "No, please don't."

Leaning over, Eranan grabs Nol and tugs him to his feet. Sora, still clutching Nol, gets dragged to her feet along with him. If Eranan moves Nol to a different enclosure, she can't pretend he got her pregnant.

"Calm yourself, Hope," Eranan says with a purr.

"I'll calm down if you leave Nol here," she offers.

Eranan reaches over to extract Nol from Sora's tight grasp. "I don't know what's going on, but it's probably simply

Commandant Holian acting out of an abundance of caution. I'm sure I'll be able to bring Nol back tomorrow after we get everything sorted out."

"No!" Sora almost screams and fights Eranan's hold on her as the large Talin pulls Nol away from her and gives him a nudge.

"Nol, go stand outside the enclosure and wait for me," Eranan orders as he holds Sora back. She stops fighting the moment Nol steps away. She's no match for Eranan or any Talin, and fighting will only earn her ill will from the keeper.

Swallowing hard, meets Eranan's gaze. "I'm sorry. I'll be good. Please let Nol stay."

"I warned Commandant Holian that this wasn't wise, but he insisted," Eranan tells her with a rattle of frustration. "I told him you needed to be kept in a stable environment because you were abused and fearful. I'll advocate for Nol to be placed back here, but until then, I need you to remain calm. Can you do that, Hope?"

Sora looks over at Nol. He looks concerned and confused but not frightened. He returns her look with an encouraging smile.

"I'll probably be back by breakfast. If you have any nightmares or get scared, call out to Henni. She's always up for a conversation."

"I'm right here, Hope," Henni calls out. "Anytime you need to talk, I'm right here."

Sniffing back her tears, Sora looks over at the other woman wrapped in her blankets and standing next to the enclosure wall. Henni gives her an encouraging smile, but Sora can't summon a smile to give her back.

"Thank you," she whispers and collapses into the nest. Eranan crouches down next to her and reaches out to run a hand over the top of her head.

"I'm sure everything will work out satisfactorily." With those words, he stands up, turns on his heels, and strides out of the enclosure, closing and locking the gate shut with a loud snap. She watches Eranan lead Nol away, staring at where they've disappeared into the dark untill when Henni speaks.

"Do you want to talk? I can answer questions or tell you stories," she offers.

"I think I'll try to go back to sleep," Sora replies, laying back down in her soft nest.

"We can chat in the morning," Henni insists. "Wake me if you need to. I don't mind."

"Thank you," Sora calls back without turning. She hears Henni settle into her own nest. It seems to take forever before the sounds of sleep are coming from the other woman.

Time to go, Sora thinks as she slowly sits up and pillows under the blanket in the rough shape of a body. *Time to go before someone comes to take me out of this cell and send me somewhere I might never come back from.*

CHAPTER 22

Searin

Searin is just about to board a ship to Meno Colony when someone grabs his arm and violently pulls him off the loading ramp. With a rattle of aggression, he turns only to find himself face to face with his enraged father. Without hesitation, Searin unleashes his claws and swipes across his father's face, leaving deep grooves in the tough flesh of his cheek.

Rattling with shock, Mavianin stumbles back and grabs his face. There's no blood, but he acts as if Searin ripped him open.

"What are you thinking?" he asks with an angry rattle of his own. "How dare you strike your father?"

"How dare you steal from your son?" Searin counters.

Mavianin rattles with outrage at his words. "I'm no thief!" he declares and then glances over at his guards, who are obviously torn. They're expected to protect the king, but none of them want to draw the ire of the Prime Son, their next potential ruler.

"Leave us," Mavianin orders, and all three guards quickly move away. Searin would've rumbled out a laugh at their obvious relief if he wasn't so busy being infuriated with his father.

"What else would you call it when a man takes something that doesn't belong to him and gives it to another?" Searin asks, his aggressive rattling increasing in tempo. If he's not careful, it will turn into a war rattle. He stalks forward until his face is close to his father's. "What you did was inexcusable!"

"I'm protecting you," Mavianin whispers with a rumble of confusion. "I heard your pet's belly is filled with your young and I was understandably disgusted. I'm saving you from yourself. Don't you understand, Searin? If this gets out, you can't be chosen to lead. You'll be exiled. Shamed."

"I don't care," Searin tells him, emphasizing his words with aggressive rattles. "I don't want to rule. I don't want to be a good Talin. All I want is my Sora back. We can go far away. Live outside the Talin Empire. I don't want to be the next leader if it means sacrificing Sora and my child."

"This is the poison of scent-bonding," Mavianin hisses. "This is why our ancestors turned away from it. You're a disgrace, but you're still my male child. I will see you cured of your attachment. Once you're thinking clearly again, you'll understand everything I've done is for the best."

Straightening up, he waves to his guards. "Escort Prime Son Searin to my estate on Rora Colony," he orders. "I will follow once I've seen to a few things here."

Backing up, Searin rattles his plates and raises his quills, ready to battle the guards. For their part, the guards don't move. Their gazes jump back and forth between him and Mavianin, clearly torn to who they should obey.

"I'm going to board this ship and travel to the Meno Colony. If you attempt to detain me in any way, it will be an act of treason on the Prime Family," Searin roars at them as he prepares to fight.

"My son is not in his right mind. This is for his own good. Do as I say or I'll send both of you back to your families in disgrace," Mavianin threatens, and that pushes the guards into action.

Both guards are military, highly trained, and kept at peak physical fitness to serve Mavianin. Searin might have training and be strong, but he's not at the level of these elite warriors. Still, he has no intention of complying.

After exchanging a glace with each other, the guards step toward him. Searin feels a presence at his side and looks over to see Tieno standing there with quills up and claws out. Tieno is in the same boat as him, but it feels good to have a friend willing to fight and bleed at his side.

"Tieno, what do you think you're doing?" Mavianin barks out.

"Acting with honor," Tieno retorts. "Unlike others." The barb hits home and Mavianin unleashes his fury on Tieno.

"How dare you!" he spits out. He turns to the guard. "He's of an insignificant family of a lesser clan. I don't care how much you wound him. But you will subdue my son now."

To Searin's relief, neither guard pulls a weapon as they advance on him and Tieno, but it's a small comfort when he knows his friend is much more likely to be seriously injured in this battle. They won't do permanent damage to a Prime Son, but they won't hesitate to hurt Tieno.

He wants to tell Tieno to go, to protect himself, but he keeps his mouth firmly closed. If Tieno's going to honor him by standing at his side in battle, he can do no less than accept the sacrifice.

Both guards rattle as they step closer. Their quills are up and claws out. Searin can see restraints dangling from one of the guard's belts. Before they can do anymore posturing, Searin charges, feinting a high attack and then ducking down.

Taken by surprise, the guard reacts defensively, falling for the feint. Searin grabs the restraints and dances out of range, landing an insignificant blow to the guard's chest and receiving a slash on his arm in the process.

He's not sure why it was so important for him to get the restraints away from the guard, but he can tell it was a good move by the way the two men glance at each other and then back at him and Tieno.

"Don't make us hurt you," one of them says. Searin can see both guards are highly conflicted. They didn't sign on as a guard to Mavianin to be put in such an untenable position. Searin can sympathize, but that doesn't change the fact that he won't go quietly with these men.

Before Searin can respond, Tieno flies past him and tackles one of the guards. Both men go down in a flurry of movement. The moment Tieno moves, Searin is in motion, swiping at his opponent. He hopes to back him up against a nearby wall of cargo to limit his ability to move.

The experienced warrior doesn't fall for it, and instead, Searin finds himself with several claw marks down his dominant arm before he can extract himself. They face off, both rattling and breathing hard. Out of the corner of his eye, he can see Tieno isn't doing well against his opponent. The guard isn't only more skilled than his friend but bigger too. He winces when he hears Tieno's muffled grunt of pain, but the fighting doesn't stop.

"You've chosen the side of a dishonorable male," Searin growls, hoping to distract the guard. "He stole my human pet, Sora. She's scent-bonded to me and breeding. This separation could kill her."

In a blink of an eye, the guard's rattle stops. He steps away and straightens. His quills relax on his forearm, and his claws retract.

"You have a human? A breeding female human?" the guard asks, shocked. "Why would King Mavianin take her?"

He's not just shocked; he's horrified. A loud grunt of pain and the sound of a blow reminds everyone that two men are still fighting on the ground.

"Release him, Gravian," the guard barks. The fighting stops and Gravian easily rolls to his feet, leaving Tieno panting and bleeding on the ground.

"What are you doing?" Mavianin screams, stepping up to his guard.

"Is this true?" the guard asks. "Did you take his human away from him?"

"It's just a human," Mavianin replies with a bewildered rattle.

"They aren't *just* humans," the guard retorts aggressively. "They are treasures. I've…" he stops himself and then draws his shoulders back and faces Mavianin. "I resign my position."

"I do as well," Gravian echoes. "A true king would never do something like this."

Obviously, these were not the guards who helped Mavianin steal Sora.

"My name's Vitrian. It would be my honor to escort you to Meno Colony to retrieve your pet."

"You will do no such thing!" Mavianin roars, and that's when Searin notices more royal guards have arrived. A dozen now surround Mavianin. Although Tieno's back on his feet and both Vitrian and Gravian hurry to stand at his side, the four of them can do little when facing down so many opponents.

"I stand with you, Prime Son Searin," Vitrian declares loudly so the other guards can hear.

"I stand with you also," Gravian shouts out with a challenging rattle.

"You stand against your king!" Mavianin screams, spittle flying as his back plates rattle aggressively.

"And you, King Mavianin, stand against your monarch," Searin's mother declares, stepping around the cargo crates. She's followed by her entourage of guards, servants, and ladies-in-waiting. The entire tableau freezes as she makes her way to them, rattling with anger.

"How could you, Mavianin?" she asks softly. "You're a disappointment to our people."

"No, I—" he starts, but she cuts him off with a motion to her guards.

"Take him to the holding cell at the palace," she orders.

"You can't do that," he objects, but she shakes her head and sounds a sad rumble.

"You might be king, but that's only because you married the monarch. Your power comes from our marriage contract, which will be dissolved soon. You are a disgrace, not our son."

"I'll make it known that Searin is suffering the Fading, and he's scent-bonded to a human," Mavianin threatens. "His life will be over!"

When the monarch only rumbles out a laugh at his words, he rattles out a sound of surprise and shock.

"He stands right there, vital and strong," she counters, gesturing at Searin. "He's not suffering from the Fading. As for scent-bonding, you have no proof while I have a witness to your depraved actions against your son."

At her gesture, Monian steps forward. His shoulders hunch with fear, but his voice is determined. "King Mavianin came to Prime Son Searin's residence and stole his pet, Sora. She's a sweet little human, and she's probably scared and maybe even getting sick." He rattles loudly with anxiety. "She cried as he took her away. Cried for her master." His rattling stops, and he sounds a rumble of desolation. "It's my fault. Prime Son Searin wasn't there, and I was too cowardly to stand against my King."

A smattering of soothing rumbles sounds through the crowd, but the angry rattles are louder. Mavianin's guards are completely silent and most of them are edging away from him.

"He's not your king any longer," she assures Monian. Turning to Searin, she rumbles out a soothing sound. Revalian steps up to stand next to her, lending her own softer rumble to the mix.

Dismissing her soon-to-be ex-spouse, the monarch addresses her son. "Your pet isn't on Meno Colony. She was given to Commandant Holian and sent to his compound on Kalor Colony. I've already contacted him and requested she be isolated from the other humans in his care. She's not in any danger, my son, so you need not fear while you travel to retrieve her. I'll see to your father's punishment while you're away."

"I'm sorry for the loss of your loyal husband," Searin murmurs.

"If he was truly loyal, this wouldn't have happened," she responds stiffly without bothering to glance at her king.

With a subtle practiced move, Revalian brushes her hand against the monarch, making it look like a casual accidental touch, but Searin can see his mother is soothed by it.

What have they become that even comforting another is a shameful act? What kind of species makes it a crime to bond with another or want to raise your children?

Things need to change.

He needs to change them.

"We will make everything different," he promises his mother. "When I get back, we'll make everything better."

"Yes," she agrees. "We will."

CHAPTER 23

Sora

It ends up being ridiculously easy for Sora to get out of her enclosure.

A Talin identifying himself as Galian checked on her not long after Eranan took Nol away. When Henni calls him over to her enclosure to help her move her nest, he closes but doesn't lock Sora's gate.

After he finishes helping Henni adjust her bed, he didn't notice that Sora's gate remained unlatched and hurried off, making Sora marvel at her good fortune.

With the nest reorientated, Henni crawled in and promptly fell back to sleep. Once Henni starts snoring softly, Sora tiptoes to the gate and lets herself out of the enclosure.

Darting from spot to spot, she waits for long periods between runs. She wants to make sure there are no roving guards or any kind of security measures she could trip.

Commandant Holian's estate is large. Before she finds a main road, she passes several sets of enclosures, all containing sleeping humans. He must have almost twenty human pets here, not including those kept in the house. Considering how sought-after humans are among the Talins, Holian must be very wealthy and influential to own so many.

No alarms sound and no lights come on as she leaves the property. Finding a main road, she heads toward lights on the horizon. The small port city she heard Nol talk about must be in that direction. She has to duck into nearby greenery several times to avoid being seen by small ground transports, but other than that, her journey is easy.

The collar proves more difficult.

She knows the collar must have a tracking device. She needs to get it off, but she's not sure how to do that. On the edges of the town, she finds a small abandoned shop and ducks in. There's not much there, but she finds a discarded energy knife on the dirty floor.

It won't turn on but after banging it a few times it sparks. That becomes the pattern. Bang the knife, make a cut, then have to bang it again.

By the time the banging stops working, she's mostly through the collar. Grabbing it with both hands and pulling it hard against the back of her neck snaps open the spot she'd been working on.

She can feel bruises forming on her neck and there's a small burn from where she'd been cutting, but those are insignificant.

Dropping the collar to the dirty floor and tucking the old knife into the tie of her wrap, she goes back outside to examine her surroundings.

She's on the edge of the city. She can see an obelisk tower that marks the port in the distance. With pre-dawn light illuminating the horizon, she's running out of time to travel under the cover of darkness.

Trotting down the road and trying to ignore the increasing pain of her bare feet, she keeps a wary ear out for traffic.

Soon she's forced to abandon the road altogether and travel through the dense forest that seems to make up most of the planet.

The underbrush is frustratingly thick. Even though she keeps a close eye on where she steps, sometimes she pricks herself on sharp roots or unyielding rocks. When she treads on some kind of plant with thorns the size of her smallest finger, she feels it impale the heel of her right foot before she's able to stop her momentum.

She manages not to cry out but ends up toppled on the ground and clutching her foot.

Pulling the thorn out, she examines the puncture. The pain is steadily getting worse. The thorn must have contained some kind of toxin to cause this much discomfort so quickly.

She prods at the small wound, trying to make it bleed to get the toxin out. Despite her effort, fiery pain is rapidly spreading from her heel to the rest of her foot. She waits, hoping the agony will ease, but it doesn't. As the pain reaches her ankle, she knows her escape plan is ruined.

She doesn't have many options. The poison from the thorn might only cause her pain, or it might debilitate and kill her. She can't know.

She could try to sneak into a health center, but she doesn't know how to use a scanner, let alone how to read one. Seeking help from a random Talin isn't an option. She might end up somewhere that isn't as nice as Holian's compound. She could very well end up with someone cruel and heartless like Mavianin.

Of course, if she returns, she knows Eranan will take care of her, but her next escape attempt won't be anywhere near as easy. The one bright side is that they're unlikely to punish her physically. They might isolate her in a cage far from the other humans, but she doesn't think they'll beat her.

That makes her mind up for her. She needs to get back to Holian's property.

With a sigh of resignation, she uses a nearby tree to get back to her feet. She tries to put weight on her wounded foot. Not only does pain rocket up her leg, but the muscles in that calf aren't responding anymore. Her foot dangles at the end of her leg, unresponsive and useless. Trying to stand on it just about causes her to tumble to the ground again.

"Why?" she cries out! Hadn't life been hard enough? Was this punishment from the universe for thinking she'd get to live a happy life with Searin?

Stifling her sobs, she hops to a branch lying on the ground. It's awkward, but she's able to use it as a walking staff and starts hobbling back the way she came.

The progress is so slow and the pain increases so rapidly that panic flares in her chest.

"I don't want to die out here," she tells the empty woods. The road isn't far. She's tempted to reveal herself and hope one of the ground transports has living people inside that she can beg to take her back to Commandant Holian's estate.

Using the stick to hobble forward takes up so much of her attention that she doesn't see the Talin until she's almost on top of him. He's standing perfectly still and staring at her. He's not making a sound, no rumble or rattle. If it wasn't for the obvious movement of his chest with every breath, she might think he's a statue.

"Real?" His voice is a shocked whisper.

Tears start falling freely down her face at the sight of rescue. "I need help."

Her words spur this stranger into action. He sounds a surprised rumble and drops the bag overflowing with greenery heedlessly on the ground.

"Human," he declares triumphantly and takes a step closer.

"Please," she begs, leaning heavily on the makeshift crutch. The pain is up to her hip now. "I stepped on one of those thorns, and now it hurts—"

Strong arms go around her, and with one swift move, he throws her over his shoulder. She gasps both from the impact of her stomach hitting his shoulder and also the pain in her leg from being jostled.

"Please take me to Commandant Holian," she begs and hears a rumbling purr come from his chest.

"No." He jogs through the forest, not hindered at all by her weight. "You're mine now. I know what to do."

She wants to argue with him, but it's taking all her concentration to stay conscious as he carries her. By the time he's lowering her onto a large pallet, she's panting and soaked with sweat. Dark spots mar her vision and she blinks rapidly, trying to focus on the male crouching in front of her.

When he reaches for her, she tries to bat his hands away, but he easily ignores her. She feels a cold metal collar click closed around her neck and whimpers. Her vision clears a little. She sees him tug out a chain secured to a wall and lock it to her collar. He makes a satisfied rumble sound.

"Stay here, little wanderer," he tells her and rushes away. As if she could go anywhere, she thinks bitterly. At least the pain is easing slightly now that she's no longer trying to stand or being jostled over a shoulder.

Carefully sitting up, she looks around. She's in a one-room cabin made of stone. There's a meal preparation area, several storage cabinets, and an area in the far corner that's used as an elimination room. The place is sparsely furnished, but the few pieces present all look to be handcrafted.

"I don't think I improved my situation," she mutters to herself with a pitiful sniff. She tugs at her tether, but it holds fast to the wall. That small amount of movement sends agony through her leg so she slumps down and works on simply dragging air into her lungs. The return of her latest owner makes her shiver in fear.

"Stay still," he orders as he sinks into a cross-legged sitting position next to her wounded side. Pulling her foot onto his lap, he probes the red and blistered puncture with blunt fingers.

With a cry of pain, she tries to pull her foot away from him, but his powerful hands hold her still. "Please don't hurt me."

"It's bad," he announces. "But not as bad as it could be."

He grabs a cleaning cloth from the pile he dropped on the floor and starts rubbing it across the wound. An astringent smell hits her nose at the same time the pain in her foot eases.

Once he's finished cleaning the heel, he reaches into a bowl full of a dark, pulpy substance. Spreading it on her heel, he works it into the wound. At first, it burns and she gasps and jerks. His firm hold on her ankle keeps her still. Soon a pleasant numbness spreads through her foot and up her leg.

Relief from the pain makes her feel giddy, and she slumps back with a sigh of pleasure.

He pats the top of her foot. "Better?"

"So much better," she agrees, letting her eyes flutter shut. Her lack of sleep and her hasty escape are catching up with her. She doesn't even fight the stranger when he pulls her into his lap, gathers her against his chest, and starts rumbling out a purr. He has the strangest rumble. It sounds rough, like an engine that isn't running right.

"I'll take good care of you," he tells her. "No collar means you have no owner, so I'll be your owner. I'll shelter and feed you. I'll keep you safe."

"I had a collar," she murmurs.

"I know," he says simply. "You cut it off and injured yourself. Holian isn't usually so careless. His loss, my gain."

Could it be this simple? Would Holian leave her here in the forest? Isn't she valuable property he'll search for? Out of nowhere, impulsive words leave her mouth.

"I'm pregnant," she says in a rush and waits for the repercussions of her words.

The male goes still, and then his arms tighten around her slightly. "Human or Talin?"

Now it's her turn to be shocked. "W-what?" she stammers out.

"Did you rut with a human or a Talin?" His tone is calm and measured. They could be discussing the weather or something equally mundane instead of something that got her stolen, almost got her unborn child killed, and resulted in her being exiled to a Talin colony.

"Talin," she whispers, afraid to say the word out loud. It almost feels like Mavianin will appear and drag her away because she dared state the truth.

"That's good," he grunts. "It'll be born smaller than a pure human. It won't be as difficult a birth for you."

"Oh," she says. Has she fallen into some alternate universe where human-Talin babies are commonplace and the fear of being disgraced is absent?

"I'll provide for both of you," he tells her. "No one will bother us out here. Holian leaves me and the other warriors in the woods alone. There's no one on the planet of higher rank than him. If he can't be bothered to bring us to heel, no one else dares touch us."

"You're not worried about being dishonored?"

"Honor," he mutters. "Honor is just a word. Actions are important. Let others have their honor. I'll take happiness instead."

For the first time since the healer broke the news that she's pregnant, a genuine smile curves her lips.

"I couldn't agree with you more," she murmurs.

Her original goal was to stowaway on a ship and make her way off this world. But, if she's honest with herself, she probably would've been caught quickly and either returned to Holian or given to another Talin. Her chances of actually gaining her freedom were remote.

But if her objective is to keep her child safe, she might achieve that here. This male might be strange and the living situation rough, but he's unfazed by the news that would appall most Talins. And more than that, he seems willing not only to let her keep the child but to help raise it. She could do a lot worse.

"What's your name?" she asks, wiggling until she can see his face.

"Dalt," he grunts as he loosens his hold enough for her to face him. It seems short for a Talin name. Perhaps it's a nickname or a shortening of his traditional name.

"Hello, Dalt. I'm Sora," she says. "I guess I'm your new human."

A rumble of humor comes out of him. "Hello, Sora the Wanderer."

She takes a moment to study his face. Something about him looks off to her. Feeling bold, she reaches out and runs her hand over the top of his head and then down the back of his neck. Where her fingers should find overlapping armor plates, there's only flesh and scar tissue.

At her questioning look, he stops purring. "Torture," he states bluntly, and she pulls her hand back as if she's been burned. He grabs her hand and presses it back down on his neck. "That felt good," he insists. "Don't stop."

Worried about causing him pain, she's cautious as she pets him, but it seems all the wounds are old and long healed. As she reaches her hands down, she can feel he's missing the armor plates at the top of his back also.

She can't reach any further but surmises the rest of the plates are probably missing. No wonder he hasn't made a single rattling sound. He literally can't. Looking down, she can see his forearms don't have quills, and his hands have no retractable claws. The scars tell a story of a horrific accident or deliberate, systematic torture.

Either way, the pain this male must have endured is unimaginable.

Feeling a strange kinship to this Talin, she drops her head down to rest on his chest. "I won't hurt you either," she tells him, and he rumbles out a laugh.

"Very good," he murmurs. "No more pain for either of us."

CHAPTER 24

Searin

The small female human regards him, Tieno, and the two guards with curiosity but no fear.

"Who are you?" she asks.

Before answering, Searin tests the enclosure gate. It's locked and much too sturdy to break without tools. As he tests the gate, she moves back.

"Go away." her words are brave, but her voice trembles with fright.

Tieno hits him on the arm, "Stop scaring her."

"Sora's here," Searin insists. "I can smell her."

"Sora?" the girl asks, sounding confused. "Who's Sora?"

"She was renamed Hope before being sent here," Searin explains and feels optimistic when recognition shows on the human's face.

"Hope? What do you want with her?"

Searin's heart thuds in his chest. "I want to take her home."

"She got here yesterday," the human explains. "But she was terrified and kept asking weird questions. And then Eranan took Nol away. I felt so bad for her. I think she was abused in her last home." Suddenly she eyes him with distrust. "Were you her last owner?"

He wants to know who Nol and Eranan are, but those questions can wait. First, he needs this girl to tell him where Sora's being kept.

"She was stolen from me," he explains, grasping the bars of the gate. "Please, if you know anything, tell me. I need to find her."

She opens her mouth to say something, but a loud, aggressive rattle draws the men's attention. They turn to find Talin standing further down the aisle of enclosures.

"Get away from her!" he says, rattling with anger. He's holding a weapon illegal on their homeworld. The thing could easily kill all four of them with one round. Searin and the men with him all freeze at the sight of this powerful weapon held in confident, steady hands.

"There's no need for that," Tieno says quickly.

"I don't know who you are, but you can't come onto Commandant Holian's estate and harass his pets." The male doesn't seem to be intimidated by Searin or the three men standing behind him.

"This is Prime Son Searin," Gravian announces, putting his body between the man with the powerful weapon and Searin.

Searin's not sure how it happened, but apparently, he has personal guards now. Neither of his new guards have any weapons except for the traditional long knives on their belts. Royal guards don't normally carry projectile weapons around on Talarian, and they didn't have time to outfit themselves for the journey to the colony.

The man rattles out another warning, holding the gun with practiced ease. "If he's the monarch's son, he should know better than to barge onto another's estate," he retorts.

Always the calm, level-headed one, Tieno steps forward. Or more accurately, stumbles forward. Even after the marks spent on the transport to the colony, he's moving poorly. The confrontation with Gravian on the homeworld left him wounded and in pain.

"I'm sure you're only being loyal to Commandant Holian," Tieno says as he rumbles out a soothing sound. "But King Mavianin has done his son a horrible injustice. Searin's pet human was given to Commandant Holian by Mavianin without Searin's consent or knowledge. She's scent-bonded to Searin and might even now be weakening and suffering from Separation Sickness. We ask for your cooperation instead of hindrance for the sake of the pet."

"We have no humans here by the name of Sora," he tells them. He's not ready to back down, but he's not rattling confrontationally any longer either.

"They're talking about Hope," the female speaks up from inside her enclosure.

That makes the man pause and lower his gun slightly. "Hope arrived yesterday," he states slowly. "But there's a problem."

At those words, bands of tension tighten around Searin's chest. He steps forward, fear sounds rumbling out of his chest unchecked.

"What's happened to her?" Searin demands. "Take me to her. Are the healers here? She's breeding. She—"

Shaking his head, he brings the weapon back up, forcing Searin to stop walking. "She can't be your Sora then. Hope, the human pet given to Commandant Holian, isn't breeding. The paperwork sent by the healers states she's fertile and ready to be rutted."

His words almost make Searin crumble to the ground. What has his father done? Mavianin must have ordered the healers to terminate the gestation. Terminate Sora's child. His child.

"No," he whispers. His rattles and rumbles cease. He hears a roaring in his ears as he tries to understand the gravity of this information.

"You should take us to her," Tieno requests. "Let us verify that this Hope is Sora and determine exactly what has happened. Then we can take her to the healers." He leans close to Searin. "If the baby is gone, she'll need you. She'll be distraught and perhaps even prone to self-harm. You'll need to comfort her, Searin. Your bond with her might help her survive this."

"Let me see Hope," Searin all but begs. "Let me hold her and comfort her. She'll need my scent right now."

The male hesitates for a long time. Searin finally comes out of his mind long enough to realize the sound rattling from the male is one of anxiety, not aggression, and more apprehension fills him.

"Tell us," he demands. The man finally drops the muzzle of his weapon, his shoulder slumping.

"She's missing," he whispers. "That's the issue. She ran away last night. We don't want to sound a general alarm because we don't want anyone visiting the colony hunting her down and stealing her away. The entire household is out looking for her." He gestures to the human female in the enclosure. "I came back to check on Henni and the other humans before returning to the search."

A crash of emotions hits Searin. He was close to bringing his Sora home, only to have her determination thwart him. He almost rumbles out a laugh. Then he realizes she's out there alone. Anyone could take her. Within a few marks, she could be off-planet and sold. If that happens, he might never find her.

He turns and addresses the men who came with him, speaking to Tieno first. "Search the port. That's the most likely place she'll go."

Pulling out a scrap of fabric he tore from one of Sora's wraps, he hands it to Vitrian. "This is hers. The scent should help you track her as you search. She might hide in the green area outside the port, waiting for an opportunity to stow away on a ship. If you find her, try not to spook her. Keep her in sight and call for me or Tieno." Both men tap their chest plates and then all three hurry away.

Turning back to the servant blocking his path, he taps his chest. "You can contact the palace to confirm my story but right now my men and I will help with the search."

The servant makes another agitated rattle. "This is my fault. I put Nol in with her. He's our most gentle male. He was to keep her calm and help her transition to her new home. She was starting to trust him, but then Commandant Holian made me move him out late last night. I should have fought him. I should have insisted Nol stay with her. She wouldn't have been so scared and felt like she needed to escape if he stayed with her."

"You put a male in with her?" Searin barely keeps his anger in check.

"We thought he might help to settle her." He sounds a rattle of frustrated. "If I'd known. If I'd only known…" He doesn't finish that statement and Searin realizes this servant was an unwitting accomplice in Sora's abduction and relocation. He obviously cares for the humans under his charge and was only trying to be a good keeper.

"What's your name?"

"Eranan of the Brix family."

"Thoren Clan, correct?"

Eranan nods in confirmation.

Not only is this man from a low-ranking clan, but his family is one of the least powerful members of the clan. Eranan must be exceptional to find a job with someone as important as Holian. This explains the male's fierce defense of both his humans and his employer.

"Commandant Holian is an excellent judge of character," he states. "I'm sure you did everything in your power to care for the humans in your custody."

Eranan powers down the gun and swings it around to hang from his back. He straightens up a little as he replies. "I do my best."

"I can tell. Now, tell me about this Colony," Searin demands. "Tell me about who settles here and tell me about all the places a frightened human might hide."

CHAPTER 25

Sora

Eyes fluttering open, Sora takes in her surroundings. She fell asleep on Dalt's lap, but must not have woken up when he transferred her to the bed. It's dark inside the cabin now, with a few glowing bowls of crystals casting weak light around the room. When she sits up the chain attached to her collar jangles, reminding her she can't get far.

Her foot isn't in agony anymore, so that's a relief. But she needs to pee so badly it's bordering on painful.

"Dalt?" she calls out softly. With no idea how far they are from anyone else, she doesn't want to risk being discovered by drawing unwanted attention. Caterwauling for Dalt is definitely out.

Listening intently, she hears leaves rustling, the faint sounds of animal calls, and the distant hum of massive ship engines.

"Dalt?" she tries again, this time a little louder. When the door opens and he steps in carrying a large basket in both hands, she breathes a sigh of relief.

"Don't be afraid." He sets the basket down inside the door and then crouches and shuffles awkwardly toward her. "You're safe."

Hunching over and trying to appear small, he moves slowly as if he's worried about scaring her, and she finds his actions heartwarming if a little ridiculous.

Huffing out a little laugh, she holds out her hand to him. "I'm not scared, but I need to use the elimination facilities. Urgently!"

His rumble of humor sounds off key and rusty. He grasps her hand and pulls her up to her feet as he stands and then casually reaches over to unlock the chain from her collar. The chain drops noisily to the floor, and she looks down at it for a moment, chewing on her lip. When she looks back up, Dalt is watching her intensely.

"You don't like that." He motions to the chain and then reaches out to run a finger over the collar.

"No."

"I don't want you to wander off and get hurt. You'd be dead now if I hadn't found you."

The collar and chain aren't something he wants to do, she realizes. If she's careful, she might be able to talk Dalt into giving her more freedom.

"I won't go outside while you're gone. I absolutely won't run away. You know about the baby. I have no reason to run."

He rumbles out his broken purr. "I'm glad you feel safe here, but be aware, there's nowhere to go. No way to get off the planet unless you belong to someone else. But this planet is dangerous."

Frowning, she puts her palm on his chest, feeling the irregular vibrations of his purr. "I'm safer here. I was a slave before I was bought by a Talin and became a pet. And I was a pet before I became a lover. Being a pet was the safest I've felt. I don't mind being your pet, Dalt. I want to keep my child, and I want to raise it. I trust you, so I need you to trust me back because I don't want to be chained or caged anymore. It's scary not to be able to leave a place if I feel threatened."

First Halieni hunted her down within her outdoor enclosure, like a canned hunt. Then the king showed up and there wasn't even any place to hide within her indoor enclosure.

Purring louder, his hand covers hers, grasping her gently and bringing her palm to his lips. He runs his lips over the soft skin of her hand several times before taking a deep breath and letting go.

"I understand feeling trapped. No more chains." He reaches up and presses his fingers to the collar. It beeps several times and then releases and drops to the floor. "No more collars or cages.

You'll stay with me, and I'll keep you safe. Don't go beyond the gardens. Nothing in the gardens can hurt you. Outside that—" He gives a little rumble that makes her think of humans making a humming sound. He didn't need to say more; she's already experienced the wild dangers of this planet.

"I'll stay on the grounds," she assures him. "You're a good man, Dalt."

His purring abruptly stops. "I'm a broken man."

She gives him a mildly exasperated look. "Good and broken aren't mutually exclusive."

She should know, in some ways she's broken too. A human carrying a mixed Talin baby in a culture that sees her as a pet can't be included in the realm of success.

"Most would argue with that statement. A broken tool has no value."

This time, her smile is brilliant. Putting her palm against the exposed skin of his neck, she rubs gently. He doesn't have any scars there and he makes a rumbling moaning sound at the touch.

"Despite what the universe has tried to teach me, I believe we are worth more than what we can produce," she whispers. "We have intrinsic value."

He stands still as she rests her hand on his skin, as if he's soaking up her touch. Unlike with Searin, she doesn't feel any desire for this Talin, only a kind of kinship. They've both been powerless and abused. While Dalt might need to hold her, pet her, and cuddle, she suspects he's not going to initiate any kind of sexual interaction.

Without any warning, nausea rises up in her, making her smack a hand over her mouth before she rushes to the elimination receptacle in the corner of the cabin. She gets there just before she vomits up bile.

When she's finally done retching, she slumps back on the stone floor and finds Dalt hovering over her making anxious noises. He snatches a rag from the wall and wets it from a nearby bucket full of clean water before wiping her face with it. The coolness feels good, and she closes her eyes and lets him care for her.

His anxious rumbles switch to his broken purring. "I wish humans didn't become ill when breeding."

She huffs out a little laugh. "You and me both. Now turn your back so I can use the elimination facilities for another reason." Obligingly, Dalt turns his back so she can urinate. A feeling of intense relief fills her as she's finally able to empty her bladder.

Cleaning herself off once she's done, she smiles when she thinks about the fact that she just emptied herself from both ends. The thought is as amusing as it is disgusting.

"Done," she calls out and Dalt turns back and scoops her up. She expects him to put her back on the bed, but he walks outside.

Her abrupt arrival the day before did not allow her to take in her surroundings. Now she has time to observe and is impressed by what she sees.

Never would she expect to see an elaborate garden surrounding Dalt's cabin. The night is well lit by a trio of moons in the sky, casting enough light to create shadows. The air is warm and perfumed by the many flowering plants around her. The garden is a mass of potted plants, raised planters, and small, heavily trimmed trees, with intersecting footpaths around everything.

Dalt carries her to a central spot where half a dozen paths meet. In the center of the path's apex is a round plot of flat greenery upon which he gently sets her down. Whatever plant is under her, it's incredibly soft and silky to the touch.

A feeling of contentment makes her sigh. "This is lovely."

Easing his bulk down next to her, he reclines and urges her to do the same. Shoulder to shoulder, they gaze up at the moon and the stars, listening to the rustle of leaves around them as the warm fragrant air fills their lungs. "Thank you," she murmurs.

"We can sleep here," he offers. "On warm nights like tonight. We can sleep in the open, no walls."

"I'd like that," she agrees. Never would she have thought her life could take so many twists and turns so rapidly. Rolling over, she snuggles into him, trying to ignore the fact that he doesn't smell like Searin.

I need to be content with this, she tells herself sternly. Content and safe are better. Much better than in love and in danger.

She wonders how many times she's going to need to repeat that to herself before she believes it.

CHAPTER 26

Sora

"Try this." Dalt attempts to shove a bit of food into her mouth, but Sora bats his hand away. Her mouth is still full of the previous bite he fed her. She's lived with him for several rotations now, and even though he's fed her half a dozen meals, he still seems to have trouble with the concept that she can only eat one mouthful at a time.

Despite his over-eagerness to feed her, it's pleasant to have someone care for her again. Plus, there's the added bonus of trust. She's not locked up anymore. She can come and go from the house at will, readily obeying his command to stay within the garden for her own safety.

For the first time since she was sixteen, she's not wearing a collar. Sometimes it feels odd, like she's missing something. When she reaches up to scratch her neck and meets nothing but skin, it's startling but never fails to make her smile.

Because the nausea is taking a toll on her, Dalt's determined to get her to eat as much as possible when she's not suffering the effects of her pregnancy. Although she occasionally voids the food not long after eating, he remains undaunted.

After she swallows the bite, she opens her mouth to ask him a question, but he takes that opportunity to shove more food in. When she finally swallows, she holds her hand in front of her face to keep him from filling her mouth.

"I'm scared about having the baby," she admits, and he purrs loudly.

His response is brutally honest. "It's a painful process for humans. And it can be dangerous."

Fear spikes through her. She and the baby could die. Her aunt died during birth. As a child, she wasn't allowed into the room and the family didn't have the money to pay to take her to a medical facility. Women flowed in and out of the room during the labor, their faces calm at first but then growing more concerned as the hours passed. A full rotation passed. Then another. Finally, with somber expressions, they whispered words of consolation to her mom.

Sora looks down at her stomach. "I don't want to die."

"It's unlikely. Commandant Holian employs a full-time healer. No one has ever died in childbirth here. I can bring the healer when the time comes. Holian's compound isn't far. He also has a human who's had several children and now spends most of her time with pregnant and birthing humans. I've been told she's very good at aiding women through the process."

She tilts her head to the side and regards him with a wry smile. "I doubt he's just going to lend you his human midwife without an explanation."

He sounds a dismissive rumble and tries to feed her another bite. She keeps her mouth closed and gives her head a little shake.

"He'll know I have you by then. It'll be fine."

That shocks her. "He's going to be fine with me running off? I'm property. I'm owned. If you have me, isn't it stealing?"

He makes another dismissive rumble. "Commandant Holian acts as a human way station. If they're abused, in need of help, or anything like that, they end up with him. Everyone thinks he's an avid collector. He's only ever bought two humans. All the rest find their way to him or are given to him. If you're happy and safe with me, he won't try to take you away. In a few weeks, I'll approach him and explain. He'll want to talk with you, but once he's satisfied, he'll leave us alone."

"You seem to know him very well," she probes.

Instead of explaining their relationship, Dalt rumbles out an affirmative noise. After so many months of hearing rattling, she's getting used to Dalt's quieter communications.

Dalt's a very different kind of Talin than she's met so far. Never once in the last few days has he mentioned his family or clan. He doesn't talk about honor or serving the Talin people. Instead, he lives quietly, working hard on his garden and cabin while diligently caring for her and planning their future.

He has demons there, buried deep. Sometimes she'll catch him staring off into the distance, lost in a memory. He'll stand perfectly still and silent and she won't be able to get his attention until the memory has run its course. It's distressing to see him that way, but he tells her nothing is to be done, and she shouldn't worry herself over him.

Talins don't dream, but it seems they can have waking nightmares. Holding her helps him recover after one of those waking nightmares. She wishes she could somehow stop him from having the nightmares at all, but once they start nothing can pull him out of them until he's relived the traumatic memory.

Even when she presses, he refuses to tell her any details about what happened to him. He claims it might cause her distress and hurt her pregnancy. She thinks it is more likely he feels ashamed of what happened and doesn't want to influence her opinion of him.

Given time, she's sure he'll share with her. He's a compassionate male who's already earned her trust. Eventually, he'll come to understand she would never judge him for what happened to him in the past.

And of course, even with all his assurances, she's still nervous about the birth, but she'd never admit that to him. "I trust you to do your best for me."

"Always." Then he pushes more food at her.

Suddenly, Dalt drops the food and bounds to his feet. He snatches her up and sprints to the door of the cabin, but several men step into sight before he's even gotten halfway there.

"Dalt, we haven't seen you for rotations," one man calls out as he emerges from some greenery. Three men stand behind him, but they all freeze as they take in the sight of her in Dalt's arms.

In a voice full of both awe and surprise, one man murmurs, "Human."

"Female," another breathes out. All four of them are staring at her and purring. She clutches at Dalt.

He can't rattle, but his snarling voice leaves no question of his emotional state. "Mine!"

"No, you have to share," the man in front states adamantly. "When we moved here, we all agreed that we'd share with each other."

"We agreed to look after each other," Dalt corrects him. "You're my comrade and friend, Iansif, but don't test me on this."

"We'll be gentle with her," another one promises as he steps forward. The four of them stand shoulder to shoulder now, blocking the path to the cabin. Dalt gently sets her down and pushes her behind him.

"This female is more fragile than most," Dalt growls. "No one touches her, Tisuran."

"This is unacceptable." Tisuran sounds an aggressive rattle. "What makes you better than us? Why do you deserve to have a dedicated human when we don't? None of us would harm her. You're being unreasonable. You know us, Dalt. How could you deny us the same comfort you're receiving?"

Peaking around Dalt, Sora can see all four men have their quills up and their claws extended. Not only is Dalt outnumbered, but without claws, quills, or back armor, he's vulnerable.

"They can touch me," she whispers to him. "Don't fight them. I don't want you to get hurt."

Without looking at her, he shouts out. "No." His answer is for both her and them.

The smallest of the four speaks for the first time, his tone plaintive. "Maka wasn't our fault. We couldn't know she was sick."

His words make Sora shiver with fear. She's not the first female to find herself among these men and whoever Maka was, it appears her captivity didn't end well.

"She was our responsibility! Ours!" Dalt roars out. "She's dead, and it's our fault."

"Holian's healer told us we couldn't have known that the vessel in her head would rupture," Tisuran argues.

Dalt cuts him off. "Holian locks down his humans. All of them. He never did that before Maka."

"Holian locked down the humans because of the attack, not because of Maka." Tisuran's voice is calm, but the claws extending at his fingertips says he's anything but.

Dalt jerks his head down to indicate where she's peering around his broad body. She flinches when all four men focus their eyes on her.

"This one ran away because of the lockdown. She almost died. Why? Because Holian doesn't trust us anymore. All of you caused this!"

Those last words are a roar, making Sora gasp. Dalt is enraged and ready to kill, but what chance does he have against so many?

"I'm pregnant," she blurts out, thinking that knowledge will make the men back off. If anything, they all take a step forward with eager rumbles.

"We'll take good care of you," Iansif coos. "I've held human pups before. When they're newly born you need to be extra careful because they don't have spine plates to protect their necks."

Tisuran nods in agreement but doesn't retract his claws. "You should have more than one Talin to take care of you."

"I only want Dalt," she tells them, trying to sound brave, but her words come out shaky instead. "Not any of you. Please don't hurt him."

"If our service together meant anything, you would leave my garden," Dalt growls out.

"If our service together meant anything, you would protect her from your instability and hand her over to us," Tisuran counters. His tone turns hard. "What happens if you have a Memory Episode when she needs you? Have you thought of that?"

Backing up slowly, Dalt moves them until she's almost against a nearby tree. "I'm going to draw them off the path," he whispers to her. "The moment you can, run into the house and bolt the door behind you. They won't be able to get in without tools. Stay safe until they're gone and then run to Holian's compound."

With a whimper, she shakes her head. "No! You promised I could stay with you."

"Do as I say, Sora. I'm trusting you."

She wants to beg him to run, beg him to negotiate with the men, beg him to do anything but fight.

"They can touch me. They can hold me. I'll get away and return to you," she pleads.

"Palforma, the man wearing the blue pants, will hurt you. He won't mean to, but he will. He might hurt the baby. He's not right in his mind. He was hit by a round in the head and can't even talk now. Narmolo is much too strong and can't be trusted to care for anything delicate. You aren't safe with them."

All four men are advancing on the two of them now, shoulders hunched and knees bent. They are ready to fight Dalt for her. Without another word, Dalt launches himself in a powerful attack. He's the second biggest of all of them and takes all four down to the ground in a tangle of limbs.

"Run!" he roars, and she does.

She's almost to the house when she hears footsteps behind her. She has no time to look.

Gasping from the effort, she grabs the door as she falls into the cabin. Pain shoots up her arm as her grip on the door checks her momentum and almost sends her crashing into a wall. Clumsily, she turns and shoves at the heavy door. She can hear shouting and rattling from the men but ignores it. Her entire focus is on getting the door closed.

Just as she swings it closed and locks the sliding latch, an impact rattles it. The violence of it makes her stumble, falling hard to the floor. Stunned, she stays there, listening.

The cabin has windows, but they are so small even she couldn't fit through them. She watches the men circle the cabin, shouting at each other as they break one of the tiny windows and test the stone frames. No opening is big enough to allow even one of their shoulders into the cabin.

Noise from the roof makes her look up although she can't see anything except for more stone. The cabin's stone walls slowly curve in until they meet at the top of a tall dome. Clawed feet scramble on the roof, looking for a weakness as pounding on the door resumes.

As Dalt promised, the cabin holds strong, and no one gets in. She crawls to one of the broken windows and stands on tiptoe to look out. Palforma's face suddenly appears, making her cry out and pull away. He makes a purring sound when he sees her but doesn't speak.

His face is violently thrust away, so she goes back on tiptoe to look out the window. Dalt and Palforma are on the ground, fighting. The battle is intense, both men bleeding, but Dalt is far more wounded.

With a last roar, Dalt brings both fists up as Palforma sinks his claws into Dalt's abdomen. Fists locked together, Dalt crashes them down into Palforma's face. Sora hears a distinct crunch and Palforma goes limp.

Instead of standing up, Dalt collapses sideways and goes still.

Crying out in fear, Sora hurries to the door and unlatches it, getting it open just far enough to slip out. She runs around the cabin to find Dalt crawling toward her. Iansif and Tisuran are also lying unconscious, but the fourth man is missing.

"Run!" Dalt cries out. When she kneels next to him, he stops trying to move and just grasps one of her hands in his bloody, broken fingers. "Narmolo went to get a breaker staff to open my door. You need to get to Holian before he returns."

The ground is darkening as blood pools around Dalt. Without answering him, she runs back into the house and grabs several pairs of his pants. She rushes back and drops to her knees on the ground next to him. The wrap he fashioned for her out of an old bedsheet rapidly soaks up his blood as she rips apart a pair of pants for a bandage.

"You need to go." His voice is weaker now, and he's not opening his eyes.

"You need to live." She doesn't recognize the fierce voice coming out of her. "I can't lose anyone else."

Determined now, she wraps the cloth around his torso, tightening it down until he gasps. The cloth is quickly saturated with his blood, but by the time she's added a third layer, the bleeding is slowed. Assessing his other wounds, she wraps one thigh but leaves the rest. She's out of time. If he's going to survive, she's going to need to get help.

Iansif groans, and she freezes in place. He tries to get up, but falters and falls back to the ground with a moan of pain. With one last glance at Dalt, she gets to her feet and starts running.

Concentrating on the crude map she pictured in her head when he told her how to get to Holian's compound, she starts down the path leading from his property marked with blue wildflowers. She can only hope she's remembering correctly and help is at the end of this trail.

CHAPTER 27

Searin

"It's been four rotations! Four!" Searin roars out as he paces in front of Holian. "How have you not found her in four rotations?"

Holian calmly watches Searin rage. Tieno, Vitrian, and Holian are all sitting together waiting to hear from Gravian and Eranan, hoping the two excellent trackers have found a trace of Sora. After the first rotations when she couldn't be found at the port or in the surrounding woods, Holian started systematically searching the rest of the forest. But instead of allowing Searin, Tieno, and Gravian to help with the search, Holian assigned only Vitrian and Eranan, forcing the rest of them to remain at his mansion.

Coming to a stop in front of Holian, Searin sounds an enraged rattle. "We should be out there, looking!"

"As I explained earlier, the forest is full of retired soldiers. If we go walking through the forest en masse, it could produce an unfavorable reaction with my men. We need to be cautious."

"What if one of your precious broken warriors finds Sora?" Searin challenges.

Standing up, Holian faces Searin's anger without any audible display of emotion. "If they're broken, they got that way fighting wars for your Empire, Prime Son Searin. Each one of them needed a safe place to live. This colony provides it."

"I heard about what happened to the human Maka last year," Searin challenges. "Current operational soldiers should be called in to sweep the forest for Sora. One of these men could have already killed her!" The last few words are delivered with a deafening war rattle.

Male members of the Prime Family are born with the ability to make extremely loud rattles, and Searin is no exception.

Holian doesn't react to his war rattle. Instead the male waits for Searin to stop and continues speaking.

"Maka had an issue none of us knew about," Holian explains again. "She had a defect in her brain that ruptured one day, causing blood to pool there and disrupting her brain functions. They got her here as soon as they could, but it was already too late by the time they realized something was wrong. The male taking care of her at the time ran his feet bloody trying to get her to me in time. I will not punish my men for something like that."

"They are—"

Holian lets loose with a decisive rattle, cutting Searin off. "One man Faded within weeks of her death, even though I told him to spend time among the other humans on my property. He was too devastated." Holian goes silent for a moment before speaking again. "I'm simply trying to help all of them. All my soldiers and all my humans."

Searin regards the commandant with a new understanding. "You do it on purpose. You have so many broken warriors and orphaned humans here because you want to save them. Both the soldiers and the humans. I didn't realize."

Holian takes a deep breath and seems to debate with himself. Finally, he speaks. "If the homeworld knew what was going on here, what was happening, I'd be imprisoned."

That brings Searin up short, "What do you mean?"

Straightening his shoulders, Holian strides to the door. "Come with me, Prime Son Searin." When the other men move to follow, Holian rattles out a warning. "The rest of you stay."

Looking to Searin for instruction, Gravian sounds nn irritated rattle. "Prime Son Searin, you shouldn't go anywhere alone."

Searin gestures for him to stay seated. "I'm sure I'll be fine. Remain here. I'll call out if I need you." He didn't point out that he'd never had a guard before but managed to survive so far.

Gravian is unhappy about that order but gives a rumble of assent. If Searin wasn't so terrified for Sora, he'd rumble out a laugh at Gravian, who's turned into his loyal shadow. He never wanted personal guards before, but now he's gained two.

Following Holian through the immense house, they get to a set of grade-four doors that require a biosignature to open. These same kinds of doors are used on ships or space stations meant to withstand direct hits from weapons fire. Searin notices other unusual things, such as protective domes over the windows and discrete weapons lockers hidden within decorative cabinets.

He only gets more curious as they go through several sets of security measures, each one with a biosignature lock. He can't imagine what treasure Holian is keeping in this wing of the building and why he wants to show Searin.

The distinct sounds of laughter hits his ears as the last set of double doors slide open. Searin's met with a sight that freezes him in place, an unwitting rattle of astonishment sounding from his back plates. Holian stands at his side silently, his gaze sweeping the children playing and the indulgent adults chasing after them. About half of the adults in the room are human women, but the other half are a mix of male and female Talins.

However, the children have Searin's full attention. Many of them are obviously products of Talin and human interbreeding.

Searin says the only thing that comes to his mind. "They're beautiful."

One little girl sees the two of them. With a cry of delight, she launches herself in their direction. "Uncle Holian!" she screeches as she flings herself into his arms.

Holian catches her and holds her tightly to his chest, rocking back and forth as he murmurs to her. She tries to rumble, but the sound is off-kilter, so she stops and just smiles instead, something Talins can't do. Her human eyes regard him curiously as her Talin teeth peek out from between her full human lips.

A surprised rumble comes out of his chest before he can stifle it. "Is she yours?"

Rumbling out an affectionate sound for the child, Holian addresses Searin. "None of them are mine, more's the pity. None of the human women have found me captivating enough to bond with me, and I'd never force anyone."

"My Sora was breeding my child."

He can't believe he just stated that out loud and boldly, as if it wasn't a secret that could destroy him.

Instead of a rattle of outrage or a rumble of disgust, Holian interrupts his purr to make the soothing sound a Talin might use with a good friend or family member.

"I guessed as much. When King Mavianin gifted me a young healthy human, I assumed some unlucky Talin was caught scent-bonding to her and perhaps even rutting with her. I didn't know she was breeding, but it wouldn't have mattered. She would have been safe here."

Searin considers his words as they turn their attention back to the children playing. "She couldn't have known. She must have been so scared. My father had the gestation ended. My child is gone."

The invisible bands around his chest tighten so badly he's unable to breathe for a few moments. A tug at his pants draws his attention down. A little boy, a human-Talin mix by the looks of him, gives Searin a concerned look.

"Do you need to be clutched? I can give you a clutching. I'm very good at it," he tells Searin with deep sincerity. "Nanni says I'm the best clutcher and clinger."

Sinking to his knees, Searin opens up his arms and the little boy presses his small body against his. When he folds his big arms around the child, he marvels at the boy's fragile little body.

This child reflects the love, kindness, and empathy he's being raised around. No cresh adults here with their special training and strict guidelines. There's no fear, no anxiety, and no reservations. The boy simply saw Searin and decided this Talin needed to be held, so he offered.

"That's Yoni," Holian explains. "His mother came to me already breeding. She and her male were discovered scent-bonding. He was sent off world in disgrace, but I managed to get her before anyone found out she had little Yoni growing in her belly."

"He saved me," a human woman says as she walks up with a smile. "He saved me and Yoni."

A sad rumble comes out of Holian's chest. "I'm sorry I couldn't save Sevorian too."

"You tried. They sent him so far away that he was probably dead from Ending before you even launched a ship," she says, then looks at Searin. "But I have Yoni, and we are safe. That's enough."

She holds out her hands for Yoni, and Searin reluctantly lets go of the boy. He watches as the two join several others in a little circle where stories are being told.

"How have you kept this all a secret?"

The little girl in Holian's arms wiggles and Holian sets her down with a little rumbling laugh before sending her on her way to join another child on an artificial climbing tree. "Because there are many more like us than you would ever expect."

A little rattle of surprise comes out of Searin. "Like us?"

Holian turns his attention to Searin and makes a derisive sound. "You were suffering the Fading before Sora." He holds up a hand before Searin can protest. "Don't bother denying it. That's why you scent-bonded with her. I know the signs well. When I first found out she originally belonged to you, I assumed she'd developed a relationship with a Talin in your household, and that the Talin scent-bonded back with her. Why else would she be sent away? Of course, I never considered it could be you. Who would ever imagine a Prime Son doing something as dishonorable and illegal as scent-bonding? And with a human no less?"

Searin's angry rattle causes several of the children to make sounds of distress. Embarrassed, he quiets his rattle, but he can't make his quills lie flat or his claws retract. He knows the commandant isn't threatening him, but his feelings for Sora are so new and his fear of losing her so great that he can't seem to keep his emotions under control.

Holian doesn't look intimidated or concerned by Searin at all. "Try to keep yourself calm, Prime Son Searin. Becoming agitated in here will upset everyone. I'm taking an enormous risk in showing you this. Don't make me regret it." He sweeps out an arm to encompass the room. "Don't make them regret it."

Hastily, Searin makes a reassuring rumble, thinking of Dorn and Dinala. "I would never. I know of others who've bonded with one of their humans. I've kept their secret too."

"That's good because they need as many of us as they can get."

"Us?"

"Talins willing to fight our own culture and idiocy. Humans are dying out. We are going to die out too if we aren't careful. Tell me something, when was the last time the Apogee Council issued birth and death statistics?"

Thrown by the seemingly random question, Searin answers by rote. "Those numbers are readily available on the UniBase. It's unnecessary to publish them as part of an annual review."

"I've heard that before. Let me ask you another question. Why are we relying more and more on trade when just a generation ago we produced ninety percent of everything we needed?"

It only takes a moment for Searin to make the connection between the two questions. "Our population is declining."

"Cresh construction has increased substantially over the last ten solars, but we can't keep up with the number of citizens we are prematurely losing to the Fading. An article was written by the Historian Umarian of the Yax Clan that clearly shows the trend's been going on for hundreds of years. In the end, if this continues, colonies like mine will survive our insanity, not the unbending and suicidal clans of our home world."

"Does everyone on Kalor know about this?" Searin can't keep the harshness out of his voice. The more who know, the greater the danger to these vulnerable children.

"Many, but that's because they moved here with their children. Or they're loyal soldiers who were under my command. I wasn't even the one who started all this."

His words stager Searin. "You didn't?"

"No. The Talin woman who founded this colony did it to keep her pregnancy a secret. She'd scent-bonded with her husband. When he died in war, she was despondent and suffered the painful effects of Ending. But she wasn't ready to give up and succumb to death. To put it simply, she founded a new colony. She bought this entire planet and moved her household here. She only took those she could truly trust to settle here because she had a bold plan. She stole his seed from a cresh facility and impregnated herself. She was determined not only to birth her own child but to raise it herself as well. She risked a great deal but decided the reward was worth it. Others found out, and a network of like-minded Talins emerged. It was a short jump from there to include humans in the mix."

"And her child, did they survive?"

"He standing next to you, doing his best to carry on his mother's legacy."

Searin is rendered dumb. He can't seem to form words, rattle, or rumble. The sounds of children playing and adults talking fills his earholes as he imagines Sora and his child. He imagines having everything. Her love. Her body in his bed every night. His child in his arms, laughing and hugging him and calling him father with a voice full of affection and joy.

Father.

Then he remembers his child was taken away before it could even breathe, and a powerful rage rises up in him again. He might yet murder his father, despite the very clear laws in place against personal reprisal.

Laws be damned. His life is over if he can't find Sora. He might as well make sure Mavianin's life is over as well.

Holian continues his explanation. "These men, the soldiers who settled here once their service was over, would die before they hurt Sora. Some are wounded, both in body and mind, but I know them. They might fight each other, but they'd never touch her with anything but gentleness. I know Sora's in the woods, housed with one or perhaps several of them. She might be scared, but she's safe. I stake my life on it. But we need to be careful approaching those soldiers. We'll get Sora back but not at the expense of one of my men."

Forcing a breath of air through the tension in his chest, emotions rioting through his mind, Searin flexes his hands until he finally gets his claws to retract. When he speaks, his voice is quiet, but his tone is heavy with promise.

"I hope you understand. She is more important to me than your life."

"I believe I understand that better than anyone."

A display on the wall near them chirps and Holian turns to tap on it. Searin takes that opportunity to watch the activity in the room, noting how content and happy everyone appears to be.

"Searin, hurry!"

No title and a voice full of stress makes Searin turn violently around. Holian is already moving through the door, racing back the way they came.

Searin sprints to catch up with the commandant. "What's happened?"

"No time. Hurry!"

They burst out of the house to find a small crowd gathered around something.

"Dalt's hurt! He's dying. Let go! We need to go to him!"

Hearing Sora's familiar voice spurs Searin into action. His aggressive rattling moves everyone out of the way, giving him a clear line of sight to Sora. She's sobbing and swaying on her feet. The hands that were holding her up withdraw because of his rattle, and she drops painfully to her knees.

"Get Mellie and Healer Vormian!" Holian commands. "You shouldn't touch her. She might be badly injured, and you could aggravate it."

Although he doesn't acknowledge Holian's words, Searin takes her into his arms.

"Searin!" she cries out, reaching for him with her small hands. "I never thought I'd see you again!"

He captures her hands before she can try to hug him. She might not even realize she's hurt and could make an injury worse by clinging to him. Transferring both her wrists into one of his hands, he cups his other hand under her chin to hold her head and neck immobile.

Her skin pales with his touch, and fear spikes through him. There'll be time for comforting touches and loving words later. Right now, he needs to make sure she survives. Worry makes his words harsh. "You're covered in blood. Where are your injuries?"

Whimpering, she tries to pull away from him. "Not mine. It's all Dalt's blood. Please save him. Please, Searin!"

"What's happened to Dalt?" Holian asks, kneeling next to Searin.

"There were four of them. I d-d-don't remember their names. But they all fought, and he's hurt. You need to go to him now!" Searin wants to demand she remain quiet and calm. But if this wounded male defended her, he deserves care. He doesn't keep Holian from talking to her.

"Where is he?"

"His cabin. I followed a path and I-I—" She tries to turn her head, but Searin's grip on her chin keeps her from being able to move. Her eyes are frantic. "Flowers," she stammers out. "The path with flowers."

Holian must understand what she's talking about because he hurries off, calling for men to come with him and others to fetch more healers. Sora is crying now, great choking sobs, and Searin badly wants to draw her into his lap and surround her in his warmth.

Then the healer is there, making Searin move away and instructing others to bring a hov-stretcher. Sora tries to resist them, tries to get up and walk, chanting Dalt's name the entire time.

When the healer announces she's going to give Sora a sedative, his little human fights against his hold. Searin's forced to hold her down.

"Don't!" Her eyes are wide and full of terror as the healer approaches with the medication. "Don't put me in a box. Don't send me away!" Her words tear at his heart, and he tries to reassure her with soothing words but she's too panicked to hear him.

"*No!*" she screams as the healer injects her because she won't open her mouth to accept a vial of liquid or medicated wafer. Tears flow from her eyes and her lids flutter shut. Her next words are barely audible, but Searin hears them and desperately wishes he hadn't.

"Don't let them take my baby."

CHAPTER 28

Sora

When Sora wakes up, she's back in an enclosure with Nol. Thoroughly disoriented, she tries to sit up. The male doesn't smile at her but helps her up, and between the two of them, they prop her up on some pillows. She shakes her head a little, trying to clear her mind, and regards Nol quizzically.

"Was it all a dream?"

"You mean did you dream that you ran off, found Dalt, ended up pregnant, and then got Dalt involved in a fight with a bunch of other ex-soldiers where he almost died? Nope, not a dream." Nol's voice isn't harsh, but there's very little sympathy there either.

"Go easy on her." Henni sounds cross and exasperated. They must have been arguing while she was asleep. "You would run too if you were stolen and afraid!"

"Eranan was frantic!" Nol retorts. "I've never seen him so scared. If he gets sent away, it's her fault!"

"He won't get sent away. You're concerned about something Master Holian would never do."

With uncoordinated fumbling, Sora sits up farther, no longer using the pillows, so she can better see. The two of them stop arguing to watch her struggles.

Regarding her with an angry expression, Nol moves back a little and crosses his arms over his chest. Sora watches him warily and asks the most important question she can think of.

"Is Dalt alive?"

When both Nol and Henni remain silent, she thinks the worst. Tears start flowing down her face. The tears make Nol relent and he moves to sit next to her.

"We don't know how Dalt's doing," he admits. "The place is in chaos. You were carried in here and then I was shoved in and told to keep you calm when you woke up. Everyone's rushing around and we haven't heard anything further. The healer should be back soon to check on you. She's been in and out several times. Maybe she'll know what's going on."

Looking down, she notices her feet and lower legs are wrapped in heavy bandages. The frantic run through the forest comes back to her. Bare feet ripped apart by stones and brambles. Calves and shins gashed from low branches. She pushed past the pain because Dalt needed her to get help.

Then she remembers collapsing just outside the manor house. The memories are vague and fuzzy, but she knows the face that filled her vision. The voice that tried to calm her. The hands that held her still.

"Searin is here!" she cries out, startling Nol.

Standing up on painful feet, she wobbles to the front of the enclosure. Nol doesn't stop her, and she ignores Henni's concerns.

"Searin!" she screams out. Why did he leave her? Did he go to help Dalt? She grips the gate and rattles it violently, putting her whole body against it. The gate doesn't move.

"Searin!" she yells loudly enough to make her throat hurt. Nothing happens.

She needs to get out. She needs to find Searin. She needs to make him understand that even if he doesn't want the baby, he needs to help her get free. Needs to help her protect their child.

Then a thought makes her go still. What if Searin knew what Mavianin was going to do to her? What if the only reason he's here is to make sure the baby is gone?

She doesn't want to believe it, but so much has happened.

Collapsing onto her knees, she leans her forehead against the bars and tries to think clearly. Fear is choking her. Suffocating her. Dalt might be dead. She doesn't know Searin's intentions. She can't just stay here and wait to find out her fate.

"Sora, you need to lie back down," Henni calls out. "The healer didn't have a flesh knitter, so she couldn't heal your feet. You shouldn't be walking on them yet."

"Let her walk if she wants to," Nol counters, flopping back on the nest. "Stupid human."

"You're human too," Henni reminds him. "And you're an idiot! Stop being so mean to her."

Sora ignores the two trading insults as she examines the enclosure. It must have another weak spot. Limping and using the bars to help her walk, she circles the enclosure, looking for some way out.

When she gets to the section where the bars meet a solid stone wall, she notices one spot where the bars sink into the ground. Kneeling, she gives the spot a hard tug, and it gives. With a grunt, she pulls hard. It starts to bend.

Suddenly, Nol is there, tugging her away. "What do you think you're doing? Stop that!"

Thankfully, he isn't a large male and doesn't want to hurt her, so when she struggles, he lets go and steps away.

"I have to find out about Dalt! I need to escape. I can't just stay here and wait."

"But staying here and waiting is exactly what you need to do," Nol argues.

"What if they send me away again?" Sora casts a desperate look at Nol and then Henni. She debates telling the two of them the truth and potentially making it worse for herself.

No, she needs to escape, not waste time confiding in others. She returns her attention to the weak section of fencing, but Nol wedges himself between her and the fence, making it impossible for her to pull at it.

Crying out in frustration, she slumps back. Then she looks up at Nol and screams. "You don't understand! They'll kill my baby if I stay!"

Henni makes a distressed sound. "No, Sora, they won't. Master Holian will keep you safe. We know you have a Talin-human child in you. It doesn't matter. You're safe here."

That they know doesn't stop her fear. Shaking her head violently, Sora pushes at Nol. If they know that much, they might as well know the rest.

"I'm not safe. Can Holian stop a king? Because that's who tried to kill my baby before. King Mavianin told the healers to end it. To send me here with an empty womb. But they lied and said they did. They told me to rut with the first human I could so everyone would assume the baby was from that match. The healers didn't know it's Searin's baby."

"King Mavianin?" Shock makes his voice a whisper. "Husband of the monarch?"

"Yes, the fucking king!" She looks back and forth between the two alarmed faces. "This baby will be part human and part Talin. But not just any Talin. The baby's father is a member of the Prime Family. The Prime Family!" she screams. "The family that's supposed to uphold all the Talin species' most honorable traits. The family that's supposed to embody Talin values. Now tell me Holian can keep me safe!"

The two other humans stare blankly at her, and she knows her answer. Then they exchange significant looks while she watches. Her feet are throbbing with pain, and her head doesn't feel much better. Adrenalin is flooding her system, making it easy to set aside her agony and focus on the task at hand.

"Holian can't risk the king paying too much attention to him," Henni murmurs. Her face is pale now, her features pinched from worry and fear. "If King Mavianin finds out about the nursery…" She leaves the rest unsaid. Sora might not know what the nursery is, but by the look on Henni's face, it's something that needs to be carefully guarded.

"She's dangerous to us. She needs to go," Nol agrees.

Those words make her sag with relief. Taking a deep breath, she tries to calm herself because these two are now allies instead of opposition.

"I need to find out if Dalt lives. Then I need to find a place to hide. I can't risk my baby by staying here."

"We all thought it was Dalt's baby," Nol murmurs. This time when she nudges Nol, he moves aside.

"I was pregnant when I got here. I needed to sleep with you so they'd think it was your baby."

He no longer looks angry. Now he looks sad and scared for her. "I didn't know. I'm sorry."."

"Help me with this," she begs, pulling at the bars. "Help me escape and save my child."

"Help her," Henni calls out. "You need to hurry. Keeper Eranan and the healer will be back soon."

Sadness gives way to determination, and Nol grasps the bars with her. Together they pull the bars far enough apart for her to wiggle out. Before she can run off, he grabs her hand through the bars.

"Go to the side of the house where the windows don't have protective domes over them. They're probably housing Dalt in the infirmary. It's at the very back, and there's a door from the outside so the ill and injured can be taken in and out without needing to go through the main house." Crouching down, he uses the patch of dirt to sketch out a symbol. "This emblem will be on the door."

She stares at the symbol until she's sure she has it memorized and then gives Henni and Nol a look of gratitude. "I'm sorry if helping me gets either of you in trouble."

Again, the two share a significant look, and then Nol gives her a tight smile. "Don't worry about us."

"If Dalt's alive, talk to him. He can hide you in the forest and then Holian can honestly claim he doesn't have you if King Mavianin comes looking."

Shaking her head, Sora blinks back tears. "Dalt might be dead because of me. I can't risk that happening to him again."

Neither of them has an answer for that, so she turns and painfully makes her way to the house. Following Nol's directions, she soon finds the infirmary door. Tucking herself into an ornate bush just next to the door, she listens closely for voices or movement. Her caution is rewarded when several Talins, wearing healer green tunics, stride out of the door.

She can't hear what they're saying, but as soon as they're out of sight, she crawls to the door and eases it open. All the beds are empty except for one. Being as quiet as she can, she crawls inside and ducks under the closest bed. Listening for any alarms or someone coming, she breathes a small sigh of relief when everything remains quiet.

Her knees hurt by the time she crawls over to the one occupied bed and stands to see who's in it.

The sight of Dalt fills her with conflicting emotions. She's overjoyed to find him alive and well, but despondent at the state of him. He's stretched out naked so she can clearly see the wounds on his abdomen, deep gouges that have barely begun to heal. She doesn't understand why the healers don't just use a flesh knitter on him, but the sight of his injuries makes her want to race after the healers and demand they do more.

"I'll be fine," Dalt murmurs without opening his eyes, making Sora startle. Climbing onto the bed, she carefully places herself at his side.

"I'm so sorry, Dalt. This is all my fault," she whispers.

His eyes slide open just enough to look at her. "I smell blood."

"You're badly wounded," she explains, wondering if he sustained a brain injury or is on pain-reducing drugs that are muddling his thought process.

"Not my blood, yours."

"Oh," she looks down at herself, noticing the bandages on her feet are soaked red. "It's fine," she lies.

"Not fine. You need a healer."

"I think they already saw me," she hedges.

Out of all the ways she saw this conversation going, this wasn't one of them. She pictured Dalt on death's door. Or angry at her for almost getting him killed. Maybe even dismissive because she's more trouble than she's worth. Having him worried about her is the last thing she expects.

She hears alarms sound outside. They must have discovered she's missing.

Or Mavianin is here.

She needs to stay focused. She needs some information. "What happened to the men who attacked us?"

"Home healing," he grunts. "Commandant Holian said we all acted badly. No one's being punished."

That tells her she can't return to the woods. Her options are rapidly narrowing. She can't get off-planet. She can't hide in the forest. Putting a protective hand on her stomach, she doesn't notice Dalt move until his hand closes around her wrist.

His hold is tight, but not harsh. "Searin owned you?"

Returning her gaze to his face, she debates what answer she should give. He must have read the indecision in her expression because he growls. "Truth."

"Yes. And he's the father of my child," she whispers before he can ask the next question.

"Searin, the Prime Son is the father?" he asks as if he can't quite wrap his head around that fact.

Sora's heart beats hard as she nods her head. "Yes."

After a slight pause, Dalt sounds his rusty broken purr. It starts and stops several times before he gives up. "Holian knows about your child. Don't run. Prime Son or not, Holian will keep you safe. We will keep you safe."

"Shhh, you need to rest," she soothes. His hand around her wrist tightens, just shy of painful.

"Don't run."

Even severely wounded, Dalt is observant. His eyes close, but his grip doesn't relax. "The healers will be back. They'll see to you."

Tugging at his grip, she shakes her head. "I need to go before they get back. It's fine. It's old blood. I just need a bath."

"Liar," he declares without heat. He takes a deep breath, and she thinks it's because he's in pain, but instead he shouts at the top of his lungs. "In here!"

Frantic, she pulls at her wrist trying to get loose. Dalt doesn't give, but he hisses in pain as her struggles jostle him. "Be still."

"Dalt, let go!" She hears footsteps on the stone path outside and slides off the bed. Her wrist still in Dalt's grip means she ends up sitting on the floor with her arm on the bed at an awkward angle. She braces her feet against the bed to use her body to pull her wrist free of Dalt's iron grasp.

The outside door to the infirmary opens. "She's in here!" a voice calls out.

She stops struggling, expecting to be rushed at and subdued by Talins, but no one comes near her. The door shuts again, leaving her and Dalt alone. She hears the distinct sound of a door being latched and looks over to the second door in the room that leads into the mansion. The lights on this display tell her it's locked.

As with Dalt's cabin, the windows of the room are too small for her to climb through, and the entire room comprises the same sturdy stone as the rest of the mansion.

She's effectively trapped.

Letting go of her wrist, Dalt shifts a little in the bed and groans. "You're stronger than you look."

"You did that to yourself," she retorts.

Suddenly, everything is too much.

Nausea hits her, making her swallow convulsively. She looks around for a waste receptacle, finally spotting one across the room. She tries to get to her feet, but the pain makes her unsteady, and her stomach heaves. Kneeling on all fours, she retches bile onto the shiny smooth stone floor. When she's done retching, she slumps sideways. The cool stone feels good against her heated skin.

"Sora?" Dalt rolls onto his side and hangs his head over the end of the bed, watching her.

Looking up at him, she gives a rueful smile. "We're quite the pair."

A door opens, and the sound of several pairs of feet tells her the reprieve is over. She lets her eyes drift shut and exhaustion takes over. She curls up in a tight ball to protect the baby in her belly and waits.

"My heart," a soft, familiar voice murmurs as arms pick her up.

"Searin?" His name is a whimper on her lips.

His purring fills the room as he lays her on one of the infirmary beds. "I'll do what's best for you," he promises.

"Best?"

"Shhh," he coos. She wants to open her eyes but just doesn't have the strength. The sounds of Dalt's broken purr and Searin's strong steady purr fill her ears as unconsciousness overtakes her.

CHAPTER 29

Sora

High-pitched giggling pulls Sora out of a dreamless sleep.

It's such a human sound she's taken back to her childhood. Until she was about ten and things started getting really bad for the human settlements, her life was full of playful cousins and a loving family. Sounds like laughter were a common occurrence. But it's been so long since she's heard a human child vocalize joy that the sound is startling.

Opening her eyes, she's met by a softly lit room. It takes a bit before she can focus. Dark brown eyes slowly coalesce in front of her. When the owner of those eyes pulls back a little, Sora can see the round face of a little girl. Short-cropped light brown hair curls around her head. She smiles to reveal pointed teeth that would do any Talin proud.

Transfixed, Sora reaches out to touch the child's face. Holding still, the girl lets Sora run her fingers down her cheek. But it's not long until she's bored with this game and rears back and screams at the top of her lungs.

"She's awake!"

Flinching at the screech, Sora sits up, moving slowly because her body feels stiff and uncoordinated.

The little girl runs off, but soon the small room is filled with a mixture of adult humans and Talins. They all talk at once.

"Do your feet hurt?

"How's your head?"

"Are you hungry?"

"Do you need to throw up?"

"I can take you to Dalt when you're ready."

"Or Searin."

Looking around at all the earnest faces, Sora's too overwhelmed to speak.

"Quiet," a commanding voice demands.

Everyone falls silent and steps back to allow a Talin male to walk in. He's as large as Searin, except he bears several scars on his face and head. His coloring reminds her of copper, darkening down his arms and legs.

Because of the way everyone reacts, this man must be important.

"I'm Commandant Holian," he explains.

"Are you my owner?" The words come out as a dry croak. Before Holian can respond, a flask of water is pushed into her hands. Greedily, she puts it to her mouth and drinks down most of it.

"That's up for debate," he comments and then addresses everyone else in the room. "Out."

They scatter, but there's no fear on anyone's faces, only respect. When everyone's gone, he shuts the door and pulls a chair closer to her bed. Sitting down, he regards her silently. Not a single rumble or rattle comes out of him.

It's unnerving. Just like a human with a face devoid of expression.

"Sir?"

"I'm trying to decide where to start," he admits. "You've created quite the complicated situation."

Deciding this man is probably the key to her future, she tries to be conciliatory. "I'm sorry I ran away."

"Twice. You ran away twice. Those outside enclosures are supposed to keep everyone in or out, depending." Now he makes a sound, the buzzing rattle of annoyance. "I can't believe Eranan didn't notice the rotten fencing. I guess I should thank you for making us realize we need to be more vigilant about those outside enclosures."

Worried that Eranan will be dismissed and Nol's heart will be broken, she slides off the bed to kneel in front of Holian. The move is uncoordinated and her slide ends up being more of a fall than a graceful transfer.

"Please don't punish anyone. It was my fault. All my fault. You can punish me." Bracing for a blow, she flinches when Holian wraps firm hands around her upper arms.

"None of that," he chides. "Back into bed with you." When she's flat on her back again, he sits back and makes a soft purring noise. "I need you to be completely honest with me right now. Your future depends on it."

Nodding, she focuses on him and wonders what he's going to ask her. "I'll tell you the truth."

Or lie. Whatever will keep her safer.

"Did you scent-bond with Dalt? You don't have his scent on you, but that doesn't necessarily mean anything with humans."

Instead of answering, she hedges. "What does Dalt say?"

"Sora, don't do that," he admonishes her without heat or anger. "Answer my questions."

How is she supposed to answer his questions if she doesn't know the consequences of her answers?

"Dalt's been very good to me."

"That's not what I asked. I know you belonged to Prime Son Searin. I know King Mavianin stole you and gave you to me to get you away from his son. Your ownership is now in question, and I've been tasked to figure out what to do with you."

He sits back on the chair, crossing his arms over his chest. "I'm going to ask you again. Did you scent-bond with Dalt? You humans call it falling in love. He's not going through any extra pain from being separated from you, so it's obvious he's not scent-bonded to you. But humans can be less obvious when they've bonded."

"I like him. He tried to keep me safe. Tried to protect me from the other soldiers."

"They wouldn't have hurt you. Those men would die before hurting you, Dalt included. The problem is, Dalt's just as damaged as the rest of them. You haven't been among the Talins long, but I'm assuming by now you're coming to realize our flaws as well as our strengths. Aggression in the pursuit of guarding others is a strong trait in our soldiers. It doesn't just turn off when they retire. That fight shouldn't have happened, but at least everyone will heal."

She doesn't know how to respond to his little speech. The other men seemed like they'd been trying their best to kill Dalt.

She'd rather Holian locked them away or sent them to another colony.

Once again her years of obedience rise up. Keeping her opinion to herself, she nods her head. "That's good."

Placing his forearms on his thighs and leaning close to her. The position makes him appear less threatening, but she isn't fooled for a moment. "Two men are claiming you, Dalt and Searin. I need to decide who you're going to end up with."

Her first instinct is to shout out Searin's name, but fear checks her voice.

Mavianin.

That one word makes her fear almost overwhelming. Then she remembers the way Searin held her at arm's length after she made it to the mansion to ask for help. Does that mean he's disgusted with her now? That he's no longer scent-bonded to her?

"I need you to decide between Dalt and Searin. I know it's asking a lot to make you chose right now, but I have a wounded soldier in need of comfort and a Prime son ready to rip walls apart. I refuse to give you to either man without your input, but I need you to name one of them right now."

So many questions flood her head, but none of them make it out of her mouth. She's so scared and intimidated she even drops her face to her lap. A desperate part of her screams to demand to talk to Searin, but then she remembers the child growing in her belly.

She only has one choice.

"Dalt." Her whisper is so quiet she's not sure Holian can even hear it.

A rattle of surprise comes out of Holian. "I'll be honest, little Sora. That's not what I expected. But I'll abide by your choice. You've suffered enough and staying here on Kalor will be much safer for you and the child. Dalt will make an excellent caregiver for you both. And Ancestors know, he deserves a human of his own after what happened to him. Many of my humans won't interact with him. They find his scars too upsetting and his inability to rattle disconcerting. But they were raised among the Talin, unlike you."

Not sure what to expect now that she's decided between the love of her life and safety, she waits and watches Holian get to his feet. When he steps up to the bed and bends over to scoop her up, she gives a little gasp of surprise but doesn't struggle.

"Dalt's in the infirmary. I'll take you there now."

Holian, like every other Talin she's met so far, seems to have no problem carrying her, but she feels obliged to protest. "I can walk, Master."

"No, you can't. The last flesh knitter we had broke several rotations ago, and more won't arrive until tomorrow. Until then, you need to be carried. Your delicate human feet are a mess."

Looking down she notices her feet are covered in fresh bandages. Despite Holian's words, they don't hurt. She must be on pain suppressors or Holian is being overly cautious.

Eranan is waiting just outside the door and falls in step next to Holian. Dozens of faces look up to watch as she's carried through a large room filled with toys, places for children to climb, corners piled high with pillows, and bright cheerful colors everywhere.

"This is the nursery," Eranan explains. "This is where the mixed children stay most of the time. You won't need to stay here because Dalt lives so far in the forest no one will accidentally bump into either you or the child. But you will need to come to us for checkups before and after the baby's born."

"Thank you, sir. What about the other men in the forest?"

Holian makes a soft rumble of reassurance. "The other soldiers have been warned they need to stay away from you and Dalt. He needs you to himself, and you're too delicate to be handed off from lap to lap."

"Thank you, sir." Her words don't match her feelings of anxiety at going back out to Dalt's cabin.

Holian must read her facial expression accurately and continues to reassure her. "I swear to you, there's no need to worry further. Don't worry about them."

"Will Searin be okay without me?" she asks, even though she doesn't want to know the answer.

"Probably not," Holian says with brutal honesty. "But he's a Prime Son, so no one will know he's suffering until he's already dead."

Those callus words make Sora cover her face with her hands and press her palms to her eyes to keep the tears at bay. Why did she have to choose between safety and love? Between her baby's life and Searin's?

Suddenly she's angry. "All of you are idiots."

She mutters it under her breath, but the men with their excellent hearing catch her words anyway.

Eranan rattles from surprise, but Holian doesn't make a sound or falter at her words. "Probably."

They make the rest of the journey to the infirmary in silence. When she sees Dalt lying so still on the bed, tears well up in her eyes again. He looks so tired and battered, it breaks her heart.

He's worth loving too, she tells herself. Hopefully, someday, she'll grow to love him as much as she loves Searin.

Holian deposits her on the bed next to Dalt's. When he opens his eyes and starts his familiar rusty purr, it makes Sora smile.

"Sora," he whispers. "You chose me. Thank you. I'll take good care of you and the baby. Everything will be well between us."

Sitting up as soon as Holian lets go of her, she scoots to the edge of the bed. These two beds have been pushed close enough together, so she's able to reach him.

"Don't leave the bed," Eranan admonishes her, and she clutches Dalt's big hand in hers.

"Both of you require rest and healing," Holian says to back up Eranan's orders. "Neither of you moves from those beds or we'll separate you." Turning his attention to Dalt, Holian slaps his hand to the natural armor plating over his pectoral muscle. "I present you with your human pet, Sora. The paperwork will be completed and filed for her under the name Hope. She's yours to care for, guard, and treasure. You'll have the same responsibilities to her young. If anything happens to either of them, you will be held accountable. Do you understand your duties as her owner and keeper?"

Raising the hand that Sora's not holding, Dalt smacks his fist to his chest. "I understand and accept this responsibility. I will act with all honor and diligence toward Sora and her pup."

Their formal words remind Sora of her cousin's marriage ceremony. It feels very similar; important and somber. She remains quiet, unsure what she should say or if she even has a role other than an observer.

Turning to face her, Holian gives a decisive rattle, like a human might clap their hands together to signal something done.

"Dalt is going to care for you now. When he's healed, you'll both go back and live in the woods in his cabin. If you're ever fearful and Dalt isn't there, you're welcome to make your way back here. I'll show you how to gain entrance from an underground passage in the woods so you won't be seen. Remember, Sora, the secrets here are important. Keeping everyone here safe and happy is my primary concern. Don't jeopardize that."

Knowing a threat when she hears one, she grips Dalt's hand tightly in her own. "I won't, sir."

Her face must have shown her fear, because Holian rumbles out a purr. "And no more escaping. You're making Eranan and me look bad with all your running away."

Trying to smile at his humor, she nods her head. "No more running. I promise."

"Very good." He turns and leaves with Eranan right behind him. Soon they are alone in the infirmary.

Dalt closes his eyes and lets the hand on his chest fall back to his side. "Feet?"

Used to his taciturn speech, Sora glances down at her bandaged feet dangling off the side of the bed between them. "I think they're fine. I don't feel anything."

"Good."

"What about you?"

"Fine."

"I don't believe you. But I'm sure the healers will make everything better."

They lapse into silence with Dalt's rusty purr the only sound in the room.

"Stay here? Don't leave me." His words might sound calm, but she can hear the underlying desperation.

"I'm staying," she promises as she lies down, keeping her arm outstretched so one of her hands can stay linked with his. "Didn't you hear earlier? I'm not running anymore."

His purring quiets, and his body relaxes a little. Soon his breathing evens out, his purring stops, and his face goes slack. She watches him sleep and finds herself dwelling on Searin.

His purrs. His gentle hands. His big, warm body. The way he makes her body heat with pleasure. The way he holds her and wants her close, even when he's attending holo-meetings.

But none of that changes the fact that she's not safe with him. Her baby isn't safe with him. He's a Prime Son, and she's a weakness his family can't afford.

She reminds herself that she made the right choice.

She made the only choice.

CHAPTER 30

Sora

Healer Vormian regards Dalt and sounds an impatient rumble. "As I told you yesterday, she's perfectly healthy."

"But she won't eat," Dalt responds, the distress in his voice making up for his lack of back plates to rattle.

Grabbing his arm to get his attention, she waits until his eyes turn to her. "Dalt, I do eat."

"Not enough. You should be bigger. You're growing young inside you. You should be bigger by now."

"The gestation is perfectly healthy," Vormian reminds him. She's repeated the same thing a dozen times in a dozen different ways this visit. It would be humorous if this wasn't the third visit to the healer in the last four rotations. Vormian turns to put her scanner away, so Sora slides off the table. Dalt grabs her mid-drop and puts her right back on.

"More tests," he demands.

"No, Dalt. Go home. She'll eat as she needs to." With those words, Vormian leaves without a backward glance.

Dalt calls out for her to come back, but the door slides with a soft click behind her. Aggravated, he looks at Sora, then the door, and then back to Sora. She knows he's debating between going after Vormian and dragging her back into the infirmary or staying with Sora.

Several dozen rotations have passed since she decided between Dalt and Searin. For the first handful of rotations, the two of them stayed in the infirmary as both healed.

Once they were pronounced fit, Dalt carried her back to his home in the woods and set about seeing to her every need. On the rare occasion he leaves her side, he barricades her in the house with enough food and water to last for several rotations, even though he was rarely gone for longer than a few marks.

They also have a small information square stored in the cabin now. With it they can contact the main house in case of emergency.

Not that she worries anymore about being attacked. The four other retired soldiers sent her recorded apologies and gifts. Dalt didn't make a sound as she watched the vids on the small information square, but later he apologized as well.

"I've lost so much," he mumbles at the end of his short, apologetic speech. "I can't lose anything else and remain sane." She didn't know how to respond to that, so she just hugged him instead.

Now, sitting in the infirmary with Dalt hovering over her, she realizes he's terrified that something will happen to her and he'll be alone again.

"Can we go home?" she asks, putting a hand on the strip of unprotected flesh on his neck. He relaxes a fraction at her touch.

Before he can answer her, a shout sounds outside. Then the door to the infirmary slides soundlessly open allowing a small body to tumble inside. She stops short when she sees the two of them. Dalt turns, putting his bulk between her and the stranger but doesn't make a move beyond that.

The creature panting in front of them is dressed in rags, and most of her skin is nothing but old bloody scabs. Sora isn't even sure what color the girl's skin is under all the old blood and dirt, but she thinks her hair might be black.

But she's certain of a few things; this person is female, human, and desperate.

Voices outside are getting louder. The girl swings around to face the closed infirmary door. She taps at the display to lock it. When nothing happens because her biosignature isn't in the system, she makes a strange keening sound and turns to survey the room, her eyes wide and fearful.

She clambers onto a counter, knocking things on the floor. She holds one arm to her chest as if it hurts but moves with amazing speed and agility despite being unable to use that limb. She opens a cabinet and uses the shelves inside like ladder rungs to climb up. Then she wiggles herself into the space between the cabinet and the ceiling.

Neither she nor Dalt have moved or made as sound as the girl makes herself disappear into an impossibly small space.

Eranan rushes into the room, slamming the door open and looking around wildly. "Is she in here?"

In a very human gesture, Dalt tilts his head to the side. "She?"

"New human arrived this morning. She's gotten out twice already. I don't know how she did it this time, but the Healer Vormian went to see her and found the enclosure empty." Eranan makes an agitated rattle. "We need to find her. She was rescued from a terrible situation. She's traumatized and needs medical attention." Eranan sniffs the air. "I can smell her in here. Are you sure you didn't see anyone?"

Interested to see what Dalt will do, Sora remains silent and forces herself not to look up at where the woman's hiding.

"We just got here," Dalt lies.

Sora's mouth drops open. The man lied! Right to Eranan's face. She puts her face against Dalt's side to hide her facial expression, sure she'll give away everything if Eranan sees her.

"She must have come through here, probably looking for a place to hide," Eranan mutters, kneeling so he can look under the beds and then moving to open up all the cabinets. "As if the day isn't already hectic enough with a royal visit from the monarch, now I have a wounded and distressed human loose on the grounds."

Feeling ill, Sora speaks up. "The monarch is here?"

"Just arrived," Eranan confirms without looking at her. "Commandant Holian and some of his men are assembling on the front garden to receive her, but I need to find Lakin before anything bad happens to her."

"Lakin is the human?" Dalt asks.

"It's the name on her paperwork," Eranan says with a shrug and a pointed look at Sora. "Who knows what her real name is." Satisfied she's not in the room, he moves to the door that leads inside the mansion. "If you see her, don't grab her or anything.

Corner her and call for help. We're going to need to sedate her or she might end up more hurt than she already is."

Both she and Dalt wordlessly nod at Eranan. The keeper is so preoccupied he doesn't spare them another glance as he leaves.

The moment the door into the mansion slams shut, a scraping sound comes from the hiding spot. The top of a head and two eyes appear. Before anyone can do anything, Dalt strides over to the display next to the door leading outside and slaps a hand on it, locking both sets of doors. Sora thinks he's locking the girl in, but his next words make her realize his intent is much different.

"They're locked out," he calls out softly. "I won't let them sedate you."

"We won't hurt you," Sora adds. "I don't know what happened to you, but I was a slave for ten years before the Talins bought me. You're safe now. This colony is very good to us." The woman doesn't talk right away. Instead, she stares at the two of them for a while, as if gauging what she should say. Finally, she comes to a decision.

"Most of the damage was done by a couple of his people." Her voice is so soft, Sora isn't sure she heard correctly until Dalt hisses beside her.

"Who?" he demands, his voice angry and low. Her eyes stare at him for a moment, but a sound outside the door makes her duck back and disappear.

The timing is perfect because the door chimes and opens, revealing Holian the only male that could override the locks. With him are a dozen other Talins Sora's never meet. Uncharacteristically, the calm, cool Holian seems agitated.

"Dalt, get Sora to the front garden." He pins his eyes on Sora. "You need to be respectful and honest."

Sora shrinks back a little. "Yes, Master Holian." She's not afraid of Holian, but whatever's going on can't be good if it involves the monarch.

What must the women hiding think of this exchange? This can't look good to someone so obviously abused and mistreated. When Dalt sounds his broken rough purr, she's sure it's for the stranger as much as her.

"We need to come back here after," Dalt insists much louder than necessary as he scoops Sora up and cradles her to his chest. Her feet are healed, but just like Searin, Dalt likes to carry her around.

"You take such good care of me, Dalt," she states loudly. "You would never let anyone hurt a human. Never. I bet you'd die to protect us humans."

He doesn't bother responding because they're out the door at the point, but he gives her a little squeeze to show his appreciation.

"Should we have told them?" she whispers in his ear so that Holian and his men following behind won't hear.

Dalt isn't one to mince words, so the answer is swift and short. "No."

Her next question dies on her tongue as she takes in the gathering in front of her. Shade tents have been erected, and tables and chairs are set out. Dozens of guards and elaborately dressed men and women are gathered under the shade, some of them sitting and some standing.

One woman with an air of command stands slightly apart from the rest. Everyone turns to them as they approach, and several guards step in their path, blocking them from the woman.

"The female is to go to the monarch. You are to stay here," the guard orders. If Dalt could rattle, Sora's sure he'd be sounding an impressively aggressive rattle at the guard's command.

"No."

"Put her down, Dalt," Holian orders him. "The monarch won't hurt her."

"No."

Holian leans in close to her and Dalt. "Put her down or I'll send Eranan and a dozen guards to pull that little human out from where she's hiding on the top of the cabinets without using any sedation."

Sora gasps at Holian's words. He knew Lakin was there and let her stay? And worse, he's using that poor girl as a bargaining chip. Holian must feel very threatened by the monarch's visit to resort to such tactics. "You know I'm good for my word, Dalt. Don't test me on this."

Reluctantly, Dalt lowers Sora to the ground. "I'll be right here."

"Everything will be fine," she assures him. She doesn't know if that's the truth or not, but it makes her feel better to say it. She gives Dalt a last squeeze on the arm and turns to the woman who must be the monarch, Searin's mother.

Neither the monarch nor any of the royal entourage make any sound as Sora walks forward. They all stare at her with expressionless Talin faces. And she thought Holian's silence could be unnerving.

When she's finally standing in front of the monarch, she wonders what the protocol is. Should she kneel? Bow? She probably shouldn't look the woman in the eye, so she drops her gaze to the ground and waits.

A strong hand cups her chin and tilts her head up, but she keeps her eyes downcast. The monarch makes a soft, considering rumble.

"You're lovely," she finally murmurs. "I can see why he's so enamored of you."

Her heart hammers away in her chest. The monarch must be talking about Searin. Sora wants to ask how Searin is doing. Is he eating? Sleeping? Has he found someone else to kneel on the pillow at his feet? Is someone else cuddling with him at night?

She wants to know everything, but fearful of stepping on a political landmine, she keeps silent instead.

"Look at me, female," the woman demands, and Sora raises her gaze. The monarch leans forward until her face is close enough to kiss. "Tell me, are you still pregnant with my son's child?"

Gasping, Sora tries to pull away, but the monarch holds her in a firm grip. "Answer me. Are you? It would be easy enough to have my healer test you, so don't bother lying."

She finds it hard to speak through the fear, but she croaks out an answer. "Yes, Monarch. His child is growing inside me."

"Do you know if it's male or female yet?"

"Female and healthy," she whispers. The hand holding her chin tightens slightly. "Please," she begs, feeling the world fall away around her. Her entire focus is on the face in front of her and the hand holding her chin. "Please don't hurt us."

"Whom do you plead for? You and the baby or my son?"

Fear makes her bold. Sora violently twists her head free from the woman's grip. "Both. Love shouldn't be punished."

Her tone must have been harsher than she meant it to be because several of the colorfully dressed people behind the monarch sound surprised rattles.

The monarch drops her hand and straightens up to her impressive height. "Tell me, little pet, what would you be willing to do to keep the child and Searin safe?"

"I have nothing of value but my own life. I'd be willing to give it up to keep those I love safe."

"What if I wanted the baby for Searin but not you?" Images of Searin holding and purring to their child fill her mind. What would she be willing to do to assure a long life for her child? Is she willing to live never knowing her daughter?

"King Mavianin wanted to kill her," she states starkly. "He tried to end the life of my child before she even got to breathe air."

A rattle of anger and disgust comes from the queen. "King Mavianin has been dealt with. I'm the monarch. He's only a king, a consort to the crown. His power comes from my benevolence, and he's destroyed any trust or kindness I felt for him." Her little speech gives Sora hope until the next words come. "And you broke my kindness also. You, who desired a nameless soldier instead of my child. You picked a broken man with no armor, quills, or claws over a Prime Son. What's wrong with you, human, that you would do such a thing?"

Incensed on Dalt's behalf, Sora curls her hands into tight fists at her side and tries to keep her voice calm. "If they were gaming pieces on a playing board, who would be more powerful, a Prime Son or a king? What about a Prime Son versus the Apogee Assembly? I felt the power of a king firsthand and have no wish to test the power of the Apogee Assembly if they ever find out about us." No one talks as Sora takes a few shuddering breaths, amazed at her own courage to talk so boldly.

"Searin is a Prime Son and needs to be on homeworld, a place that might mean my child's death. But here, we can be safe and Dalt would die to protect me." She looks down at her belly and covers it with her hand. "He'd die to protect both of us."

A rumble of realization sounds from the monarch. "Searin didn't keep you safe."

"He can't," Sora whispers.

"But I can," the monarch declares. "What would your choice be if you knew that the might of the monarch will protect your child? If you understood that every man and woman standing with me today knows about the mixed children and loves them as their own? That everyone here wishes our culture to change and will risk possible death in order to live a life full of scent-bonding instead of devoid of it?"

Jolting in shock at the monarch's words, Sora's heart lifts, but the monarch isn't done yet.

"You need to decide, Sora. Give up Dalt or give up your child. My son is dying and I'll do anything in my power to keep that from happening. I can't force you to be with him, to bond with him, but I can take your child away if it means giving my son something to live for."

At those words, Sora feels the blood drain from her face and her legs go weak. She sways a little as panic engulfs her, narrowing her vision. She worries she's going to faint.

Suddenly Holian is there, grabbing her arm to steady her. No rumble or rattle comes out of him as he keeps her standing and addresses the monarch himself.

"I wonder if the rumors of your generosity are exaggerated because no one with any decency would threaten a breeding human. They are delicate to begin with and while they're breeding, they're even more vulnerable."

Waving him off with a dismissive hand, the monarch issues an irritated rattle. "I can assure you, they're far hardier than the literature would have you believe." She levels her gaze back at Sora. "And I need this one to understand the dire consequences of her decision. I can promise that there's no longer a threat to you on Talarian. I'll make you safe if you return with me. But make no mistake, I will be returning with you and the child, or the child alone."

"After my child is born, you mean," she whispers, afraid she already knows the answer. The monarch points to one member of her entourage outfitted in healer green.

"No. We'll extract your child and put her in an artificial womb. It's not optimal for you or the child, but I'm determined."

Flinching at those words, Sora whimpers in fear at the idea of her baby being ripped from her before she's even born. Only Holian holding her keeps her legs from giving out from under her.

Angry shouts and warning rattles sound behind her. She turns her head to see Dalt being held back by four guards.

"Stand down," Holian commands, but Dalt's too far gone to hear him. Three more guards join the fray, and soon Dalt's shackled hand and feet, struggling hard and making the restraints cut into his armored flesh. He struggles so hard, she can see a hint of blood forming under the shackles.

Sora turns back to the monarch. "Please don't hurt us."

"For my son, I'd burn this colony to the ground," the monarch says in a calm tone, as if discussing the weather. "Female, you are it. He'll never scent-bond to another. You've killed him. Bringing his daughter back with me might not even be enough. If I could, I'd put you in chains and drag you back to Talarian to care for my son. But if you struggled against him, if he didn't think you wanted to be there, it would just kill him faster. You might have saved him from the Fading, but now you've doomed him to die of the Ending instead. Suffering from the Collapsed Scent Disease isn't a pleasant way to die, so I'll do everything in my power to help, even if it only eases his symptoms."

Finding out Searin's dying from a broken scent-bond is like a knife through Sora's heart. Between that knowledge, the monarch's assurance, and her cold calculated threats, Sora can only do one thing.

It's the one thing her heart wants her to do.

"I love Searin," she whispers, afraid to say the words too loudly. "His face fills my dreams, but his voice is missing from my ears and his scent from my nose. I want it all, monarch. Searin, my child, and safety. Your threats aren't necessary. You're offering all I could hope for but feared would never happen."

The monarch rumbles with satisfaction. "Excellent. Prepare for our journey. We leave in a quarter of a mark." Looking over to where Dalt is still screaming and struggling, she rumbles with sadness for the first time.

"I wish I didn't have to hurt others to save my son, but I won't be dissuaded. The soldier stays here, so say your goodbyes. My guards will be with you. Don't do anything that'll force my hand."

With those words, she turns and strides off, all but six of her entourage falling in step with her. The remaining take up positions around Sora, giving her a very clear message of strength. Not only to Sora, but to anyone who might try to take her. Holian slowly lets go of her, as if making sure she can stand on her own feet. Once she's steady, they both turn to face Dalt.

"I have to leave."

Holian doesn't rattle or rumble. "I know. Talk to Dalt. He'll understand."

With a heavy heart, she walks to Dalt, still struggling on the ground. When she kneels by him, one guard makes a warning rattle, and she glares up at him. The guard doesn't back up, but he stops rattling.

Placing a gentle hand on Dalt's shoulder, Sora leans close so she can whisper in his ear hole. "I need you to help that girl."

Her words make Dalt freeze and when she pulls back, his eyes are tracking her with his usual calm intensity.

"I'm leaving, going back to the homeworld, but I'm going to be safe. The monarch herself is going to keep me safe. I'm cared for, but that girl in the infirmary doesn't have anyone. I'm worried about her. Can you look after her? Protect her? She's going to need someone patient."

Sora thinks about the blood and dirt covering the Lakin's skin, the pain she must be enduring, and her intense determination to survive. Her actions were clever and quick, first finding a hiding spot and then getting herself in position despite the agony it must have caused. She didn't get to see her for very long, but what she saw was telling.

The woman's eyes held determination and grit. In a flash, Sora realizes Lakin might have a lot in common with Dalt. "She's going to need someone who knows what it's like."

At Dalt's questioning rumble, she gives him a small sad smile. "What it's like to be tortured."

Comprehension makes his rumble go quiet. "You'll contact me if you need me."

"I won't need you," she promises. "But maybe, someday, we'll visit."

With a nod, he turns his attention to the guards. "Let me loose," he demands. "I have a life to look after."

CHAPTER 31

Searin

Talins don't dream, but in the strange place between full sleep and wakefulness, Searin finds he can conjure memories that are so vivid they feel real. It's the only place he can see Sora again. Remember the softness of her skin under his fingers. The gleam of her hair in the sun. The sound of her laughter. The delightful smell of her.

The smell is the rarest memory, the hardest for him to bring out. Her scent is so special, so perfect, especially mixed with his own. On the rare occasions he's able to get her scent to surface, he'll lie still for marks, quiet and motionless, just experiencing every nuance of the memory until pain or some outside influence forces him from his bed.

The staff mostly leave him alone now. His mother and sister both tried to get him to eat, but neither managed it. A healer provided numbing drugs, which Searin listlessly swallowed. With the pain slightly muted, he's better able to remember Sora.

Then they all left, and he's been blissfully alone with his thoughts for rotations. He doesn't know how much time he's spent almost motionless in his bed, all moments blending together now.

He knows he's dying. His body has grown weak from lack of sustenance, but he's in too much pain to eat. Besides, if he doesn't eat, death will come for him sooner and the anguish will end.

The technical term is Collapsed Scent Disease. It's what happened to his ancestors when they were separated for too long from a scent-bonded partner. But really, everyone calls it the Ending.

And now he's dying from it. Painfully. Slowly. Agonizingly.

But at least his memories keep floating in when the drugs for the pain are strong enough. Despite the pain, he doesn't regret Sora. For a brief time, he understood why so many break the laws. He understands why the ancient ancestors wrote poems about scent-bonding. The wonderful memories of Sora will follow him into the afterlife.

He'll join his ancestor in the Domicile of Souls with full understanding of what it means to be Talin.

"Searin, I've been told you need to eat."

Sora's voice is so clear she could be in the room with him. This memory makes his body shudder involuntarily causing pain to tighten all his muscles.

"Easy." Small soft hands touch the armor plates on his chest and then trail lower until they get to the flesh of his abdomen. A face nuzzles his neck and warm breath blows across the tender strip of exposed skin there.

"If I lay down, will you hold me?"

His visions were never so real. Never so perfect. Perhaps this is an effect of dying. A last pleasure to ease him into the realm of the ancestors.

Small hands grip his arm and pull it around a small body. His eyes fly open. His hazy monotone vision takes in Sora's face, wet with tears and full of fearful concern. "Please, Searin, don't leave me."

Still half convinced that what he's experiencing isn't real, he wraps her in his arms and rolls on his back, dragging her onto his chest as he moves. Her weight feels real, but the scent that fills his lungs isn't right.

"Sora?" It's the first thing he's said in rotations and the single word makes his throat burn with pain.

"Yes, it's me," she answers. "I'm really here."

The scent glands in his cheeks are so full they ache. Obeying instinct, he rubs his face on her, releasing his overfull scent glands into her hair.

She gives a little gasp and wiggles on top of him until she can bring her hands up. The moment he pulls his face away from her, she sinks her fingers into her hair and starts combing them through the curly mass. Soon their combined scent fills the air, and Searin feels something powerful and profound release in his mind.

The overwhelming pain vanishes.

"Sora." This time the sound slides out of him more easily.

"I'm here. I'm sorry I picked Dalt. I was only thinking about our child. Please don't die on me. Please don't leave me. Don't leave our daughter."

"Daughter?"

Sitting up, she places her hands protectively on her belly, her eyes shining with tears. "Yes, our daughter. She wants to meet you. You wouldn't deny her a father, would you?"

Purring fills the room for several moments before he realizes it's coming from him. "My daughter." He places a gentle hand over hers. "You both came back to me."

She collapses onto him, clinging to him tightly. The pain is gone, but his body is exhausted from the effort of just trying to survive the agony. His eyes close and he lets sleep overtake him.

When he opens his eyes again, the bright colors of the ceiling register and the drive to live fills him. Sora is still on top of him. Her slight weight is warm and reassuring. He tightens his arms around her and she shifts a little, telling him she's awake.

"You came back to me," he murmurs, a rumble of contentment and affection pouring out of him. He hears her sniff and feels a drop of wetness hit his chest. "Don't cry, sweet Sora. I shouldn't have left you, but I thought you scent-bonded to Dalt. I didn't want to hurt you. I didn't want to hurt your child."

"Our child, Searin. Dalt was kind, but I love only you," she tells him, her voice thick with emotion.

"Everything's going to be well," he whispers to her, believing it with his whole heart now. "We'll make everything perfect."

CHAPTER 32

Sora

As she clumsily lowers herself to a thickly padded sofa made especially for her, Sora isn't sure she ever wants to have children again. She was due days ago, but her daughter is stubborn and doesn't want to leave the comfortable confines of the womb.

She's looking forward to holding her baby in her arms, and maybe not suffering from swollen ankles. Or needing to use the elimination facilities three million times a rotation.

"Sora?" Searin strides into the room with a concerned rattle, and she smiles up at him, despite her discomfort.

"Everything's fine," she assures him. If she thought he was protective before, it was nothing compared to now. They're rarely parted, and on the infrequent occasions he leaves the palace, he locks her in their quarters and puts a dozen guards outside the door.

Mavianin has long since been exiled to a distant colony, but the fear and shock of Sora's abduction has stayed with Searin.

"Halieni's here," Searin tells her with a distinctly unhappy rattle. He hasn't forgiven his sister yet, but at least he allows her to visit and everyone is civil to each other.

"Finally!" Sora crows and struggles to get off the sofa.

Searin moves to kneel in front of her, blocking her from rising. "She's on her way here. You don't need to get up."

Knowing better than to argue, Sora points to a nearby table. "Could you hand me my information square, please?"

Without needing to stand, Searin casually reaches one long arm out and snags it from the table before holding it just out of her reach. She cocks an eyebrow at him and then laughs.

Leaning forward, she kisses him. She takes her time and only pulls back when a rumble of lust comes out of his chest. "Now give me the pad and you can have more of that after Halieni leaves."

He practically shoves the information square at her, making her laugh again. She taps a few things on the pad and sets it down just as the door to their private quarters opens to admit Halieni. She walks in slowly as if waiting for Searin to dismiss her or some other poor reception.

"Sister," Searin greets her coldly and Sora pinches him where Halieni can't see. There's no way her little pinch could cause Searin pain, but he grunts in acknowledgment and gets to his feet to greet his sister.

"Greetings, Halieni. Won't you sit? May I call for refreshments for you?"

Visibly relaxing, she takes the indicated seat. "I'm in no need of sustenance at this time, but thank you, my brother." Her words are formal and her tone stiff. She turns her attention to Sora, and a soft purr starts up in her chest. "How's your human and the child?"

"Both are well."

An uncomfortable silence fills the room. Normally Sora would settle herself down next to Halieni and force Searin to make conversation, but today she lets them stew in their own awkward quiet, enjoying the way these two powerful Talins can't seem to figure out how to have an affectionate relationship.

When a tentative knock sounds at the door, Sora gives them both a brilliant smile and then addresses Searin. "Holian sent a human here to join us. He arrived this morning. He's shy and lonely. Would it be alright if he joined us?"

Blinking in confusion and surprise, Searin doesn't even hesitate to accommodate her. "Of course, my heart."

"Come on in, Hale," she shouts out, startling Halieni who's never experienced her at full volume.

The adult male human who comes into the room is gorgeous, and if Sora's heart didn't already belong to Searin, she'd be tempted to consider spending some quality time with him.

His long, light brown hair reaches down to the middle of his back, gleaming and thick. High cheekbones and a slender nose should make his face look too narrow, but instead he looks captivating. Bright blue eyes take in the room as he stands in the partially open door, his lean muscled chest on display because he's only wearing a loincloth instead of the ubiquitous wraps that all the humans wear.

The loincloth was her idea.

"Sora?" he says hesitantly, and she gives him a wide smile and waves him in.

"Come in. You can sit down on the kneeling pad next to Searin's sister, Halieni." She looks to the Talin who's let out a rumble of surprise and then pleasure at the sight of Hale. "None of the females on Kalor Colony wanted to settle down with Hale, and no one here is interested, either. Poor Hale is very lonely and could use a little companionship. I hope you don't need to rush off today, Halieni."

Not even acknowledging Sora's words, Halieni sits, transfixed by Hale as he walks over and settles himself down at her feet with an effortless grace Sora envies.

"I thought he was here because you bought him," Searin whispers in her ear.

After several rounds of discussions, Searin gave Sora a budget and access to information and communication off-planet so she can keep tabs on all the auctions. All her years as a slave and going through auction twice gave Sora special understanding of auction houses making her very good at sorting through sellers' jargon to find actual humans.

The moment she finds a human she snatches them up and either keeps them at the palace or sends them to Kalor.

Hale is her most recent find. She had him purchased and brought directly to the palace. The human never saw Holian's planet, let alone met any of the females there.

"Shhhh," she whispers back. "Telling Halieni I bought a human for her might not go over well. She's got a lot of pride. Not unlike someone else I know."

Resting her gaze across the room, Sora sees Halieni leaning over and talking to Hale. Her voice is too low to hear, but her body language is eager, and her rumbling purr hasn't stopped.

Rubbing her distended belly, Sora gives a little sigh. "He might be the best thing to happen to Halieni."

Searin rubs a scent gland on her head, filling her nose with the comforting smell of cinnamon. "Your love is the best thing that's ever happened to me."

Picking her up as he stands, he cradles her to his chest, ignoring the other two in the room. "I think perhaps we should take a nap." Sora snuggles into him with a little sound of happiness. Neither Halieni nor Hale even look up as the two of them leave.

Sora can't imagine her life could ever be any happier. "Thank you for buying me, my love."

Searin's purr fills the hallway. "Thank you for saving me. Without you, there's no air to breathe."

Dear Readers,

Thank you for reading *Loving Captivity*. Don't worry, the next book in the series, *Escaping Captivity*, gives Lakin and Dalt their HEA!

I hope you enjoyed *Loving Captivity* enough to leave a review! As an indie writer without the support of a publishing company, I need all the help I can get. Your good reviews keep me writing.

Want links to my social media sights or to some free novellas? You can find everything on my website:

www.rk-munin.com

Have a fruitful rotation,
Rye

Other books by RK Munin

-Science Fiction-

Hissa Warrior Series
Rescuing Halin (Mian and Halin)
Buying Tiran (Mara and Tiran)
Tempting Selon (Lara and Selon)
Defying Kilan (Deena and Kilan)
Healing Mavito (Raleen and Mavito)
Claiming Yopin (Mouse and Yopin)
Teasing Woken (Safena and Woken)
Defending Revin (Kamaril and Revin)
Trusting Warik – Coming soon

Human Pets of Talin Series
Loving Captivity (Sora and Searin)
Escaping Captivity (Lakin and Dalt)
Negotiating Captivity (Nalia and Derani)
Fighting Captivity (Zia and Palforma)
Tender Captivity (Jinna and Holian - This is a novella you can get for free by signing up for my newsletter)
Craving Captivity (Lasha and Tamerin)
The Twelve Nights of Halloheen: A holiday mashup novella (Isla and Tisuran)
Stealing Captivity (Kasi and Ignatias)
Redeeming Captivity – Coming soon

Origins (A Human Pets of Talin Series)
Creating Captivity (Ari and Bazium)
Gossamer Chains (Rain and Hesarium)
Golden Cages – Coming soon
Purring, Presents, and Parties – Coming soon

-Paranormal /Urban Fantasy-

Ours Evermore Series
Two Wolves for Soren (Soren, Kalli, and Quinn)
A Hacker, Vampire, and Chimera Walk into a Bar… (Tobias, Briar, and Memphis)
When Darkness Meets Dawn (Imani, Lex, and Mac)

Tag, You're It (Novella)
Kidnapping Their Third (Cora, Pike, and Kimble)
Pastries on a Plate and Blood in a Mug – Coming soon

Alpha Series
Alpha Mage (Emma and Kade)
His Alpha Mage (Avery and Jason – Novella)
Alpha King (Cathleen and Lazlo)

New Clan Series
Stray Wolf (Steph and Eli)
Lost Lion (Maeve and Cyrus)
Reluctant Cervid (Tavi and Donovan)
Broken Thorn (Sabina and Theodosius)

www.ingramcontent.com/pod-product-compliance
Lightning Source LLC
Chambersburg PA
CBHW060438310726